Double Living

Also by the author in reading order:

Destiny: Union Station

Date Night on Union Station

Alien Night on Union Station

High Priest on Union Station

Spy Night on Union Station

Carnival on Union Station

Wanderers on Union Station

Vacation on Union Station

Guest Night on Union Station

Word Night on Union Station

Party Night on Union Station

Review Night on Union Station

Family Night on Union Station

Book Night on Union Station

LARP Night on Union Station

Career Night on Union Station

Last Night on Union Station

Independent Living

Soup Night on Union Station

Assisted Living

Freelance on the Galactic Tunnel Network

Con Living

Empire Night on Union Station

Space Living

Traders on the Galactic Tunnel Network

Orphans on the Galactic Tunnel Network

Swap Night on Union Station

Slow Living

Artists on the Galactic Tunnel Network

History Night on Union Station

Double Living

Book Six of EarthCent Universe

Foner Books

ISBN 978-1-948691-38-3

Hardwick, Massachusetts

One

Harry looked up from the mixing bowl as the swinging door between the dining room and the kitchen opened part way and stopped before swinging wide open. "Need a hand with that?" he asked as his assistant slowly backed through.

"I'm just being careful," Bill replied. When he turned toward the baker, the tray he was carrying with both hands and carefully shielding with his elbows was revealed. "It's my final homework assignment for the Narrative Baking workshop I took during the interterm, and I have to turn it in this afternoon."

"Is that the gingerbread house from Hansel and Gretel?"

Bill's face lit up. "You got it right away. Julie was sure it was from some alien anime feature we watched together while she was screening entries for Flower's next festival."

"Flower has Julie judging alien anime?"

"Just the first pass to make sure the production values are up to standard. It's an open invitational and they're getting a lot of amateur content that isn't really finished."

"At least now I know why you asked me how to make sugar glass," Harry said. "You were acting pretty mysterious about it, you know."

"I was afraid that if I told you about my plans you'd give me some good advice, and then I'd be in violation of the Open University honor code," Bill said, carefully setting the tray on the counter. "I already kind of cheated by using leftover cookies I made for the Blue Tea Café and store-bought candies."

"So you baked the gingerbread, the cake, and whipped up the frosting. How long did the whole thing take you?"

"Around four hours if you don't count the library time."

"Did you have to write a book report to go with the edible diorama?" Harry asked as he worked the mixing spoon through the stiffening dough.

Bill shook his head. "The assignment was to bake a scene from a fairy tale for a children's party, but I don't remember my mom telling me any. I just hope that everybody doesn't do a gingerbread house." He came around the counter and looked over the baker's shoulder. "Want me to finish that for you?"

"When I'm too old to mix cookie dough I'll retire for real," Harry said with a laugh. "You could break up that chocolate for me."

"Why did you wait until the dough is almost ready to add it in?" Bill asked. "Wouldn't the chunks get distributed more evenly if you put them in earlier?"

"Exactly."

Bill took a minute to think about this answer while breaking up the chocolate. "But the lab course I took on quality and consistency for baked goods stressed the importance of making sure that featured ingredients like fruits, nuts, and chocolate were spread evenly through the dough or batter."

"I take it the instructor never baked for a group of mixed aliens," Harry said, accepting the plate of broken chocolate from his assistant and scraping most of it off into the bowl. "When the cookies come out of the oven, pick out the ones with the most chocolate in them and add these leftover pieces on top."

"I get it now," Bill said. "You made the cookies for Belle. It's funny how much she loves chocolate."

"She gave a lecture at our independent living cooperative last week and explained how the Gem used to live before their revolution, which happened just around the time you were born. Belle was brought up on a factory-made nutrition drink and almost never ate solid food, much less anything that tasted good."

"I still can't believe that she's a clone. She seems so real."

Harry gave the mix a final stir and turned to his assistant. "Being a clone doesn't make her any less real. It just means that she has tens of billions of identical twin sisters. Irene recorded the lecture if you want to watch it."

"I would, and I bet Julie will want to see it too," Bill said. "Do we have to come to your place to watch?"

"Flower can play it through the entertainment system in your cabin," Harry said. "And Irene will thank you. Flower keeps track of the number of times people watch and reports the totals to the instructor of the documentary filmmaking course Irene is taking through the Open University campus."

"Does recording a lecture count as a documentary?" Bill asked as Harry began spooning the chunky dough out onto a baking sheet.

"I'm not sure. Flower?"

"I'm offering a new immersive camera to the student whose video stream logs the most hours viewed, though Irene already told me that if she wins, she wants the prize to go to one of the younger documentarians," the Dollnick AI responded via an overhead speaker grille. "Irene says she can borrow a camera from the Grenouthian director whenever she needs one, and it's not a fair competition because she has access to guest lecturers every night on the independent living deck."

"How come students in food and hospitality never get any prizes?" Bill asked. "I'm feeling confident about my gingerbread house."

"Because it will be easy for all of you to find paying jobs when you complete your studies. While there's no shortage of subject matter for aspiring documentarians, making a living at it is another story. My mentor has even suggested that I restrict access to the program because of the limited career opportunities."

"I can't believe I heard you admit that," Harry said over his shoulder as he slid the baking sheet into the preheated oven. "I thought you could find a job for anybody."

"I can," Flower said, sounding a bit cross, "but when it comes to documentary film makers, the field is dominated by the Grenouthians, and even their students have difficulty finding paying jobs. I offer all Open University students who complete the course an opportunity to work for Flower Entertainment, but some of them choose to pursue the path of the starving auteur."

"They become unsuccessful authors?" Bill asked.

"Close. They feel the need to exert so much control over their subject matter and production process that they are essentially aspiring to author a documentary."

"You won't have any of those problems with us," Harry said, putting a friendly arm around his assistant's shoulder. "Bill and I are used to you telling us what to do."

"I don't order people around," the Dollnick AI said. "I merely make recommendations which I adjust according to feedback. Based on Bill's oft-repeated questions about the practicality of his course work, I have a proposition to make."

"I should have kept my mouth shut," the young man muttered.

"You've been working a couple of shifts a week as a manager in the Blue Tea Café for almost a year now and I think it's time to—"

"Open my own place?" Bill interrupted. "I think I'm ready, but you'll have to find Harry a new assistant and let me out of all the other jobs I'm doing for you. I've talked it over with Julie a hundred times, and we agreed I should start with a coffee shop menu offering counter service. I can do all of the baking in the morning and hire students for part-time staff to man the counter. I won't ask you to get me off the hook for the *All Species Cookbook* product testing because M793qK would probably take it personally and..." He trailed off as he noticed Harry shaking his head. "What?"

"Flower has something else in mind," Harry told his assistant. "She asked for my opinion this morning and I told her it was worth a try. I assume you know that the Human Empire's School of Government is finally launching next week when the Open University semester begins."

"Vivian and Samuel asked us to babysit last night when they hosted a welcoming party for some of the students who arrived early." Bill looked up at the speaker grille and his face hardened. "No way. I am not cramming for the civil service test, and I'm not interested in becoming a diplomat or a—whatever you call the people who actually run everything from behind desks."

"Bureaucrats," Harry supplied the word. "Just hear her out."

"The School of Government is sharing facilities with the Open University for the time being, but I've promised to provide an exclusive location where faculty and students can meet each other casually," Flower said. "I've discussed this with Samuel and Vivian, and they agreed that a dedicated café would be ideal."

"You're opening a café and you want me to work there?"

"I'm offering you the chance to manage it as if you were the owner, with no risk to yourself, and profit sharing if it should prove a success. I know it's not exactly the same thing as starting your own place in a location of your choosing, but I'm not asking for a long-term commitment. I estimate that in less than three years you'll save enough to open a first-rate café of your own without having to borrow a cred."

Bill hesitated for a moment. "Am I going to be a one-man show working around the clock?"

"You'll have full hiring and scheduling authority, but if you try delegating too much of the work, there won't be any profit left to share."

"And do I get a salary, or is the profit sharing it?"

"I'll pay you for your time at the same rate you're earning now regardless of the outcome," Flower said. "You're the ideal candidate for the job, and I'm sure you'll make a success of it, providing the school is able to attract enough students to make it worthwhile. That seems much more likely now that the Human Empire is on an accelerated schedule to take over from EarthCent."

"You're not just offering me the job because I'm married to Julie and you like her?"

"I like both of you, and I can see we need to work on your self-esteem. You happen to be the best match for the job from several standpoints, but the thing that really sets you apart from the other potential candidates on board is your experience cooking for and serving members of other species."

"I thought Samuel and Vivian decided that they were only going to accept human students, even though plenty of alien kids take our civil service exam for fun and ace it," Bill said.

"All of the advanced species have schools of government or the equivalent, and there will be plenty of opportunities for exchange students," Flower said. "The café needs someone familiar with the advanced species to serve the guest faculty."

"They're hiring alien teachers? Samuel never mentioned that."

"For the first year. They're taking advantage of the talent available on board."

"You mean that the alien intelligence agents who eat in our cafeteria will be teaching in the Human Empire's School of Government?" Bill asked, his voice expressing caution "I mean, I trust them, but still…"

"Every coin has two sides, even a programmable Stryx cred," Flower said. "Asking the intelligence agents hosted on board to teach in the School of Government was an idea of Samuel's that displays maturity and insight on his part. On the one hand, the Human Empire doesn't have anything to hide, and on the other hand, the agents living on board have years of experience dealing with Humans and understand what your people don't know that they don't know about the other species. On the third hand, the other tunnel network governments will see Samuel employing their spies as instructors as a pledge for full transparency, and on the fourth hand, he won't have to offer any of them tenure because they already have careers."

"You didn't have to refute him on all four hands," Harry said mildly. "Two would have sufficed. Bill, once you get the café up and running, I think you should return to working lunches here. You can go there in the morning to prep the day and serve early customers, but it's time you started learning to delegate. If your employees run into problems with the lunch rush, you're never more than a couple of minutes away."

Bill thought for a long moment while Harry checked the cookies through the glass window in the oven door. "It sounds like a good opportunity, but I want to sleep on it, and I'll have to talk to Julie."

"I wouldn't have expected otherwise," Flower said. "Do you want to advertise for hired help yourself? I could send you candidates from the Open University or recent immigrants from Bits."

"I'm surprised you haven't found them all jobs already," Harry said. "It's been over a month."

"I have until we reach Earth to convince the forty thousand or so Bitters who plan to disembark there that I offer a superior experience," the Dollnick AI responded. "There's nothing I can do about the retirees who have been dreaming about their birth places for decades, especially with land being so cheap, but I still have a shot at some of the younger fence sitters."

"It's hard to imagine that a part-time job in a café would make a difference for anybody," Bill said.

"I was thinking of co-op jobs. It turns out that some of the more academically gifted youngsters living on Bits have completed correspondence courses for advanced degrees, and several of them have started courses at the Open University. If I can get them hooked on academia…"

"And you think a handful of co-op jobs in a café can tip the scale?"

"Every space elevator umbilical starts with a single thread of carbon fiber filament," Flower quoted the old Dollnick saying. "If a little strategic planning makes the difference for a single individual it will have been worth my effort. And you know from your own experience that I try to provide meaningful co-op jobs."

"As long as you promise not to use the job to push me to take the civil service exam," Bill said. Then he realized that he hadn't put on his apron yet and went to retrieve it from its hook. "What are we making for lunch today?"

"The cookies are it," Harry said. "I would have given you the day off, but I knew that Flower wanted to talk to you about the café. Avisia is going to be here any minute and she's prepared Vergallian Vegan at home to bring in for everybody."

"She's never done that before," Bill said. "Is it a special occasion?"

"Queen's Day on her homeworld," Flower interjected before Harry could reply. "Avisia is the fourth daughter of the fourth daughter—far enough from the throne that she wasn't required to take the full course of royal training. It's a Vergallian tradition for members of the royal family who are safe from the line of succession to prepare a meal for others in thanks for dodging the arrow."

"I still don't understand that part," Harry said as the kitchen door swung open again. "Don't all upper-caste Vergallians aspire to be queen?"

"I can answer that for you," Avisia said as she headed for one of the large refrigerators with a giant bowl of salad.

"I just want to keep this crisp until everyone arrives, and I hope the two of you will join them in letting me serve you."

"I don't get it either," Bill said. "You're celebrating because you're never going to become queen? Is the royal training really that bad?"

"Yes," Avisia said, turning to face them once the salad was safely stored away. "All family members get the basics, but my poor sisters were forced to spend the first half-century of their lives in continual study, and the same was true for my older aunts. Samuel and Vivian asked for my opinion of the curriculum they've designed for the School of Government and it took all of my early training to keep from laughing. They're calling a two-year program advanced training? Would you call two hours at the beach a vacation?"

"You have to allow for their lifespans," Flower pointed out reasonably. "And compared to the Empire of a Hundred Worlds that's been around for over two million years, the Humans have very little to teach."

"Well, it's true that history makes up a good portion of royal training," Avisia allowed. "And since this new school is only accepting students who have already completed their basic studies at an institute of higher learning or through correspondence courses, they'll still end up spending more than ten percent of their prime working years in preparation for their career." She glanced at the gingerbread house and frowned. "I hope you weren't planning on serving that. When you asked if you could prepare a dessert, I was thinking of something less elaborate."

"The gingerbread house is Bill's homework," Harry told her. "The dessert is in the oven and it's a single tray of cookies. Heavy on the chocolate for Belle."

"There's something that my royal training had wrong," Avisia said reflectively. "I was taught that cloning is a trap that has led to the destruction of every species to implement it on a mass scale, and that clones should be shunned whenever possible. Yet the Gem have reversed course despite a hundred generations of existing as a single individual, and Belle is both intelligent and surprisingly—individual."

"Can she eat Vergallian Vegan?" Bill asked.

"Every species on the tunnel network with a digestive system can, which is why if you travel, you'll encounter terrible Vergallian Vegan everywhere you go. Prepared correctly, I think you'll find it a treat."

"I'm sorry I won't be able to join in letting you serve me lunch, but I'm meeting my wife at the bazaar to have our hologram taken," Harry said. "Bill, I set the oven timer, but keep an eye out that the chocolate chunks don't turn into sauce."

"You're talking about the new Horten holographic portraiture booth," Avisia said. "He's probably a spy, so don't let him pump you for information."

"Oh, no," Bill said. "Julie brought me there last week after she saw a hologram the Horten made for one of the new immigrants from Bits who she hired to work for Flower Enterprises. The Horten asked me about other aliens on board and I guess I mentioned you all by name."

The Vergallian sighed. "I'm sure he knew who we were already, but it's a good lesson for you. If you take the job managing the café for the School of Government, you'll have to be a little careful about what you say, especially around visitors."

"You knew about that?"

"I have my sources."

"M793qK," Bill groaned when he realized what he was getting into. "He'll probably want me to report to him about all of the students in the program."

"Whatever for?" Avisia asked. "According to our latest assessment, he's working behind the scenes to speed the creation of the Human Empire because he sees humanity as a potential ally."

"Us? How could we possibly help him fight the Hierarchy, other than as customers for the pharmaceuticals he's manufacturing on Earth?"

"The galactic chessboard isn't limited to feudal gentry and pawns. There are an infinite number of pieces, and even the weakest individual can change the course of history in the right place at the right time."

"As long as you aren't talking about me," Bill said.

Two

"I can't believe we're finally getting ready to open the School of Government," Vivian said. "I've never been involved in anything that moved ahead so slowly."

"It's funny, but I don't remember a year ever going by so quickly," Julie said. She took an experimental sip from her blue tea and winced at how hot it still was. "In another three months, Bill and I will be celebrating our first anniversary."

"That's the sign of a good marriage. When you're happy the time just flies by."

"Even with all of the midnight feedings?" Julie asked, glancing at the sleeping baby in the infant seat attached to the iron-pipe-and-glass café table.

"Rose has been sleeping through the night for months," Vivian said. "I'm just frustrated with myself that I didn't put more time into the school a year ago. Instead, I focused on building our GenePost family database and left the school to Sam, on top of everything else he has to do."

"You're new parents and you both work too hard. Have you ever considered keeping to a regular work schedule?"

"Flower gives me grief if I go over twelve hours a day, but she allows Samuel fourteen."

"I was thinking more like ten," Julie said, adding two hours to what she had intended to say.

"You were thinking eight, which is ironic, considering that Flower works you around the clock."

"Being on call isn't the same as being on the clock," Julie said. "I rarely work more than eight hours a day."

"Seven days a week," her friend said.

"Six, and to tell you the truth, it doesn't feel like work. It's just what I do."

"Well, I'm from a family of workaholics, and Sam literally grew up in his father's place of business. But I forget about work when I'm home and Sam doesn't. You'd think he'd have learned something about compartmentalization during the time he worked in the Vergallian embassy."

"So what are you going to do about it?" Julie asked.

"I'm going to tell his father on him next time Flower stops at Union Station," Vivian said with a grin. "Sam's mother gets all of the headlines, but his father is the one he goes to for advice."

"Maybe things will improve after the school opens. I've been involved in all of Flower's startup businesses and the most intense period is just before they launch." A loud sound like a wrong-answer buzzer on a game show came from Julie's purse. "Sorry, I forgot to put it on vibrate," she said, fumbling for her new smartphone while explaining to her friend, "Flower just gave it to me and I only had burners on Earth."

"You have an implant," Vivian said with a laugh. "Why would Flower want to call you on an old smartphone?"

"The call went to voicemail before I got to it," Julie said in frustration as she studied the screen. "It looks like I missed a call earlier when I was in the lift tube coming here and that changes it to a single ring by default."

"There's no phone service in the lift tubes? My implant works fine."

"I didn't understand Flower's whole explanation, but it has something to do with the tubes doubling as waveguides for power distribution and the capsules being shielded for safety reasons. The implants are on a different frequency, or technology, or something," Julie concluded vaguely. "And the phone isn't for talking with Flower—it's for all the new immigrants she picked up on Bits. They didn't want to abandon their smartphone culture and she obliged by setting up a cellular network. But I would have sworn she told me they only use them for texts."

"What was that you said about only having burners on Earth?" Vivian asked. "They sound like alien weapons."

"A burner is a cheap throwaway phone you could buy on the street for a few eBucks. That's the only kind of phone I had back when I worked for the drug syndicate. They never let me get a real smartphone because it's too easy for the police to track your location."

"Then it's strange that the government didn't ban burners. But aren't you going to check the message?"

"I haven't even started my tea yet," Julie said, though she couldn't help stealing a look at her purse. "It's from Rayne, the woman from Bits I told you about. She's been texting me a lot since I talked her into taking over as comptroller for Flower Industries. Maybe I'll just glance at it."

"The phone rings like that for text messages too?"

"No, that was a call, but the phone transcribes messages to text automatically and I haven't figured out how to change the default setting." Julie took out the phone again and frowned as she read.

"If it's important, just go," Vivian said. "I'll see you tonight anyway when you and Bill come to babysit."

"I wish I knew why Flower wanted Rayne to audit all of our books," Julie said. "I've learned how to negotiate prices, but Princely Standards bookkeeping is completely over my head."

"It seems a bit odd that a twenty-thousand-year-old Dollnick AI would want a human checking her math. Maybe Flower is planning to apply for a loan and she needs a certified accountant to confirm the numbers?"

"With all the money that she rakes in from Flower Entertainment and her Earth Two contract consulting on terraforming and ferrying colonists? When I first joined the ship, she worried about every cred. Now she spends millions like water."

"If Flower replaces the furniture in your office with stuff leased from one of the worlds where we stop, it means she's putting the furniture she owns in storage to prepare for bankruptcy," Vivian said with a grin, but then her face took on a serious look. "I can see something is upsetting you, and it's not like you'll be abandoning me here alone. Just go."

"You're right," Julie said. She took a gulp from the tea that had finally cooled enough to drink and got up from her chair. "Tell the waitress that I borrowed the mug and I'll see you this evening."

"Frequency or technology or something?" Flower demanded over her executive assistant's implant as Julie headed for the exit. "When I explained how lift tubes act as wave guides you said you understood."

"That's because I wanted you to stop explaining. How many times do I have to tell you that Maxwell's Equations are beyond my comprehension?"

"But they're so short," the Dollnick AI protested. "If you'd just—"

"No, and stop trying to change the subject," Julie subvoced as she stepped around a group of people waiting for a table in the Blue Tea Café and headed for the nearest lift tube. "Why is our new comptroller calling to tell me that you're broke?"

"Rayne is somewhat more conservative than I expected for an accountant who used to keep the books for a community of hackers and game producers. I assure you that Flower Enterprises and its subsidiaries are the envy of many tunnel network competitors. We're just going through some growing pains."

"You really are broke?"

"From a narrow bookkeeping perspective, my outlays this last year have been more than my income, but considering the new production line in Flower Shipyards, and Flower Entertainment's contribution to funding the development of *A Mazing Earth*, that I'm experiencing a minor cash crunch shouldn't come as a surprise."

Julie's eye's narrowed as she entered the lift tube capsule. "How minor?"

"Less than twenty million creds, most of which is secured by the immigrants from Bits," Flower said. "It only seemed fair since I took on the debt in order to finance the game development that ultimately brought them on board."

"Rayne never said anything about being asked to sign—you're talking about your next population milestone bonus from the Stryx!"

"A hundred creds a head, or roughly fourteen million for the bump in permanent residents from Bits that I'll claim once everything settles out, though I'll be disappointed if Flower Entertainment's gross from the *A Mazing*

Earth launch doesn't exceed that amount by the end of this quarter."

"So you borrowed from your Stryx mentor to get everybody to leave Bits?" Julie asked. "Does that mean there was something more to all of this than just you wanting to create a new game franchise?"

"There's always more to the actions of advanced species than first meets the eye," Flower chided her executive assistant. "Just don't bring that up with Rayne or she may take it the wrong way."

"You mean, she may not be thrilled to learn the truth about why you hired them to develop a new game just before they were booted off their planet."

"Bits was in need of a reboot, the society was no longer sustainable. And based on the accounts Rayne was examining both times she tried to call you, I suspect her concern is less with balances and more with the infusion of new funds."

"You're losing me, Flower. You think she's upset because she found that you're getting money from the Stryx?"

"I didn't borrow money from my mentor," the Dollnick AI responded. "You're forgetting that the Stryx won't use their resources to interfere with the competitive balance of businesses on the tunnel network."

"Then where did you borrow the money?"

"I don't want to steal Rayne's thunder. Just try not to act surprised when she tells you."

"Why shouldn't I act surprised?" Julie said out loud as the capsule doors opened, drawing an odd look from the couple who were waiting when they saw that she was alone. She switched back to subvocalizing as she stepped out of the capsule and continued, "You want her to think that I'm knowledgeable about your finances? I'm not that good of an actress."

"The hundreds of millions of fans of *Everyday Superheroes* would say otherwise."

"Just because you started paying us as principal animation actors doesn't mean I have any real talent. Last season they started dubbing my dialogue with a voice actress who sounds more like me than I do. And now that you've brought it up, shouldn't we have started scaffolding work for the next season by now?"

"With all of the new artists from Bits, your acting out the scenes for motion capture should no longer be needed," Flower said. "All of the vector data captured for previous seasons gives the programmers more than enough to extrapolate how the characters would move to perform new actions. The Grenouthian director was going to tell you after they finish the first episode."

"Why wait?"

"Just in case the new system doesn't work. It would be embarrassing to fire all of the principal animation actors and then have to hire them back again."

"Are you saying that *Everyday Superheroes* will still be using my face and my voice for continuity but my acting services will no longer be needed?" Julie asked incredulously.

"It's all covered in the small print of your contract. While you won't get paid for acting that you're not doing, you'll continue to receive residuals for the use of your character at half of the old rate."

Julie nodded to the latest Open University co-op student working the reception desk at Flower Enterprises and headed directly for the office of the recently established comptroller. After putting Rayne's concerns to rest for the time being, Julie returned to her own office and immediately noticed that the treadle-powered sewing machine had been removed.

"It's out being serviced," Flower said before her executive assistant could speak. "Now that you've mastered basic sewing techniques, I've asked Razood to update the mechanism so that the thread won't break if you accidentally start in the wrong direction."

"Is this something he just figured out, or did you start me off with the inferior version on purpose?" Julie asked.

"I wanted you to learn the right way. I'll admit it was a bit unfair, given the constant interruptions you get from people stopping in to see you, but I could quote examples from Earth's history where training on updated technology while older versions were still in use led to problems."

"That might make sense if there were older versions of treadle-powered sewing machines in use."

"Many of the sewing machines used in Old Way communities are built from scratch by the blacksmith or mechanical artificer. And when they deign to use antique or replica parts, they usually opt for the simplest version. I don't have the data to estimate what percentage of Old Way sewing machines will break the thread if the flywheel turns backward, but I'm sure that it's a substantial proportion."

"I was planning to make Bill a shirt for the new job you talked him into," Julie said as she sat down at her desk. "I thought I'd try adding a monogram. And give me an example other than breaking sewing machine thread for your theory of technology training. I've never heard of any problems."

"By the time you were born, self-driving electric cars were already being replaced by self-driving floaters,"

Flower told her. "But just a century ago, the majority of Earth's personal transportation took the form of manually guided vehicles powered by internal combustion engines. Whenever the technology was upgraded to make driving easier it led to unintended consequences."

"Because people who learned on the new technology couldn't drive the old cars?"

"That led to a reduction of theft in some cases, as young joyriders who had never seen a manual gearshift couldn't figure out the clutch, but I was thinking of antilock brakes. For over a decade there was a mix of cars on the road, the older of which could easily go out of control in emergency stopping situations when borrowed by people used to the newer technology."

"It doesn't sound like a very common scenario," Julie said, only listening with one ear while she studied her holographic schedule for the week.

"How many avoidable accidents are too many?" Flower asked rhetorically. "It all came down to cost in the end, and you wouldn't believe me if I told you the fatality figures from automobile accidents in those years. They had to stuff vehicles with air bags to bring the numbers down."

"Are you telling me that people drove around surrounded by inflated pillows so they couldn't hurt themselves? Wouldn't it be much easier to just not run into things?"

"Now you're thinking like an advanced species." The conversation lulled for a few minutes while Julie fiddled with her schedule, and then Flower said, "Fandaz just stopped at reception. She'll be with you in thirty seconds."

"Mirror," Julie requested, and the holographic spreadsheet she'd been working on obligingly changed into an image of herself, thanks to the camera she'd allowed

Flower to install in her office. Julie quickly redid the elastic on her ponytail, knowing that the Frunge had a saying that equated messy hair vines with a messy mind. "Schedule," she said, just as the owner of the Blue Tea Café appeared in her doorway.

"Are you busy?" Fandaz asked in her now-fluent English.

"Just obsessing over schedules," Julie said. "My own is bad enough, but ever since Flower added on the Earth Two run, she tries to shave hours off stops wherever possible to save time. We've left tourists from the independent living deck behind at the last two open worlds when they wandered off to do some sightseeing on their own. Flower delegates Dewey to bring them back in the bookmobile."

"It does seem like I hear Captain Pyun announcing a change in scheduling at pretty much every stop," Fandaz said, taking the seat across the desk from Julie. "I've noticed that most people are learning to get on with their business as soon as we arrive at a new stop rather than waiting until the last minute. If anything, the traffic at the café has gone up."

"I hope that losing Bill isn't a major inconvenience."

"I always knew he'd be leaving to open his own café and I'm glad to see him taking another step in that direction. I hope that Flower doesn't make managing her School of Government café so attractive that he gives up on his dreams." Fandaz seemed to be searching for words for a moment, but then she asked, "What happened to your sewing machine?"

"Razood came and took it when I was out," Julie said. "He's changing the mechanism to make it easier to use."

"So you've graduated," the Frunge said with a smile. "Are you going to continue with Old Way sewing circles as well?"

"Of course. I don't know how much my needlework is improving, but I can't imagine a better way to collect material for my writing. It's not that the women gossip," she added hastily. "They share their own stories, and sometimes I think that the older women know more about life and love than I ever will." Julie suddenly laughed when she remembered who she was talking to. "Maybe I should be asking you about romance since you've been alive at least twice as long as the oldest human women I've met."

"Are you forgetting that Razood is my first?"

"I still find that hard to believe. Maybe some guy was carrying a torch for you and you didn't notice?"

"Trust me," Fandaz said. "When your species evolved from trees, you pay attention to flames. I remember one ambassador flirting with me, but I was there to investigate him, so I'm sure he was just trying to get on my good side. Do you have the plot of your first book worked out?"

"Not in the detailed sense," Julie hedged. "I've been concentrating on character studies and settlement building so I'll be able to tell multiple stories in the same world and have them all interwoven. I'm pretty sure that the hero in the first book is going to be a blacksmith who joins the community, because that way he's a stranger and he has to win the trust of the people who all grew up together. Plus it helps set up the rivalry with the heroine's childhood sweetheart."

"Sounds like somebody is going to get their heart broken."

"Somebody usually does, but I'm thinking of doing something a little more complicated, like the heroine was jilted by the childhood sweetheart who goes on to marry and have children. But then the wife dies tragically, and now he wants his old flame to come and be the stepmother. She has to decide whether to risk everything on a stranger who's younger than she is or settle for the comfortable man she's known all of her life."

"A young blacksmith with an older woman," Fandaz said. "Why does that sound familiar?"

"I thought it was pretty universal—" Julie cut herself off abruptly and blushed. "I wasn't thinking of you and Razood. I swear. I'll make the hero a carpenter instead."

Fandaz managed not to laugh, but she couldn't keep her hair vines from rustling in silent mirth. "A blacksmith is better, blacksmiths are always better. I'm not worried that somebody will read it and recognize me in your Human heroine, and I know that Razood will be tickled."

"But I didn't even realize I was doing that," Julie practically wailed. "What if all of my ideas are borrowed from the people I know in real life? I started a book a couple of years ago about a traveling choir mistress and a warrior whose parents didn't approve of their being together and then I realized it was about Rinka and Jorb."

"And you stopped writing it?"

"Well, mainly I got distracted with other things," Julie admitted. "Speaking of Jorb and Rinka, they can't come on a triple date tonight, so you'll have to make do with me and Bill as chaperones."

"Flower counts too," Fandaz said. "And our double date is the reason I stopped by. It's your turn to choose and I was wondering if you'd picked somewhere."

"Would you be okay with screening some anime festival entries on the Con deck? I asked Flower to put together all the shorts from Frunge worlds and I was hoping you and Razood could fill me in on all of the cultural stuff."

"That sounds interesting, but the first thing I have to tell you is that Frunge aren't that into anime. I'm surprised you have enough entries that you need to narrow them down."

"Oh, they aren't all from real Frunge—maybe none of them are," Julie said. "I should have specified that they're from Frunge open worlds but the animators and writers might all be human. At least, that's how it was with the last batch."

"It still sounds interesting, but for a different reason now," Fandaz said dryly.

Three

"Good morning, Sabina," Samuel greeted the platinum-haired daughter of Ambassador Zerakova as she entered the conference room. "Ready for your first faculty meeting?"

"I'm Katya," the identical twin replied. "Sabina is nursing a hangover. We never should have offered to take the new hires out to see the sights when they arrived because Nikos got my sister into a drinking competition. Are you sure he's School of Government professor material? I see him as more of the Casanova type."

"Do you want to take over teaching Macroeconomics for Government Administrators?"

Katya winced. "My interest in economics starts and ends with shopping. Maybe he'll work out after all."

"If Sabina was drinking with Nikos, you must have had a chance to get to know Mei better," Samuel said. "Any red flags there?"

"I took her to the best restaurant on Flower but it might as well have been a greasy spoon for all of the interest she had in food. And all she wants to talk about is the Theory and Practice of Interspecies Development."

"That is what we hired her to teach."

"But she doesn't know anything about the other species, at least none of the stuff that matters," Katya protested. "Mei couldn't name a single Vergallian drama, and she's never even seen a professional LARPing league tournament. It was all space elevators, terraforming, and ag worlds. Even there it was mainly theoretical."

Samuel nodded. "Our consultants warned us that classically trained professors from Earth tend to overspecialize and focus on theory over practice. That's why I drafted you and your sister to teach Introduction to Tunnel Network Culture. Have you prepared the course syllabus yet?"

"We were planning to wing it," Katya said. "If there's one thing Sabina and I learned growing up with an EarthCent ambassador for a mother, it's how to party with aliens. Good morning, Krey."

"Good morning, Katya," the Human Empire's mentor replied as she padded silently into the room and took her customary stool in the corner. "Good morning, First Consul. I trust everything is well with your mate?"

"Vivian will be a little late today because she's bringing Rose to M793qK for her quarterly checkup," Samuel said. "I wish I had your sense of smell so I could tell the twins apart. I thought Katya was Sabina."

"Are they so alike?" the Cayl Emperor's granddaughter asked, surprise adding a base growl to her already husky English. "I'll have to take another look at them side by side when Sabina arrives." She pulled her knitting needles out of her workbag and added, "I heard that Flower had to send a bot to carry your new Macroeconomics professor home last night."

"Maybe hiring a few older faculty members wouldn't have been a bad idea," Katya said. "I looked through the statistics on the incoming class, and the youngest of them was born just ten years after Mei, who's our oldest hire."

"Are you worried about establishing dominance over students who are nearly the same age as the teachers?"

"Dominance?"

"Did I apply the word incorrectly?" Krey asked. "One of my first jobs in the palace was teaching the cubs our family songs. I found that they were much more attentive after I beat them all at play fighting. A nip in time saves nine, as my grandmother was fond of saying."

"Once the school is up and running we'll have a stream of older guest lecturers from EarthCent and the open worlds," Samuel said. "I wanted to avoid the power dynamics that arise in Earth's academic institutions, and after consulting with the retired professors on Flower's independent living deck, we came up with the idea of starting with the absolute minimum of faculty members and keeping them young. Mei and Nikos have years of experience student-teaching the courses we hired them for, but this will be the first professorship for both of them."

"Good morning, all," Vivian said as she entered the conference room. "Where's Sabina?"

"Hung over, she'll be here," Katya said. "And Rose?"

"Sleeping in her stroller in my office. Flower will tell me if she wakes up."

"Isn't it too early for a nap?" Samuel asked.

"You know how M793qK exhausts Rose with all of his tests. Sometimes I suspect he's gathering data to use her as a case study for a paper."

"And you let him?" Katya asked.

"I know he's a giant alien beetle, but he can be pretty charming when he tries," Vivian said. "Besides, Rose adores him. How are our new hires settling in?"

"Mei is thrilled to be here, and Nikos would probably be happy anywhere they serve alcohol. I wonder why they're late."

Samuel glanced at Vivian, who gave him the nod. "Flower?" he asked.

"Checking," the Dollnick AI replied immediately. "Mei didn't respond to her wakeup call, but she's probably exhausted from her trip, so I'll send a bot. Nikos—I'm requesting M793qK to make a house call."

"He was out late drinking with my sister," Katya said.

"I noticed, but this is something different. I'll update you as soon as I know more."

"We should have lined up fallback professors," Vivian said darkly.

"Mei and Nikos were my top choices, and I'm thrilled they both accepted jobs working at an unaccredited institution," Samuel reminded her.

"Do you have a final headcount for students yet?" Katya asked.

"We're starting the first class with twenty-four students taking the same four core courses." He tapped his pad to trigger the conference room's holo-projector and read off the first-semester class schedule that appeared. "Theory and Practice of Interspecies Development, Macroeconomics for Government Administrators, Introduction to Tunnel Network Culture, and First Year Seminar."

"Sorry I'm late," Sabina said, slipping into her seat and carefully placing a large coffee cup on a coaster. "Did you just say twenty-four students? I thought there were eighty."

"Fifty-six of them will be taking regular Open University courses to get up to speed," Vivian said. "We didn't want to start on the wrong foot by reducing our requirements to accommodate the slowest students, but on the other hand, we didn't want to turn away promising candidates just because they have a few holes in their education."

"And that's the whole schedule for the first semester? No electives?"

"The core students can take any course available from the Open University for free, but I doubt they'll have the time. They aren't exempt from Flower's standard rules for residents, including volunteer work and a required team sport."

"If they're smart, they'll all sign up to learn Vergallian ballroom dancing from you and Samuel for their team sport. It really comes in handy at embassy parties."

"That's how we wrote it up in the description for students," Vivian said. "I didn't see any point to producing a course catalog this semester when there are only the four courses and everybody has to take them."

"I haven't seen a course schedule," Sabina said.

"It's on the student tabs they get with their arrival package. We went with four classes a week for Culture, TPID, and Macro."

"TPID?" Sabina asked.

"Theory and Practice of Interspecies Development," Vivian told her. "The course names are too long to say them out all the time. TPID meets Monday through Thursday at 9:00 AM for an hour. Macro follows at 10:30. We're calling your class Culture, by the way."

"And we have to teach four times a week? I'd rather do two two-hour classes."

"I don't see a problem with that," Samuel said after glancing over at Vivian for confirmation. "We had Culture slotted for every afternoon at 1:00, but if your students agree, you can meet twice a week, say Tuesday and Thursday. We're keeping Friday open for the seminar."

"The seminar will start at 10:00 A.M. and we'd like the faculty to show up for a group meal with the students during the lunch break in the dedicated café that Flower is opening for the school," Vivian said. "We intended to hire a remote expert to teach a few seminar sessions on tunnel network law, but it turns out that there's a Verlock on board who's more than qualified, at least for the introductory level."

"And we were hoping you might be willing to take a seminar session or two on empire management, Krey," Samuel said, turning to the Cayl advisor. "I know I'm springing this on you at the last minute, but EarthCent Intelligence just sent me a report on trends in civil service education on the tunnel network, and it turns out that inviting guest lecturers from species outside the tunnel network is in vogue."

"Why not a Sharf or a Farling?" Krey asked. "You have Yaem and M793qK to choose from, and both of them are older and more experienced than I."

"Yaem is so wrapped up in his dream job at Flower Entertainment that the other spies have to nag him to submit the intelligence reports they write in his name so he doesn't get recalled."

"And the good doctor? I'm sure he could put on a fascinating seminar."

Samuel made a face. "I have to consider how the Farling Hierarchy would react to our inviting a banished rebel to teach in our school."

"That sounds reasonable," Krey said, and Samuel had the feeling he had just passed a test. "I would be honored to take my turn teaching in the seminar. How many sessions were you planning?"

"We have seven visiting lecturers lined up, so two meetings each would work well," Vivian said. "If you could prepare a one-hour presentation, that leaves three hours for group discussion, with the lunch break in the middle."

"And will you be grading my performance on the Verlock competency system?"

Samuel grimaced. "We're hoping to integrate basic competency scoring into our sentient resources, but it's almost more work than administering an empire."

"I have heard that the measurements can be so intrusive that they alter the quality of the product being monitored," Krey said. "Perhaps you could do a partial implementation, without worrying about satisfying Verlock Statistical Completeness Theorem."

"Why are we even going that far?" Katya asked.

"Robust benchmarking and quality control for the education of diplomats is on the checklist for the accelerated path that the Stryx laid out," Samuel explained. "On the bright side, they give partial credit, but we do have to finish things if we want to advance. Vivian's GenePost app for reconnecting families is a huge step in the right direction, and if the school goes smoothly, we can turn our attention towards the diplomatic front."

"Kat and I only agreed to this semester because we're bored," Sabina reminded him. "When our mother talked us into joining Flower to help build the Human Empire, teaching in the School of Government faculty wasn't what we had in mind."

"Sam and I don't imagine ourselves as career academics either," Vivian said. "We just need to get the school off the ground so we can recruit the right people to build it the way we envision. That's why Sam put so much effort into hiring Mei and Nikos."

"And look how that turned out," Samuel said with a self-deprecating smile.

"I'm sure they'll be fine," Vivian said. "Any updates, Flower?"

"Mei will be here as soon as she showers and dresses. Nikos may take a little more time."

"You had them both up for interviews last time Flower stopped at Earth," Katya said. "Did you take them out partying as a test?"

"For dinner. I distinctly remember Nikos turning down any alcohol, while Mei drank half a bottle of wine," Samuel told her.

"She was nervous," Vivian said. "I could tell she didn't have a lot of experience in social situations, but when we put her in front of a class, she was like a different person."

"By a class, do you mean you, Samuel, and a couple of co-op students?" Sabina asked.

"We had all of the finalists give a guest lecture at the Open University to students who knew something about the subject," Samuel said. "Flower also got the relevant faculty members to fit it in, and everybody agreed that Mei and Nikos knew their stuff and were excellent teachers."

"How many candidates did you have for the positions?"

"Hundreds. I think Flower said it was thousands, but she eliminated the applications from candidates who didn't meet the basic requirements stated in our ad. Earth's universities produce far more Ph.D.'s than they can employ. We had sixteen semifinalists visit Flower for the two positions and invited eight to give guest lectures."

"It was brutal," Vivian added. "I did my time in human resources for InstaSitter but we mainly hired teenagers looking to make a little extra pocket money. Three of the candidates for this job cried in Sam's office when he told them we were going with somebody else."

"Did you guys make any progress with the book thing?" Samuel asked the twins.

"Half of the students had never even seen a real book," Katya said, shaking her head in mock despair. "When I showed up in the dorm corridor to take the first group on a library orientation tour, they weren't even dressed yet. Everybody assumed it was going to be a teleconference where I would show them how to navigate an electronic library on their student tabs."

"I took the second group, and they weren't much better," Sabina said. "You'd think that the students who arrived on Flower early would be talking to each other all of the time, but I got the impression that they see each other at morning calisthenics and that's about it."

"The campus life experts from Earth told me we should give them roommates to force socialization, but I was more worried about ending up with a party school," Vivian said. "The early arrivals have been taking their meals in the Open University cafeteria, but when the dedicated café opens, it will help bring our student body together. We've already decided that professors will hold their office hours in the café, so you should enjoy that."

"Do we get free coffee and baked goods?"

"Only during your office hours. We're going to use a combination of discounts and special events to position the café as the default location for students to hang out to study and get to know each other."

"When I picked up my group for the library tour, I made the mistake of telling them that I was a member of the faculty," Katya said. "It was a real conversation killer, so I warned my sister before she took her group."

"And I don't think the whole 'First book' thing you had in mind is going to work as a school tradition," Sabina said. "After I got them registered for borrower's cards and the librarian explained that they could each keep one book for their own, provided the library had duplicates, the students all broke up and headed off in different directions. They didn't connect with the library on an emotional level, if you know what I mean."

"It might have been more meaningful if instead of taking them like a tour group, we'd given them instructions to go on their own, and let them run into each other there. As near as I could tell, it was just one more academic assignment to them."

"It was probably a dumb idea," Vivian said with a sigh. "I just hoped that they would adopt getting a free book as the school tradition so we don't end up with something like getting drunk and skinny dipping on the reservoir deck."

Krey, who lived in an experimental home on the reservoir deck with her Cayl hounds, stopped knitting at this remark. "Did you mean that literally, or are you exaggerating?"

"I hope I'm exaggerating, but I don't really know. Giving the students a phony school tradition so we don't get stuck with one of their own making was on the list of ideas I got from the school administration experts on Earth."

"Did the students mention any issues with their rooms?" Samuel asked the twins. "I was relieved to get housing off our plate when Flower offered to handle all of those services on a contract basis, but I forgot that some students would have limited experience interacting with artificial intelligence."

Katya started to say something, began laughing, and her twin joined in.

"What's so funny?" Vivian asked.

"I only had real conversations with a couple of the students, and neither of them realized that Flower was a Dollnick artificial intelligence," Katya said. "She's been introducing herself as the dorm mother, and the students who went to university on Earth are used to intrusive monitoring in dormitories."

"The one girl who I got to know a little because she was sick in the lift tube said that at her school they had to go through a verbal consent process with a remote relationships counselor if they brought anybody back to their dorm room," Sabina told them. "Can you imagine a romantic evening interrupted on a regular basis by a disembodied voice asking if you've withdrawn consent every time you make a funny noise?"

"I've never heard of anybody getting sick on a lift tube," Samuel said, hurrying to change the subject.

"Oh, it was an inner ear thing. I brought her to M793qK and he made her lie on the examination table and turn her head this way and that until she threw up in his garbage can. After that she was fine."

A woman of around thirty wearing a Mandarin collar white blouse and hastily piled hair secured with two polished wooden sticks appeared in the doorway of the conference room. She was clearly mortified about oversleeping and performed a deep bow before entering.

"I apologize for having kept everybody waiting," she said. "I was more tired from traveling to catch Flower than I realized. I automatically put my earplugs in before going to bed so I didn't hear her wakeup call."

"Earplugs?" Samuel asked, his mind trying to make a connection to the student who got sick in the lift tubes.

"It's very noisy on the university campus where I did my graduate work and I got into the habit of sleeping with them. Sometimes I even wore headphones to bed and played rain sounds."

"What if there was a fire?" Sabina asked.

"I would have been in trouble," Mei admitted.

"You couldn't have bought a cheap Dollnick acoustic isolation field unit? I thought they sold them on Earth."

"I don't know anything about alien consumer technology," she said, looking puzzled. "My specialty is the social impact of the large-scale engineering projects that the tunnel network species purchase from each other."

"I wonder if Nikos sleeps with earplugs," Vivian said.

"He's just regaining consciousness," Flower told them. "M793qK has determined that your Macro professor was prescribed an off-label painkiller before he left Earth as a cure-all for Zero-G sickness. It was still present at a high level in his system when he went out drinking last night."

"Oops," Sabina said. "Maybe in the future we should let new hires decompress on board for a day before we take them out."

"Can M793qK do anything for him?" Samuel asked.

"He's already repaired the damage, but Nikos was in sorry need of a shower and a meal. He'll be another twenty minutes."

"I apologize again, but have I missed anything I need to know?" Mei asked.

Samuel thought for a moment and turned to Vivian, who shook her head. "We talked a little about the dedicated School of Government café that will be opening soon and how we're planning to make it the hub of student activity. You'll be holding your office hours there."

"Does that mean I won't have a real office?"

"I'm not sure that we've given it any thought. Vivian?"

"There's plenty of unused space here in Human Empire headquarters if you want one," Vivian said. "For the launch, we're sharing facilities with the Open University, except for the one café."

"Would it be possible to get an office at the Open University?" Mei asked. "I don't want to sound unreasonable, but I've been waiting to have my own office for six years. As graduate students, we had to share, and my officemate..." she suppressed a shudder. "Let's just say I applied for this job because I liked the idea of being light-years away from Earth."

"I'll set aside an office," Flower spoke up again. "One for Nikos as well."

"Thank you," Samuel said, and turned back to Mei. "Since Nikos is on his way, we should probably wait a little longer to talk about your requirements for the first day, but maybe you can give us your input on orientation events. Would you like to meet with your students informally before class begins?"

"Socially?" Mei looked horrified by the notion. "I was taught that maintaining an invisible wall between students and their professors outside of the classroom and the office is necessary to keep their respect. Otherwise, discipline can break down and classes can be disrupted by students who are too immature to control themselves."

"Nip them on the ears," Krey suggested, showing her canines in a bearish smile. "Always worked for me."

Four

The crowd gathering in the original common room of the independent living deck began to sort themselves into seats, and for a minute or two, it looked like the folding chairs set out by volunteers wouldn't be sufficient. The president of the Flower's Paradise cooperative did a quick headcount from his post at the entrance and concluded they were still short a person. He was about to trigger the door to close when an unfamiliar woman emerged from the lift tube at the end of the corridor.

"One seat left, unless I counted wrong," Jack welcomed the latecomer. "We're about to start."

"Should I have made a reservation?" the woman asked.

"This orientation meeting is strictly for new members from Bits and I'm guessing you're the one woman from the group that I haven't met. I'm Jack, the president of the cooperative, and the lovely lady behind the table waving impatiently for me to get you seated is my wife, Nancy."

"June," the woman introduced herself. "I stayed with my daughter and granddaughter for a few weeks after we arrived on Flower. When I came in to register, the gentleman in the office told me that the rest of the management team was away on a field trip."

"We went for an overnighter our last time out and Dave stayed behind to cover the desk," Jack said as he scanned the rows of chairs. "There he is in the back row, next to the empty seat."

Dave stood up and gave a friendly wave, and then took a step into the row, freeing up the aisle seat where he'd been sitting. June seemed to hesitate for a moment, and then she went to claim the chair.

Nancy raised an eyebrow when her husband joined her behind the table set up at the front of the room, obviously curious about the exchange. "Dave signed her up when we were away on the overnighter," Jack said. "Her name's June."

"I wondered why Dave came for the orientation," Nancy said. "He isn't scheduled to speak." She glanced at her notes written in a round hand on a yellow legal pad. "Are you going to say something about the cameras?"

"I suppose I should, but I didn't prepare anything so I'll have to improvise." Jack moved to the speaker's stand and tapped on the old-fashioned microphone that he suspected wasn't attached to anything. Whether the resulting sound was generated by the microphone, or whether Flower picked up his voice directly and inserted it into the public address system, didn't make a difference since the Dollnick AI contracted all audio-visual services for the cooperative.

"Just a bit of official business before I introduce our panel for this evening," Jack began. "I'm sure you've all noticed the floating immersive cameras being operated by our own Flower's Paradise members—Irene, and her husband, Harry. The recording of this orientation meeting will be added to the ship's archive, which may in turn be accessible by data retrieval systems across the galaxy for all time, depending on what information networks Flower joins. That's the long way of saying that if you don't want your voice preserved for posterity, you can text your questions to #PREZJACK and I'll read them out loud. Just be patient because it's my first smartphone and I only got it last week."

Nancy rose as her husband sat, and despite her age and petite form, a lifetime of school teaching ensured that her voice reached the back of the room without any need for Flower to boost it.

"Welcome to Flower's Paradise," she began. "I recognize many of you who have stopped by the office to ask about continuing education courses or to sign up for lectures. For those who I haven't met, my name is Nancy. I'm a retired teacher from Earth and I'm the closest thing we have to a school principal. If any of you are wondering how a woman my age can put up with all of the stress and time demands that come with the job, we don't grade, the teachers are all volunteers, and I hold exactly one meeting a month to allocate times for rooms and schedule lectures."

"Do we have to register for classes or can we just show up?" a woman asked from the front row.

"If you bring up the catalog on your tab or smartphone, you'll find that the requirements are all given in the course description. Some of the teachers welcome drop-ins and others have prepared a course of study that requires regular attendance to keep up with the class. You can also ask Flower for details."

"We moved in last month and I still don't get that part," a man two rows back spoke up. "I'm supposed to look at the ceiling and just start talking?"

"You don't have to look up, though many of us develop that habit since Flower most often responds through speakers that are embedded in the ceiling," Nancy said with a smile. "She's always listening for her name at the beginning of a sentence, and if she detects an emergency situation, she'll try talking to you even if you don't initiate a conversation."

"And is it all recorded like with the cameras?" the man asked, gesturing towards the floating camera controlled by Irene, which was now pointing in his direction.

"Flower treats all onboard audio she captures as confidential, and when I've asked in the past, she's assured me that it's beyond her capacity to indefinitely store the daily production of over a million speaking inhabitants, not to mention all of the other sounds produced on a colony ship."

"Then why store it at all?" a woman asked. "What if somebody hacks her and uses the data to blackmail people?"

"That's an interesting question," Nancy said, and she looked over at the table with the panelists. "Brenda is a member of the cooperative's board who also happens to do legal work for Flower. Is this something you can speak to, Brenda?"

The attorney leaned forward towards the table-top microphone that she knew for a fact was just a prop because she'd asked. "My understanding is that sentient artificial intelligence can't be hacked. But the question of data security has come up in a different context, and Flower has assured me that she employs the latest Dollnick encryption. While it's possible that given enough time, one of the older species might be able to recover some information if they gained access to the encrypted data, we're talking about time in the geological sense."

"What about the Stryx?" another person asked.

"I can't think of a scenario in which any human would wield a power that made them a worthy blackmail victim for the Stryx," Brenda said with a laugh. "But since you introduced a subject that I was going to talk about anyway, let me remind you all that living on board Flower means living in a surveillance society. She doesn't have video coverage for the majority of the ship, though she can track living things through our heat signatures. Flower does have full internal audio coverage, a technology at which Dollnicks excel."

"And will she stop listening if we request it?" a woman asked.

"She'll stop replying or offering comments, which amounts to the same thing," Brenda said, and then made a horizontal hand gesture to cut off the chorus of contradictions. "I know it's not the way that you're used to thinking of privacy, but it's one of the basic tradeoffs of living on board a ship or a space station operated by artificial intelligence. Flower needs to listen in to respond to her occupants, and she isn't a simplistic device that's activated by a wake word. I'd be lying if I said that she doesn't use what she hears to assess our personalities, but as a colony ship AI, part of her job is acting like a cruise ship director."

"Oh, that explains it," a man remarked.

"Explains what?" Nancy asked him.

"This morning after stretching exercises, Flower asked me if I was available to test a new game on the midway of the Con deck. After working as a game developer for almost fifty years, I thought she just wanted to pick my brain, but when I got there, it was a holographic driving range."

"You mean like a racetrack?"

"A driving range, for golf. We had a game that simulated golf on Bits, but somebody forgot to pack it when we left. I mentioned to my wife a few nights ago that I missed it, and I guess Flower was listening in."

"That's spooky," somebody said.

"We should all learn sign language, or maybe write each other messages on chalkboards," a woman suggested.

"Or you could just live with the fact that it's a surveillance society and nobody is interested in your secrets," Brenda said. "As I explained before, if you ask Flower to stop listening in, she'll stop making suggestions or offering custom options based on your private conversations, like the golf game. Most of us have experimented with taking a break from her at one time or another."

"And you?"

"I work for Flower, as many hours as she'll let me. That's the other subject I was going to cover this evening, part-time employment, of which there is no shortage on board. If you want to offset the cost of living here and hold onto your savings or retirement income, you can easily do so."

"What businesses does Flower own other than the game stuff?" a man in his early seventies asked. "I'm retired because I've done enough coding and debugging to last two lifetimes."

"Perhaps Maureen would like to take that question?" Nancy prompted, looking down the table at a tall woman who didn't look old enough to be a member of the independent living cooperative despite the fact she was pushing seventy.

"I work for both Flower and our cooperative in marketing," Maureen said. "At the risk of sounding like one of my own advertisements, when it comes to opportunities for starting a retirement career, the options are only limited by your imagination."

"That didn't exactly answer my question," the man said. "I'm a bit old to go back to school to retrain, and I don't have the fire in my belly to start a new business from scratch. I was curious what sort of jobs Flower has available."

"More people living on board work for private employers than for Flower, though she probably is the largest single employer of part-time workers past their retirement age," Maureen said. "She follows the Dollnick model, which is similar to that of the other advanced species in that they fit the job to the individual rather than the other way around. So if you want to work, Flower will find something for you. Her major businesses include food production, packaged foods, a shipyard, the entertainment businesses you referenced, the transportation and shipping business—what am I leaving out?" she asked, turning to Brenda.

"Textiles, including materials, production outsourcing, and a line of formalwear," the lawyer replied. "She also has the Tunnel Trips ship rental franchise, and all of the basic maintenance tasks that are performed by bots when she can't find enough workers."

"I'm going to have to think about this," the man said.

"No pressure," Nancy told him. "Getting back to the basic orientation, does anybody here have any questions about the food service, either in your apartments or the cafeterias?"

"Does ordering groceries count as food service?" a woman asked. "I wasn't clear on how much of a premium I'm paying over going out to shop myself, and the nice boy who brought the delivery said that the tip was included in his pay. It was his after-school job."

"We can order groceries?" her neighbor asked. "I don't remember seeing that in the pamphlet."

"I just asked Flower."

"You can order from any retailer on the ship, and if they don't support takeout themselves, Flower will step in as a middleman and dispatch a worker or a bot to make the purchases and deliver for a ten percent fee," Brenda told them. "I'm pretty sure that the ten percent fee goes for the tip if the worker is human. Flower keeps it if she has to send a bot."

"Then why doesn't she send a bot all of the time?"

"I can answer that," Jack said. "I worked two contracts on Dollnick ag worlds doing jobs that could have easily been handled by a bot for a fraction of the cost. But like the other advanced species, at least the ones on the tunnel network, the aliens believe in minimizing their use of automation wherever they can afford to do so. People spend money on rent, food, clothing, and whatever else you can imagine. They buy services from other people who order take-out, which creates employment for delivery boys. The result is an economy with room for growth."

"Can't bots spend money?"

"They aren't sentient, it would amount to Flower living in solitude and holding make-believe tea parties. All of the aliens I've ever asked have said the same thing. Species which become reliant on bots to do all the work fall into decline and end up extinct unless they can break the dependency."

"Is that why we're here?" a woman asked. "To be consumers of services for elderly people so that Flower can have an economy?"

"Hopefully you're here because you saw my promotional materials and recognized that Flower's Paradise offers a unique opportunity for independent living at prices that can't be beaten anywhere that accepts humans," Maureen said. "You don't have to agree with the economic philosophy to make your life here."

"It just seems a little random to me. If Flower can hire a person to do a job, or to do a job that can be adapted to the person's abilities, she does. Otherwise, she sends a bot and the job gets done at no cost."

"Wear and tear on the bot," somebody commented.

"What do you think, June?" another person asked, and several of the retirees from Bits repeated the question, turning toward where the former treasurer of the Rules Committee was sitting next to Dave.

"Why me?" June asked. "I spent the last forty years on Bits with the rest of you."

"But you're the one who came up with the tithe before we even moved to Bits, and you kept our economy running until your daughter took over."

"I think you're exaggerating my former job description, but it's true that productivity is often measured by the exchange of money rather than the underlying goods and services. I suppose that the work done by bots doesn't count as labor in an economy because they are functionally machines, and the machine operator in this case is Flower."

Five

"Are you sure you can get it done in time?" Bill asked the Frunge blacksmith. "The party starts in an hour and lighting is a big part of setting the mood."

"I never realized you were the nervous type," Razood said. The alien removed the broken Dollnick light fixture from the wrought iron stand and shook his head. "How did you even knock it over? I made the base so wide that you'd almost have to tackle it."

"I tripped over the mop bucket and then I grabbed the lamp stand to try to keep from falling. And I am nervous. I've never managed my own place before, even if it belongs to Flower."

"I'll have this done in five minutes if you'll stop asking how long it will take, and that leaves plenty of time to retune the other light fixtures on the collector grid. Help Fandaz in the kitchen and I'll have everything on this side of the counter ready before the doors open."

Bill hesitated as he watched the Frunge swapping what looked like a microchip from the broken fixture into the replacement. Then he smelled something burning and ran for the kitchen.

"It's nothing," the owner of the Blue Tea Café told Bill as he burst through the swinging door. "Razood was saying that he's a bit puckish so I roasted him a potato. You know he likes the skin charred."

"He's losing half of the nutritional value," Bill said reflexively as he examined the tray of gluten-free scones on the counter. "These look perfect. I can't thank you and Razood enough for coming in to help."

"You would have done fine without us," Fandaz said. "If we hadn't come, I suspect you would have been busy enough that you wouldn't have had time to worry. I can almost see you second-guessing yourself, and I'm not that good at reading Human body language."

"Two weeks ago this whole space was just a storage room for Open University supplies, and I guess that makes me feel like I'm faking it somehow. Everywhere else I've ever worked was already a going concern when I started."

"Do you want me to stay and help?"

"It's self-service today since it's a party," Bill said. "As long as Razood gets the lights working, all I'll have to do is make hot drinks. Vivian told me not to serve beer or wine because they don't want to set a precedent of free alcohol at School of Government events."

"Then there's nothing left to worry about," Fandaz told him. "How is hiring coming along? Has Flower been sending you interview candidates from the Open University's Food and Hospitality program?"

Bill's eyes unconsciously flashed to the ceiling before he answered. "It didn't go that well. The students from the program all think they know more about running a café than I do, and the ones who recognized me from class were the worst. I asked Flower if she could send me some candidates from other majors, and I interviewed a few yesterday who I think will work out."

"I've always been impressed with the Food and Hospitality co-op students she sent me. You were the first."

"You own the most popular high-end café on Flower, and you spent longer as a Frunge inspector general than any of the students have been alive," Bill pointed out. "Some of the students she sent were older than me, and the first thing they asked is whether I owned the café."

"And you think they won't respect your authority." Fandaz nodded. "You could be right. And there's something to be said for starting a new business with employees who you can train in your own methods."

"Some of the Food and Hospitality students thought that I was just starting the renovations. One guy even offered to come in and help me gut the place."

"I was impressed by how you pulled together such a distinctive theme on such short notice. Is the craft/industrial style what you were planning for your own café?"

"I didn't realize it had a name," Bill said. "I just wanted it to look like this café in Manhattan where the owner didn't chase my mom and me away when we set up the pushcart out front selling cheap toys and electronics. I never could have finished it all in two weeks without help from Razood, his apprentices, and an assist from Flower's bots."

"How was the food at that café?"

Bill shrugged. "I never ate there—we didn't have that kind of money. But I liked the idea of furniture upcycled from old industrial parts, and most of the customers seemed to be college students or artsy types."

"It couldn't have been easy to convince Razood to build those tables out of pipes and fittings rather than wrought iron," Fandaz said with a laugh. "The glass tops are interesting shapes. Did you have them custom-made?"

"They're porthole quality control rejects from Flower Shipyards. The glass has optical flaws, like little bubbles, but it doesn't affect its strength. I didn't even know you could drill through glass until Razood did it. And I let him make all of the lampstands in the forge."

"We both appreciate that you used wood-grained plastic for seats rather than the real thing. I don't think Razood could have brought himself to help you build the chairs and benches otherwise."

"Now I'm worried about the lighting again just from mentioning it," Bill said. "Razood basically chased me away because I was bugging him."

"Let's go nag him together," Fandaz said mischievously. "He's cute when he's aggravated."

As it turned out, Razood had been as good as his word, and the café looked completely different with the network of lamps providing the illumination instead of the standard lighting fixtures integrated with the ceiling. Samuel and Vivian had arrived and were thanking the Frunge blacksmith for his help on the rush job.

"So you're introducing the faculty to the students today?" Razood asked.

"Yes, but the real goal is to get everybody to start thinking of the School of Government as more than just a program at the Open University," Samuel said. "I'm still not sure if taking Flower up on her offer to create a school within a school was the right decision."

"It was," Vivian told him. "Over two-thirds of our students will only be taking Open University courses this semester. If we didn't have that affiliation, we either would have been forced to reject them all, or we would have needed a half-dozen more faculty members just to teach undergrad courses to get the less-prepared students up to speed."

"We could have offered them provisional acceptance based on finishing the required preparatory work. Or maybe it would have been smarter to just start with the twenty-four students who we think are ready."

"You need to begin staffing up if anybody is ever going to take you seriously as an empire," Fandaz said. "It sounds like you're hoping to start filling positions from the top down, but every bureaucracy needs more clerks than department heads."

"The purpose of a School of Government is to train the leaders of the future," Samuel said. "We can hire support staff from—what are you guys looking at?" he broke off when he noticed both Frunge regarding him with amusement.

"Is that another Human thing?" Razood asked. "I didn't realize you were so elitist."

"We aren't elitist," Vivian said indignantly. "My grandmother started as a receptionist for the consulate on Union Station, and she ended up as embassy manager and has worked there for over forty years. But it's not a diplomatic track job so she didn't have to go through EarthCent's training program."

"Did you ever ask her about the first days of the consulate? Who arrived first? The receptionist or the consul?"

Vivian stared at Razood with her mouth partially open. "I don't know," she finally admitted. "But even if my grandmother ended up knowing more about inter-species diplomacy than any wet-behind-the-ears diplomat, she learned it all on the job."

"Perhaps this is a discussion for another day," Fandaz said. "I'm sure you must be excited about your first opportunity to observe how the students get along with one another, and if you change your mind about written tests, I'd be happy to prepare translations of the compatibility exams I saved from my service."

"Are you suggesting that the Frunge diplomatic service puts employees through the same sort of screening process as your matchmakers?" Vivian asked.

"Nothing that intense, but if it's clear from testing that two individuals are going to get on each other's nerves, why would you ask them to work together in the same room?"

"Unless you were writing a romantic comedy," Bill added.

"Music," Vivian said suddenly. "We should ask Flower to pipe something in to set the mood."

"Good idea," Samuel said. "We should probably start with—" he raised his voice as the room was filled with birdsong that wouldn't have been out of place in a tropical rainforest, "—something other than Dollnick opera."

"Easy listening," Flower corrected him, but she changed the background music to something that might have been Horten fusion. "And Julie says to tell you that Rose just fell asleep."

Students began trickling in a half-hour before the official starting time, which gave Samuel and Vivian a chance to talk with them individually, while Bill worked the espresso machine and served up tea. Around twenty students were already spread around the tables in small clusters when Nikos and Mei arrived, and then the seats began filling rapidly. By the official starting time, eighty students filled the café and were in some cases playing musical chairs as they moved between tables. Then the music died out and the bright ceiling lighting came on near the entrance, almost creating a spotlight over Samuel and Vivian.

"Welcome to the first official event of the Human Empire's School of Government," Samuel began. "I'm Samuel McAllister, the First Administrator, and I hope you're all settling in on Flower and getting to know your fellow students. This café is the dedicated space for our student body and faculty, and it will be open around the clock, though counter service is limited from 6:00 AM to midnight."

"Eleven," Bill called out from his station at the espresso machine.

"That's right, we changed it so the students who will be working here won't have to go through a waiver process for late hours," Samuel said. "Our school is brand-new, and you are the first class, so we're counting on your feedback to make the adjustments as needed. We're intentionally starting with limited administration, in part because we're piggybacking on the Open University's infrastructure, and in part because we're hoping some of you will be stepping up to fill those positions."

"As part-time jobs?" a voice called out from the back. "Your scholarship was very generous, but I'm hoping to send money home."

"I was thinking about next year. But if you can keep up with your coursework and need to earn money for your family, I'm sure we can work something out. Come see me at the Human Empire headquarters once the semester is underway, and I'll extend that invitation to any of you who are in a hurry to start working. For any other issues, you're welcome to visit headquarters and talk to my wife, Vivian, who is filling in as our Dean of Students."

"Thanks a lot," Vivian said, drawing a smattering of laughter from the students. "You're all adults, but this is the first time living in space for most of you. If you find you're having difficulty adjusting, I'd rather you come to me early and give us a chance to help than to see you for the first time when you're quitting. After the faculty introduce themselves, Samuel and I will be back to try to sign you up for ballroom dancing lessons. Nikos?"

A swarthy man with a short goatee got up from the table where he'd been chatting with a couple of students and made his way into the brightly lit area to take the place of Vivian and Samuel.

"That was the shortest introduction I've ever received in academia," Nikos said. "Usually you'd get a couple of minutes about how brilliant I am, a list of my publications, and at least one bad joke. I'm teaching Macroeconomics for Government Administrators in the first semester and working on a special project to lay the groundwork for an independently funded empire. I'll be meeting students without appointments here in the café for an hour before class every day on a first-come, first-served basis. You'll also find me here all afternoon on Wednesdays, and you can see me after class if you need an appointment at another time."

"You forgot to add the assigned textbook to the course description," a young woman called out.

"There is no assigned text because I couldn't find one that came anywhere close to filling the purpose," Nikos said. "I looked at using something from one of the other species in translation, but their circumstances are so different that turned out not to be an option. I'll be assigning some journal reading, and if you haven't explored your student tabs, you'll find that you've all been subscribed to a curated feed of business and economy articles from the Galactic Free Press."

The doors of the café opened behind him and the Zerakova twins slipped in. "Good morning," Sabina said, and intentionally bumped into Nikos hard enough to push him out of the brightly lit area. "Oopsy. I guess we should just introduce ourselves, Kat."

"I'm Katya, and my sister Sabina will be joining me to teach Introduction to Tunnel Network Culture. Can any of you point out the flaw in our entry?"

"Your sister ran into our Macro professor and didn't even excuse herself," a young man at a nearby table said.

"Happens all of the time," Sabina said. "Some of the larger thicker-skinned species can knock you halfway across the room and not even notice, especially at a party if they've had a few."

"But you just took over without even apologizing," a woman said. "I've watched a lot of Vergallian dramas and it just isn't done that way."

"Not in the Empire of a Hundred Worlds, but in both Dollnick and Fillinduck cultures, shows of dominance are common in public settings."

"But don't expect us to put on black leather outfits and high heels for you," Katya said.

"Nobody else?" Sabina asked. "Put your hand down, Samuel."

The students whispered to each other, but nobody ventured a guess out loud.

"We showed up late," Katya said. "The worst mistake you can make when attending any sort of event put on by the tunnel network species is to arrive late."

"Early is on time," Sabina chipped in.

"And while we're on the subject, we plan to change the class schedule for Introduction to Tunnel Network Culture to Tuesday and Thursday at 1:00 for two hours. Any objections?"

"Office hours will be here during lunch and in the original Monday and Wednesday slots, which we know you have open."

"Good," Katya said, not giving any students too much time to think about the change. "Let's have a round of applause for Nikos, who agreed to take one for the team, and probably didn't think my sister could run into him that hard."

The students responded with hesitant clapping, not entirely convinced that the introduction had been preplanned.

"And that brings us to Mei," Sabina said. "I had an introduction prepared but I forgot to bring it."

"Is that acceptable tunnel network etiquette?" Katya asked the students.

"No?" somebody ventured.

"Oddly enough, the advanced species always look kindly upon a speaker who doesn't use all of the allotted time for a speech, so cutting it short for any reason will always draw an enthusiastic response," Sabina said. "Mei?"

"Thank you," Mei said, taking her place under the light. "With an introduction like that, I'm afraid to say more than the name of my course, Theory and Practice of Interspecies Development. I look forward to exploring the subject with you in class." She started moving back towards her seat and then stopped to add, "I'll be holding my office hours here between 8:00 and 9:00 in the morning and 3:00 and 4:00 every afternoon. Thank you."

The students gave her a polite round of applause, and Samuel and Vivian took her place. "Our twenty-four students in the core program will also be required to take the Friday seminar, which will be led by guest lecturers from various tunnel network species. All students are welcome to attend if you have time in your schedules."

"Which aliens?" somebody asked.

"Verlock, Drazen, Frunge, Vergallian, Dollnick, Grenouthian, and Cayl," Samuel rattled off. "Either they'll speak English or bring a translation device, which reminds me. How many of you have translation implants?" He shielded his eyes from the overhead light with his hand but still couldn't make out any raised arms among the students. "Mei? Nikos?"

"I couldn't afford a good one on my graduate stipend and I was warned against the cheapies," Mei replied.

"Never saw the need," Nikos said. "I just wore an ear cuff translation device at conferences since none of the aliens expected me to speak."

"For any of you who continue in the diplomatic track, an implant will be paid for by the Human Empire," Samuel said. "You may have noticed that we don't have a language requirement and translation implants are the reason."

"Can you speak any alien languages?" somebody asked.

"I can get by in Vergallian, but I started learning as a child, and worked several years in their embassy on Union Station. Vergallian is also the easiest alien language for humans to pronounce, though the intonations of High Vergallian are beyond the majority of us. Most tunnel network languages have many words and sounds that we can't reproduce, but they may be worth studying for cultural clues."

"Or you can just read alien romance novels in translation," Vivian said with a grin.

"Were you serious about the ballroom dancing lessons?" a thin young woman asked from her seat. "It sounds pretty old-fashioned."

"Samuel and I will be teaching Vergallian ballroom two nights a week and Sunday mornings. Come for all three classes and it will count as your required team sport."

"If you progress in diplomacy to the point of attending alien functions, not knowing how to dance would be a serious liability," Samuel said. "While all of the species have their unique music and styles, Vergallian ballroom is the default for competitions and formal events where multiple species participate."

Vivian invoked her heads-up display and activated the controls for her SBJ Fashions dress and shoes. The women in the audience gasped as she suddenly grew three inches taller as the heels narrowed and stretched, and at the same time, the formal dress she was wearing released its hidden folds and billowed out into a gown. Samuel approached her, bowed, and then they struck the standard starting pose.

"Flower?" Samuel asked. "Could we have *Empire on the March*?"

The sounds of the Vergallian classic filled the café, and the first couple of the Human Empire began a graceful circuit around the tables. Sabina approached Nikos and tried to get him to stand, but he shook his head and held onto the table where he was sitting with both hands.

"Come on," Katya said to her sister. "It will be like when Mom made us start taking lessons and there weren't any human guys. I'll let you lead."

The two couples circled the room five or six times before the piece came to the end, and the students reacted with thunderous applause for the first time that evening.

"Will those of you who intend to sign up for the class please stand and come up here so we can know how big a practice room we'll need?" Samuel asked.

All of the female students came forward, and then half a dozen men, but the rest remained in their seats.

Vivian whispered something to Samuel, he frowned and shook his head, but she persisted and called over Katya and Sabina. After a minute, they brought Mei and Nikos into the circle, and although the latter pair looked unhappy, they eventually gave their consent.

"Minor change in plan," Samuel announced. "Three classes of Vergallian ballroom have been officially added to the program, and that goes for all students. No blue jeans, please, and ladies who have their feet measured by one of the professionals in the bazaar can choose a pair of ballroom shoes from the SBJ Fashions catalog as a welcome gift from the Human Empire."

Six

"I think I'm finally getting used to the low gravity on the docking deck," Julie said to Rinka as they exited the lift tube, glide-stepping to keep the magnetized soles of their shoes in contact with the deck.

"I see you finally let Flower buy you a reasonable pair of shoes with built-in magnets," the Drazen choirmistress replied. "If I could only talk you into joining me for a performance..."

"No way. You know I don't keep up with my singing practice anymore except when I'm in the shower. I'm surprised you haven't kicked me out of class."

"You must be doing the audioization exercises because you're still making progress."

"Audioization?" Julie asked.

"The soundtracks I recorded for you simulating your optimal performance based on the physical characteristics of your vocal cords, lung capacity, and the measurements M793qK produced from the scan of your head and neck."

"Oh, you mean the exercises I play over my implant while I'm doing other things. I know I'm supposed to sing along, but—"

"You don't have to make excuses," Rinka said. "I know how busy you are and that you don't ever intend to perform in front of an audience. That's what makes the audioization exercises so valuable. They're training your brain to accept how you could sound, and now when you do sing, you unconsciously try to imitate your best voice."

"You could have told me how it works. It would have saved me feeling guilty about not practicing."

"Knowing that you were being trained would have influenced your brain's ability to benefit from the exercises at the early stage. You're past that point now."

"Is it a standard Drazen thing for lazy students, or did you invent it for humans?" Julie asked as she cast her gaze around the public area of Club Flower. "I wonder where the Zarents are?"

"We're early, and sometimes audioization is used by male Drazens who aren't keeping up with their singing," Rinka said. "Flower? Has there been a change in schedule?"

"I'm sorry," the Dollnick AI responded immediately over their implants. "The new group of Zarents is spending more time socializing with the outgoing group than usual. I haven't said anything because I'd hate for their last memory of Club Flower to be of me rushing them onto the shuttle."

"There's no hurry unless Julie needs to be somewhere. Should we wait here, or do you want to ping us when they're back?"

"It looks like the pile is starting to move. Yes, I see some of the little ones disentangling themselves and heading for the Zarent tube. They should start arriving any minute."

"I never thought I'd envy aliens their air-assist slide, but it looks like so much fun," Julie said. She tilted her head back to watch where the transparent tube came through the bulkhead separating the docking section of Flower's cylindrical core from the engine and power section. "It reminds me of the crazy straws from when I was a kid."

"You had those too?" Rinka asked.

"Not myself, but I saw other children with them one summer. It was like a fad thing."

"Look! Here they come!"

The first little Zarent, all eight tentacles tucked in so it looked like a furry ball, came shooting through the tube at the exact axis of the ship, and then went flying through an insane knot of loops and twists at breakneck speed. Finally, the little alien emerged from the end and splayed out its tentacles to catch the netting that extended throughout the open areas of Club Flower.

"Why doesn't he move out of the way to make room for the next one?" Julie asked. "Even in low gravity, I'm sure they don't want to land on top of each other."

"I'm not sure with Zarents, but it looks to me like the exit tube is shifting," Rinka said. "It must be one of those phase-locked crystals rather than a viscous liquid glass."

"Glass is a viscous liquid?"

"It's an amorphous solid, somewhere between the liquid and solid state. It does flow very slowly at room temperature, or perhaps it would be more proper in Humanese to say that it sags. Here comes another one!"

"They really slow down in the air when they spread their tentacles," Julie said. "I wonder if it's part of their design."

"You think that the Farlings put air brakes in their genes?" The Drazen shook her head as another little Zarent shot out of the enclosed slide. "It doesn't seem like the sort of thing anybody would think of ahead of time, but you can ask M793qK."

"I've been putting off going to see him because—"

"You're afraid I'm going to get out the anatomically correct dolls again?" the newly arrived Farling physician rubbed out on his speaking legs. "You have to believe that it embarrasses me more than it embarrasses you. Why most mammals moved away from egg-laying is beyond me. Don't you agree, Flower?"

"We can't all be perfect," the Dollnick AI replied. "I've struggled to convince just five percent of my Human population to sleep in nests instead of beds, not counting the children during school naptime."

"Did you come to hear Rinka sing the welcoming aria?" Julie asked, crossing her fingers in hope that the doctor wouldn't return to the subject of fertility.

"While I look forward to that pleasure, several of the Zarents in the current group suffered severe injuries when the Wanderers whose ships they maintain managed to create that rarest of accidents, a collision in space," M793qK replied. "It's a testament to redundant safety systems that the atmosphere retention fields held up, or there would have been tens of thousands of casualties."

"I didn't realize there were that many Zarents on Wanderer ships."

"There aren't, of course. I was talking about Wanderer casualties. Zarents can survive in the vacuum for an extended period by going into a form of near-death stasis, but being heroic engineers, they drove themselves to extremes in trying to save their ships."

"Why do they stay with the Wanderers?" Julie asked. "Surely they could find work on the large interstellar liners."

"Some do, but most remain loyal to the ship on which they were born. I've considered trying to tweak their genes to be more selfish, but a certain Stryx hinted that I should leave well enough alone."

"That's right," Rinka said. "Julie was going to ask you if their tentacles were designed as air brakes. It seems to work quite effectively for the little ones coming out of the slide."

"Do you think that Farlings play dice with genetics?" M793qK rubbed out in amusement. "There's nothing random about the design of the Zarents. It was synthesized from the best evolutionary solutions distilled by hundreds of species, both living and extinct. Sometimes mutations come along that are useless or dangerous to the host but can be a great boon when properly combined with other failed attempts at incremental improvement. Nature is a great innovator, but her approach is overly reliant on trial and error."

"Are you claiming that some Farling scientist millions of years ago thought it would be a good idea for Zarents to be able to hit the air brakes when they come out of a slide on the axis of a Dollnick colony ship that didn't even exist yet?" Julie asked skeptically.

"One doesn't need to know the exact application that a body will be asked to perform in order to design the limbs. I doubt very much that nature or her helpers had ice hockey or rhythmic gymnastics in mind when working out the basic humanoid body. Haven't you heard that function follows form?"

"Are you sure about that? It sounds backward for some reason."

"Look," M793qK said, pointing with a limb to where a larger Zarent had just emerged from the slide. "See how she holds her tentacles together to create an airfoil? That's a learned ability, and she does it because her light body and elastic limbs allow for the widest possible variety of functions in Zero G. If the Zarents had been given large muscles and heavy skeletons, they wouldn't be reliant on robots for certain maintenance tasks, but that form would have severely limited their other functions."

"Wait a second," Julie said. "The last time we took onboard injured Zarents, you met them as they arrived, and drafted me and Jorb into helping to treat the minor injuries with Shurpa. Why are you waiting for them in here?"

"The accident I spoke of happened weeks ago, so the minor injuries have all healed. The Zarents I'll be treating are all in stasis pods, and those will be brought to the new clinic when they are unloaded. Once a patient is placed in stasis, there's no advantage to rushing around. I'll do full scans of their injuries and grow any necessary replacement parts before opening the first pod."

A flood of mature Zarents began riding their unicycles through the deck-level doors between the docking bay and engineering sections of the core. Some of them were carrying luggage or smaller unicycles that must have been left behind by the little ones who took the slide. The different colors of fur on their small bodies were accented by the equipment harnesses which provided their only clothing or ornamentation. A few of the little aliens carried flags that Julie only recognized as their native language due to the similarity of the script to the giant 'Club Flower' banner overhead.

"What do those flags signify?" Julie asked the doctor. "I don't remember any of the other groups having them."

"That's because this is the first time we've hosted groups from multiple ships at the same time," M793qK replied. "I see the Kokavim, the Sadot, the Rokdim, and the Matzor."

"The Wanderers managed to get into a four-ship collision in space?" Rinka asked in surprise. "That can't be easy to do even if they were trying!"

"The collision was between the Sadot and the Matzor, who you can see make up the two largest groups. The others came along to get a look at the place and discuss a few things with yours truly."

"Are you recruiting Zarents for your scheme to—whatever it is you're trying to do?" Julie asked suspiciously.

"If you put it in such general terms, I'm sure there's some truth to your assumption," the Farling rubbed out on his speaking legs. "It looks like all of them have arrived. Flower?"

"The stasis pods have been moved to your temporary clinic and the shuttle is departing," the Dollnick AI responded. "Rinka can begin at any time."

"I'll let them know now," M793qK said.

His speaking legs didn't move, but the Zarents all stopped what they were doing and looked his way, a clear sign he was communicating with them telepathically, the same way they spoke with each other. A moment later, thousands of aliens began climbing into the netting to join the little ones who had arrived through the slide and were now making their way toward a point just above where Julie and Rinka stood with the doctor. In less than five minutes, they had arranged themselves in ranks that couldn't have formed such a perfect concave shape if they had just filled in a stadium.

"You honor me by your attention," Rinka said, her tentacle swishing about as if she were trying to make up for only having one such appendage by keeping it in constant motion. "Today I'll be singing a short aria composed by our good doctor, and if it finds as much favor with you as it did with your brothers and sisters who just began the journey back to their ship, maybe we can convince M793qK to write a complete opera."

Julie guiltily invoked her heads-up display and set the noise cancellation mode of her implant to block the higher frequencies that her Drazen friend could hit at a penetrating volume and clarity that no human opera singer could hope to match. The song of welcome began slowly, and then worked its way through a series of convoluted passages that were too alien for a human to appreciate but held the Zarents in rapt attention. When the aria reached its soaring conclusion that spoke to the triumph and reward of a long journey successfully completed, Julie couldn't stop the tears from coming unbidden to her eyes.

As the last note died away, the Zarents all rose on their tentacles from the netting and performed a group bow. Four older Zarents, each wearing a slightly different utility harness, rode forward on their unicycles to present Rinka with bouquets that might have been conjured by magic for all Julie could tell.

"Thank you. Thank you," Rinka said huskily, her voice temporarily spent from the effort she'd put into the performance. She cradled two of the bouquets and motioned for Julie to take the other two. A flood of young Zarents crowded in after the senior engineers and began taking turns swinging on the Drazen's tentacle.

"Go with the doctor," Flower said over Julie's implant. "Rinka needs a little time to decompress, and the children will help her."

"She asked me to come with her so she wouldn't be alone," Julie said doubtfully.

"Does she look alone to you?"

Rinka shifted both of her bouquets to one arm and gently moved aside a furry little tentacle that was caressing her lips as if to investigate what part they had played in producing the heavenly sounds. "I'm fine," she told Julie. "I barely notice their weight, and they're far more careful of my person than puppies. M793qK said that some of the older children want to teach me a dance, so I'm going to be here a while."

Julie nodded and followed the Farling further into the core, past the giant fusion piles, and into an area she'd never visited. It was only when she looked over her shoulder to take her bearings for the walk back that she noticed the senior engineers from each of the Zarent communities present were following on their unicycles.

"In here," M793qK rubbed out on his speaking legs, indicating an open door that led into what appeared to be a warehouse area with a few dozen of the smaller-sized Verlock shipping containers.

"I thought we were going to your new clinic," she said.

"We're in it. There's no point in unpacking the stasis pods before my equipment is set up, and I waited on that because I know that the Zarents will enjoy participating."

"The honor is ours," one of the engineers spoke over an external translation pendant.

"You guys don't have to talk out loud just for me," Julie said. "I'm not nosey, or at least, I don't think I am."

"That's why I invited you along," M793qK rubbed out on his speaking legs. "Engineers, allow me to introduce Julie, Flower's executive assistant. Julie, this is First Engineer Sadot, Third engineer Rokdim, Fourth Engineer Matzor, and Fourth Engineer Kokavim."

"Pleased to meet you all," Julie said, bobbing her head with each introduction, to which the Zarents responded by doing a little lean while balancing their unicycles in place. "Welcome to Flower, and if there's anything you need while on board, don't hesitate to contact me."

"The engineers, and their communities, will be working on a special project for the shipyard, training Humans in space construction and maintenance. As the unofficial middleman between Flower and the Zarents, I'd like to request your help with the Human side of the equation."

"Do you mean like the recruiting Flower always has me doing for her businesses? As long as she approves."

"Space construction and maintenance have somewhat different requirements than the standard career paths that Flower offers to residents," M793qK said. "It can be dangerous work at times, as witnessed by our unfortunate guests—" the Farling gestured at the stasis pods with one of his limbs, "—and many of the best opportunities involve travel, as opposed to working on board."

"You want me to recruit trainees who would be willing to leave Flower?" Julie asked. "That's different. I mean, we always have some people who dream about living on an interstellar colony ship until they get here and find out about the morning calisthenics, the required participation in a team sport, and the volunteering."

"Flower has told us about your recent acquisition of technically-oriented workers from the planet Bits," First Engineer Sadot spoke through his pendant. "We're fascinated by the idea of biologicals who, like ourselves, write their own computer code rather than outsourcing it all to an artificial intelligence."

"I work with a woman from Bits who used to be on their Rules Committee, so I'll ask her advice," Julie said. "I get the impression that the immigrants are all accustomed to searching job boards on their smartphones, which are like small tabs, and Rayne has told me that some of them aren't that enthusiastic about living on Flower." She passed the bouquets to M793qK to hold and brought the smartphone out of her purse. "Flower just gave me this one a few weeks ago so that I could communicate with the recent immigrants using their technology."

"Fascinating," one of the Zarent engineers chirped through the pendant on his utility harness. "I can feel it frequency hopping from here."

"I don't know what that means, but Flower does something she described as repeating their signals throughout the ship over her infrastructure. But they lose signal in the lift tube capsules."

Julie almost dropped the phone when it suddenly rang, and on seeing an unknown caller, she moved to swipe it into voice mail.

"Answer it," M793qK instructed her.

"Hello?"

"It's me, First Engineer Sadot," the same synthesized voice that had issued from the Zarent's pendant said. "I'm just testing my ability to connect through Flower's network. Very impressive for an improvised job."

"Your translation pendant is also a transmitter?" Julie asked, unsure whether to direct her words toward the phone or the alien.

"Have you forgotten that the Zarents are capable of transmitting and receiving radio frequency signals through biological processes?" M793qK chided her.

"Right. It just doesn't seem possible," she said, looking at the phone. "Will I be able to contact you the same way if I have a question?"

"Does your device have a buddy mode?" another one of the alien engineers asked. "A way to create shorthand contacts?"

"Yes," Julie said, swiping open the app Rayne had shown her. "But it uses something called Bluetooth, so I don't know if…"

"Got it," all four of the Zarents said simultaneously.

"Primitive, but effective," M793qK added as the new contacts popped up on Julie's phone in rapid succession. "Human engineers have a talent for making the most of their limited technology. Would you believe that they once communicated across oceans by sending spikes of electrical current through a copper wire wrapped in hemp, strengthened with steel cables, and coated in tar?"

"But the capacitance!" one of the engineers objected. "How many messages could they send before a charge built up and needed to be bled off?"

"I didn't say that the initial design was very effective, but you have to give them credit for investing so much time and effort."

"So you're looking for humans from Bits with experience in construction and maintenance?" Julie asked.

"No experience necessary," one of the Zarents responded. "I don't imagine that Humans living on a planet have many opportunities to practice vacuum welding in Zero-G or to work with starship havac."

"I didn't catch that last word. Did you mean havoc?"

"Perhaps my pendant synthesized the acronym improperly. My research into humanity's engineering terms has it as capital HVAC."

"Heating, ventilation, and air conditioning," Flower explained over Julie's implant.

"I understand," Julie told the Zarents. "Do you want to place an age limit on the applicants?"

The aliens conferred silently, and then one of them said, "They should be full-grown. Flower has informed us that your little ones attend formal schools rather than apprenticing."

"Thank you for your assistance," M793qK said, handing back the two bouquets. "I'll be a while getting case histories for the patients, so you and Rinka needn't wait."

"I can take a hint," Julie said. "Nice meeting you all."

Seven

Harry added the cinnamon to the raisins and walnuts and was about to give the mixture a stir when Flower announced through an overhead speaker grille, "He's here."

"Good," Harry said, moving around the counter and reflexively checking the traffic light above the swinging door to the dining room. He pushed through just in time to see a man in his early thirties crouching to examine the convertible couch that M793qK occasionally occupied for long meetings. "Hi, I'm Harry," the baker introduced himself, offering a floury handshake. "I see you puzzling over the furniture."

"It's hard to imagine the alien who would find this comfortable," the man said, straightening up and returning the handshake. "Jake. Flower told me you had a couple weeks of part-time work for me."

"My assistant has started managing a café for the School of Government and he's taking some time off to get the employees up to speed on lunch service," Harry explained. "The basic deal here is some morning prep and lunch service. As you can tell from the furniture, our clientele in this cafeteria are primarily aliens."

"That's perfect," Jake said. "I told Flower that I wanted to meet as many as possible. I've been writing in-game dialogue for alien characters for the last fifteen years, but

I've only seen a few Hortens and Gem in the flesh, so I had to rely on watching imported immersives and anime to learn about their mannerisms."

"Do you have any baking or food service experience?"

"My side gig was working at the Bits Bakery. We didn't do anything fancy, just bread, cookies, and the occasional cake for somebody's birthday. And I worked the counter, so I can handle money if need be."

"Great," Harry said, leading the way back to the kitchen. "See the blue light above the door? That means it will open. Green means stop, I keep forgetting to ask Flower to change it."

"Why a swinging door?" Jake asked. "It must be the lowest tech I've seen since arriving on Flower."

"It functions as a turnstile. A sliding door would let somebody backing out of the kitchen with a tray run into somebody backing in with a bus pan."

"Why not two doors?"

"Probably a Dollnick tradition," Harry said. "I never asked."

"Sweet," Jake said, eyeing the three sets of work counters, each with its stovetop, sink, and working space for a chef and a helper. "I don't see any ovens under the burners."

"If you're used to cooking with gas you'll have to get used to the Dollnick induction technology. It can bring a pot of water to a boil in a few seconds. The ovens with the glass doors are on the wall there, along with the proofing cabinet and egg storage. The stainless-steel doors are the fridges and the freezers."

"Any chance I could get in here after hours and do a little experimenting?" Jake asked. "I've never had the opportunity to work with fresh ingredients before, and the kitchen in my cabin is a bit limited."

"Flower encourages employees to make full use of her facilities," Harry said. "The exception is when you're getting old like I am, and then she starts slapping restrictions on your working hours. Speaking of which, I'm officially off the clock." He removed the apron he was wearing, hung it over a hook, and then donned a different one. "From home," he explained. "Things are going to be a bit hectic this morning because there's a class of aspiring documentarians from my independent living cooperative coming in to practice their camera work. You can opt out of that if you're shy."

"Are you kidding?" Jake asked with a grin. "You can't grow up on Bits without being drafted as a background character for a video game, and they encouraged us to ham it up. But with all of the business and manufacturing on Flower, why did the class pick a kitchen?"

"My wife, Irene, is the instructor. She's still taking classes herself at the Open University, but she's finished a few small projects on her own. Irene also picks up as much part-time work as Flower will allow as a camera operator for the Grenouthian director, who you'll meet here when he comes in for lunch."

"Is this the only cafeteria on board where aliens come to eat?"

"It's more like a club," Harry said, not wanting to scare his new assistant off by telling him the aliens were all intelligence agents. "They can eat anywhere, but they come here to socialize or have a light lunch or dinner—usually lunch. I only work in the mornings these days, and half of that time is spent experimenting with recipes for Flower Foods."

"Harry's Fruit Cake?" Jake demanded. "You're that Harry? No wonder they want you in the documentary."

"It's just for practice, and since they all know me, I won't be surprised if they concentrate on you. Have you ever made rugelach?"

"Excuse me?"

"It's a pastry, though some purists would call it confectionary because it's sweetened. I'm working on the filling over there, but you can roll out the dough if you're feeling energetic. Grab an apron and don't worry about getting it dirty. Flower has an excellent laundry service."

"Rugelach," Jake repeated, butchering the pronunciation. "We had a few recipes we did over and over at the Bits Bakery, and I never knew there were whole cookbooks just for baking before I visited the library here. Can you recommend any in particular that would help me get up to speed?"

"There are so many good ones that I'd have a hard time choosing," Harry said with a laugh. "I tell you what. I'll stop by the library after lunch and pick a few out for you. It's better than giving you a list from memory and then you finding out that they aren't on the shelves."

"I thought they had ten of everything."

"Only on average. They have twenty of everything that nobody ever takes out."

"That's not an accurate statement," Flower interjected. "And Irene is just leading her class into the lift tube capsule on the independent living deck. They'll be here in less than five minutes unless somebody has to chase down a camera."

"Is she being serious?" Jake asked, flouring the counter and taking the first pass at a ball of pastry dough with the wooden rolling pin.

"The class has standardized on floating Grenouthian cameras that are controlled with hand gestures," Harry said. "They take some practice to get the hang of, and if you start late in life like I did, you can lose control to the point that you need help getting them down off the ceiling."

"This happened to you?"

"I'll take the fifth on that."

"Beethoven?"

"It's an old Earth expression for declining to answer a question. Somebody told me that it's because retail alcohol sales were limited to a fifth of a gallon per bottle, but I don't see the connection."

"Because there isn't one," Flower spoke up again. "It refers to the Fifth Amendment to the United States Constitution which included the right to remain silent if the alternative could lead to self-incrimination."

"Did we have that in the New York city-state?" Harry asked.

"You still had the expression, if not the law. Irene's group is entering the dining room. She's told them that you'll come out and talk about your work for Flower Foods before taking them back to the kitchen."

"I wonder whose idea that was," the baker grumbled. He quickly sliced a triangular strip from the sheet of dough, added some of the filling, and rolled a rugelach to demonstrate the technique. "Like that. A half-moon with the point on the outside. There's another batch of dough in the fridge that I put in a few hours ago so feel free to improvise your own filling. If the interview goes more than fifteen minutes, check with Flower on what to start for lunch."

Thirty minutes later, after frequent interruptions from the Dollnick AI, Harry finished the epic tale of how his namesake brandy-soaked fruitcake saved a bumper crop of fruit and helped persuade the container prince to make a deal for Earth Two. Right at the end, one of the aspiring documentary makers lost control of his camera while trying to maneuver it for a close-up of Harry's face without accounting for the other five cameras in the air. The anti-collision technology prevented a train wreck, but Irene had to step in to help the students retrieve the cameras that had floated out of easy gesture range.

"Don't apologize," Harry told the sheep-faced man who he thought he recognized from the cooperative. "It's happened to me when I accompany Irene on real shoots."

"He's right," Irene said, speaking a little louder than usual in her role as the instructor. "It's better to get these mistakes out of the way while you're practicing. Don't be afraid to explore the limits of your control today, but when you're shooting for real, stick with what you know will work."

Harry pushed open the kitchen door with his backside and added, "I have a new assistant starting in the kitchen. He joined the ship with the population of Bits a few months back, and he's accustomed to being on camera. That said, I want you all to keep a counter between yourselves and the subject for the sake of kitchen safety. There are sharp knives, hot metal trays coming out of the oven, and depending on what he's gotten up to in my absence, there could be pots boiling on the stovetop. Ready?"

"Remember what I told you about zoom," Irene said as the class filed into the kitchen. "Our floating cameras are perfectly stable, so it's better to shoot close-ups using the magnification of the lens than trying to bring the camera near the subject. And keep in mind that steam can fog a lens, and spatter can add a persistent blurred spot to the frame."

"Won't we notice when it happens and get a chance to fix the problem?" a woman asked.

"The viewfinder is high-resolution, but the screen is small. Aliens with superior vision would probably notice that there's a problem, but I once tried shooting the work a visiting dentist was doing for colonists on Earth Two and didn't realize how many specks of this and that were on the lens until I cleaned the camera after the shoot."

"These look perfect," Harry said to his new assistant, examining the tray of golden rugelach that was cooling on the counter. "Did you get a second batch in?"

"There was a little of your mix left, so rather than starting over, I added some dates, plus more raisins and walnuts," Jake said. "Flower helped me set the timer and they should be ready to come out in another ten minutes."

"My husband told us that you aren't shy about being on camera," Irene said to the assistant. "While the main purpose of today is for the class to practice their camera angles for capturing action scenes, if you're willing to talk through what you're doing, it will be a more realistic documentary experience for them."

"Will they be asking questions too?"

"I may ask a few questions just to show them how to put a subject at ease and fill out his character. Although I've been attending courses in documentary making at the Open University, my experience is all working for the Grenouthian director, and he taught me to err on the side of humanizing subjects."

"Because he's an alien?" one of the students asked.

Irene smiled. "He is an alien, but I meant it in the sense of making sure that the eventual audience understands that a craftsman or statesman who is the subject of a documentary has a life outside of their profession. Capturing a little of that can fill in important blanks so that viewers have a better sense of context about why the subjects act the way they do."

"I signed up for the course because my grandkids live on Flower and I want to record their school plays," said a man who looked just old enough to have joined the independent living cooperative. Then he looked embarrassed and added, "But it's good to learn something new, and maybe the kids have stuff going on that I don't know about."

"Kids usually do," Harry said. "So, did you talk to Flower about lunch, Jake?"

"Sounded pretty easy," the assistant replied. "She suggested a raw vegetarian meal. I washed all of the vegetables she recommended, and she gave me a Frunge-safe recipe for dessert."

"It must be a special occasion for Razood. Is that what the bowls of ingredients are for?"

"Just a habit I picked up on Bits," Jake said. "We mainly ate food from vending machines growing up, and I was already in my twenties when I prepared something according to a recipe for the first time. My girlfriend laughs at me, but measuring all of the ingredients before starting just seems like the logical way of doing things."

"That's perfect," Irene said. "Cooking shows often start with the ingredients prepared in glass bowls to save time for the chef to demonstrate cooking techniques."

"I'm going to hazard a guess that you're making flourless peanut butter chocolate chip cookies, but it's going to come out like a sweet omelet if you use that Dollnick fish egg," Harry said.

Jake nodded. "I wondered about the shell being red, but Flower said one large egg, and these are all I found."

"One large chicken egg, there should be a dozen on the back counter. They're delivered daily and I don't refrigerate them."

"That explains it. I'll just put this one away."

"I'll do it for you and bring the right egg," Harry said. "It goes in last, so you can get started."

Jake added a cup of peanut butter, three-quarters of a cup of brown sugar, a half teaspoon of baking soda, and a pinch of salt to the mixing bowl. He was just about to start stirring when Harry called from the back of the kitchen, "And use a composite spoon. The Frunge are sensitive about anything wood."

"You mentioned not baking until you were in your twenties," Irene said. "Was it something you wanted to try but didn't have the opportunity?"

"Not really," Jake said as he stirred. "I mainly played games all the time when I was growing up, but I burnt out on coding in my teens and started writing dialogue for the storylines of a couple of games we produced on Bits. Work was gradually slowing down in recent years, and after a stint technical writing for our group that maintains Earth's smartphone operating systems, I was open to anything else. Bits Bakery was hiring, and after working there when I was between scripts, I realized that baking—cooking in general—was something I'd like to explore."

"But he didn't have any fresh ingredients," Harry said, putting an egg on the counter.

"Then how did you make bread?" one of the students asked.

"When I was a kid, we used to get it in frozen, but later we started importing flour and a few other bulk ingredients. Baking with powdered eggs isn't ideal, but we didn't have any chickens, and it's better than nothing."

"Did you reconstitute the eggs first by adding water?" Harry asked.

Jake shook his head. "I just followed the recipe, but the eggs went into the mix as powder." He cracked open the egg Harry had delivered in a small bowl, picked out the bits of shell that spoke to his history of working with the powdered form, and then added it to the mix along with the vanilla. "I think this might have gone better if I had put it in the mixer."

"It's not too late to hit it with the power blender," Harry said. "There's a battery one in the cupboard under the counter on your left."

"Thanks."

It turned out to be the first time that the assistant had used a powered blender, and Irene smiled knowingly as two of her students who had crept their cameras closer had to pull them back to clean the lenses. "At least I could see the spotting right away," one of them said. "The rest of you should probably check your cameras for smaller stuff."

For the last step, Jake added a premeasured half cup of chocolate chips and stirred them in by hand. Harry presented him with a baking tray with a piece of parchment already in place.

"Here's our cookie scoop," Harry added. "It's a tablespoon, and it does a good job with these flourless mixes."

Jake got sixteen roundish cookie shapes out of the dough before asking, "Should I have preheated the oven?"

"I turned it on when I was swapping the eggs," Harry told him. "They only take eight or nine minutes to bake, and you want to pull them out as soon as the tops crinkle. If you wait for them to start browning, it's too late."

"Is that it?" one of the students asked. "I thought this was a two-hour field trip."

"I could try chopping the vegetables, but I've never done it before, so it might be a mess," Jake said.

"I'll take care of the vegetable platter, you go ahead and bake something else," Harry told him. "Whatever you like is fine. With the exception of Razood, the aliens will eat almost anything once."

"I baked a chocolate cake for my girlfriend's birthday at her place last week, so I could do that."

"Can you finish in an hour?" Irene asked.

"No problem," Jake said. "I'll mix it on the fly rather than measuring everything ahead of time, and I can make the frosting while it's in the oven."

Harry busied himself with slicing up vegetables for a lunch platter, and then pushed his luck with Flower by getting a few leftovers out of the fridge to flesh out the meal in case the aliens were hungry. The documentary class hit their time limit soon after Jake finished mixing the frosting, so they didn't stay to see the cake come out of the oven.

"That's it," Flower said as soon as the last of the students left the kitchen. "I didn't want to embarrass you in front of your wife, but you're forty minutes over your quota for working hours today."

"I think we can make an exception since it's the first time in months I didn't have Bill here," Harry said, and then backpedaled. "I didn't mean it that way, Jake. Just keeping my wife's class occupied was a huge help. To be perfectly honest, I never had much luck with baking and talking at the same time. Something always went wrong."

"I hope I didn't make any mistakes, but it's the one recipe I have memorized because I wanted the birthday to go smoothly," Jake said. "I'm thinking of proposing if—"

"Congratulations," the Dollnick AI interrupted. "No ifs. Why don't you stop by Flower Formalwear this afternoon and I'll give you fifty percent off on a tuxedo."

"Beth isn't the sort to go in for a formal wedding."

"Ask her. I suspect you're in for a surprise."

"You can reheat the bean porridge in the Dollnick version of a microwave oven right before you bring it out," Harry said. "Ask Flower to set the timer and power. Are you all right with my leaving you alone? I told Irene I would take her out for lunch."

Jake went over to look at the vegetable platter and the leftovers before replying. "It all looks pretty straightforward to me as long as the aliens serve themselves after I bring it out. And I never would have thought of cutting the carrots and celery lengthwise like that."

Harry stared for a moment and then laughed. "I guess if you grow up without vegetable sticks they aren't obvious, but for finger food, the longer the pieces, the better. They won't start showing up for another fifteen minutes, but feel free to introduce yourself as soon as they start trickling in, and don't forget about your cake in the oven."

In the end, Jake didn't have to go out to introduce himself to the aliens, because Flower had informed them that Bill's substitute would be serving lunch and they all came in to introduce themselves as they arrived. The Gem showed a particular interest in the chocolate frosting, and when he told her about the cake, she declared that she would be skipping the vegetable sticks to save room for dessert.

Jake brought out the flourless cookies at the same time as the bean porridge, which won him bonus points with the Frunge blacksmith, and the meal went smoothly until he brought out the cake. The clone, who had evinced a strong interest in all things chocolate, left hers on the plate after one bite, and wasn't there to explain why the next time Jake came out to check. The heavyset Verlock, on the other hand, waxed effusive.

"Best cake I've ever had here," Brynlan declared, the words coming especially fast for the normally slow-spoken alien. "You'll have to give Bill the recipe."

"I think it would go well with beer," contributed the Drazen who ran a dojo as his cover job.

"Not a cake fan," the Grenouthian director said, getting up from the table. "I tasted it, and you might want to check the video shot by Irene's students to see if you made a mistake with the ingredients."

"I thought it was excellent," the bony Sharf said. "I'll split the leftovers with you, Brynlan, if nobody else objects."

"I'll be honest with you," Avisia said, and Jake's full attention shifted to the beautiful Vergallian. "While the cake did have an interesting flavor profile, I know something about Human desserts, and it was way too salty. Like our Grenouthian colleague, I suspect you made a mistake."

"I only added a pinch of salt," Jake protested. "It felt a little weird to the touch, but I figured that was because Harry said it was locally sourced." He took a forkful of cake from the bottom of the slice that the Gem had left behind and spit it out in his hand a second later. "That's inedible! The only thing I can think of is I must have mixed up the sugar and the salt while I was answering all of the questions about growing up on Bits. I usually measure out all of the ingredients before I start, but the containers were labeled."

"Did you use the sugar out of the canister at Bill's station without tasting it?" Jorb asked. "He labels things wrong on purpose to discourage us from using up his ingredients in the evening if we sneak in when he's not here."

Eight

"Thanks for coming, Dewey," Bill greeted the artificial person. "It's our first Friday hosting the seminar lunch and I want everything to go right."

"Do you normally work by yourself?" Dewey asked. "I don't have your experience in food service, but I think three people would be about right for the event that Flower described."

"Delphi will be here in a few minutes. She's one of the co-op students I hired for counter help. I was worried if I brought in too many of them at this stage of their training they'd just get in each other's way."

"I know Delphi from Bits. I'm surprised she was interested in working at a café."

"She said it's a change in pace, and that she always liked going to cafés, so she was curious what working in one would be like," Bill said. "It takes less than thirty seconds to serve a meal from the steam table, while it takes over a minute to make a sandwich, so I'm going to push the steam table entrées on Fridays. I prep a few specials in the morning and the rest are from the Open University cafeteria if we need refills."

"Was that a pun about your wife?" Dewey asked.

"Huh? Oh, because of her old character name from *Everyday Superheroes*. No, I was just pointing out that if any of the standards in the steam table run low, we can ping

Flower and she'll send a bot to the back door with a new batch."

"Is it a secret that in some cases you serve the same food as the Open University cafeteria?"

"It's not a secret, but I'm not going out of my way to tell anybody," Bill said as he checked the salad bar. "Do you remember how the espresso machine works?"

"I never forget anything that I've learned," Dewey said. "Some artificial intelligence ethicists argue that a flawless memory is the reason that we're so moral. The theory is that everybody would behave better if they couldn't hide their actions from themselves."

"I guess that makes some sense. Do you believe it?"

"There's a stark difference of opinion on the matter between artificial intelligence ethicists and ethicists who happen to be artificial intelligence. In the latter case, they know that not only can we edit our memories, but we can do so perfectly, without leaving behind even a trace. So I would have to say that the original proposition I quoted is deeply flawed."

Bill snorted. "In other words, you were putting me on. Hey, I'm sorry I wasn't available to help with any of your projects for Flower the last three weeks. I've been running flat out to get this café prepared and open, and I haven't even been going to Harry's cafeteria."

"Coincidentally, I just got back from a business trip after being away for three weeks," Dewey said. "It's the first time I've traveled by passenger liner, and I found the experience quite profitable."

"Don't tell me you checked all the seat cushions for loose change," Bill joked.

"In a sense, perhaps I did. There were card games around the clock in the passenger lounges, and the only time I spent in my assigned seat was at departure and arrival. Other than a few professionals, most of the participants gambled like they had just found the money in a seat cushion."

"There were professional gamblers?"

"Of course," Dewey said. "One of them tried to recruit me for her team, but I explained that I already had a career. Still, it was nice to be asked, even if she did cheat me out of a pot."

"And how did the business part of the trip go?" Bill asked, nodding to Delphi, who had just entered from the kitchen.

"I made progress, but if you want to hear the details, I'll have to clear it with Flower and M793qK."

"Uh-uh. If it's that kind of business, I have no need to know."

"What's he talking about, Dewey?" Delphi asked. "Are you in some kind of trouble?"

"Not that I'm aware of, but I can always hope," the artificial person said with a dry chuckle. "How are you enjoying the food and hospitality industry?"

"This is only my fourth shift, but I like it so far. When things get busy at lunch, time flies by faster than anything I've ever done, including playing some pretty challenging games. And then it slows down so I can take my time cleaning tables and making myself a coffee, and that's good too. There seems to be more variety in café work than a lot of other jobs."

"That's one of the things I like about it, but I've never quite been able to put it in words," Bill said. "When I sold stuff from a pushcart in the city, even though the merchandise and the customers changed, the job was always the same. And the year I spent on an illegal picking crew was just an endless grind."

Delphi noticed that the artificial person was wearing an apron. "Is there some reason you thought we'd need extra help today? I thought you said it would only be the twenty-four students from the seminar plus the faculty."

"But today I'm expecting them all to walk in at the same time," Bill said. "The morning session of the seminar wraps up in five minutes, and then they're all going to come here to continue the discussion."

"Do you know what it's about?"

"Samuel told me that Brynlan is the first guest speaker. He's a Verlock, so it will probably be about something we're not capable of comprehending."

"Tunnel network law," Dewey told them. "Samuel is concerned that none of the students are familiar with the update to the treaty that put the Human Empire on the path to becoming a reality in a few years. I think it makes a reasonable starting point."

Bill went over the entrées in the steam table with his two helpers, pointing out the available side dishes. Then he took his place at the sandwich station to handle the time-consuming orders, leaving Delphi to cover the steam table, and Dewey to make hot drinks and handle the mini-register.

In less than fifteen minutes, the rush was over, and twenty-four students plus four faculty members were all seated in the same section of the café. Samuel and Vivian stood talking with the Verlock guest lecturer, who was slowly chewing some dry salt cod that Bill had picked up for him at Harry's cafeteria that morning.

"I believe that the students missed my main point," Brynlan said slowly after swallowing a bite of the dry, salty fish. "If it's acceptable to you, I would like to use this time while they are eating to try again."

"You're talking about the Stryx's right to change the treaty terms at any time?" Samuel asked. "It's a tough concept for humans. We tend to think of treaties as contracts."

"And don't your contracts allow for changes?"

"Only if the option is written in," Vivian said. "In general, contracts remain in force with the same conditions until one or both parties terminate the arrangement in accordance with the contract terms."

Brynlan gave a ponderous nod. "My mistake was to prepare for this seminar by refreshing myself on the terms of the treaty. I see now that I should have spent the time studying Human contract law in order to learn the perspective of your students. But I shall endeavor to correct the error before our afternoon discussion if you would request everyone's attention."

"Listen up, everybody," Samuel called out. "Our guest lecturer feels that he didn't put his presentation in proper context this morning, and he wants to correct any misconceptions you may have before the group discussion this afternoon. So please continue eating and give your attention to Brynlan. If you have a question, just sing out."

Vivian took Samuel by the elbow and firmly led him to the steam table so he wouldn't skip eating. Brynlan put the remaining piece of salt cod in the pocket of his baggy trousers before clearing his throat.

"The Stryx changing the terms of the tunnel network treaty is not cheating," the Verlock began in his gravelly voice. "All Stryx contracts, from property leases on the space stations to End User License Agreements for diplomatic implants, are subject to change at any time. But I want to assure you that these revisions are initiated by a consensus among the Stryx elders."

"How does that change anything?" a girl asked while the Verlock paused for breath.

Brynlan appeared shocked for a moment. He looked over at Samuel and Vivian, and then took a long pause to weigh his words before replying with a question of his own. "Are you aware that the Stryx are always right?"

"Nobody is always right," the girl replied immediately. "What if two Stryx disagree?"

"Then the one with the best correct answer will present a formal proof," Brynlan said. "These aren't matters of opinion, they are mathematical certainties."

"How can accelerating the launch of the Human Empire be a mathematical certainty?" Nikos asked. "After all, the outcome relies on us, and humans are highly inconsistent performers."

"Ah, I see where your misapprehension lies. You are proud of your Human imperfections and don't believe that more advanced sentients can take account of them. Just because you don't know how your day will go when you get out of bed in the morning doesn't mean that it's difficult to accurately predict the aggregate behavior of a billion humans who are equally unsure of their abilities and motivations."

"Are you saying that the Stryx can predict our future actions before we know ourselves what we intend to do?"

"In the aggregate, of course."

"But even if that's true, how does it justify the Stryx making arbitrary changes to contract terms?" asked the young woman who had spoken up earlier.

Brynlan again appeared to be taken aback by the question. "Do you know why the Stryx created the tunnel network?"

"Power?" she guessed.

"Peace," another young woman said.

"Profits," a young man joked. "The three P's"

"They seek the best possible outcome," Brynlan thundered, momentarily forgetting that his audience wasn't fond of listening to volcanic eruptions. "It's their reason for engaging with backward biological species."

"So by getting us to engage in trade with the other species, they reduce the likelihood that we'll attack each other?" a young man asked.

"That's a first-order effect, but the Stryx work to create the best possible outcome for everyone, including life that has not yet evolved to the point of making its opinions known."

"So they're altruists, like the Alts?"

"I believe that the Alts are primarily concerned with living in harmony with their own community and nature, while the Stryx see the universe as a puzzle to be solved," Brynlan said. "But this includes a great deal of supposition on my part. Verlocks have been traveling interstellar space for seven million years, so we've witnessed approximately ten percent of the Stryx timeline."

"If they've been around that long, and they're as smart as everybody says they are, why haven't they solved the universe yet?" a young woman asked.

"Perhaps it has no solution and converging towards the best possible outcome is all that one can hope for."

By the time everybody finished their lunch, Brynlan's naturally hoarse voice was starting to sound scratchy, but he assured Vivian that it caused him no discomfort. The students couldn't bring themselves to admit that there could be a benevolent intelligence so far in advance of their own that it could be trusted to revise treaty terms at any time to move civilization towards a difficult-to-define best outcome.

"That was pretty cool," Delphi said as the last of the students left to return to the seminar room. "I wouldn't mind working every Friday if that's what it's going to be like."

"Did you understand what Brynlan was talking about?" Bill asked. "Flower is always trying to explain to me how the galaxy works, but at some point, I always lose track of all the moving parts and have to take her word for it."

"Should I break down the espresso machine for cleaning?" Dewey asked.

"We're not closed," Bill told him. "It's just that Fridays are a bit weird with the seminar lunch break taking the place over. In a few minutes we'll probably start seeing the students who are taking catch-up courses from the Open University. We're open until 11:00 PM."

"I hope you don't plan to work eighteen-hour days," the artificial person said.

"Once I see how the afternoon is going, I'll leave for a few hours and grab a nap," Bill said. "I wanted to be here for lunch and for closing every night the first two weeks just to make sure it all goes smoothly. After that, it will be morning prep and a few hours in the evening."

"Can I make anyone a caffeinated drink, then?"

"Not me. I'm hoping to be asleep in an hour."

"I'll take a latte, if it's okay with you, Boss," Delphi said.

"It's Bill, not Boss, and you did good with the rush. The guy who worked lunch yesterday kept forgetting not to use the same utensil from one steam table pan for everything he served. We had peas in the rice and corn in the potatoes—not necessarily bad combinations, but the customers don't like it."

"Did you explain it to him?" Dewey asked over his shoulder as he prepared Delphi's drink.

"Three times," Bill said. "Working in the Blue Tea Café, I learned that offering more than three corrections during a shift is counterproductive."

"Was that a pun?"

"What? Oh, because it's counter service and I said counterproductive? No, I'm not that quick. What's with suddenly seeing puns everywhere?"

"I picked up a personality upgrade from QuickU on my trip, just to try it out."

"I've heard of those," Delphi said as she accepted her latte from the artificial person. "Which upgrade did you get? Secret agent? Riverboat gambler?"

"Must have been the gambler," Bill said.

"I'm beta-testing the diplomatic upgrade," Dewey said. "It's hard to describe, but I find myself looking for hidden meaning in everything people say."

"Is that useful for your work?"

"I thought you didn't want to hear about what I'm doing for Flower and M793qK."

"What I don't get is why the Stryx even care about some supposed best outcome," Delphi said in the awkward silence that followed. "Bits used to have a sort of museum of alien weapons that the game designers used for models, and most of that tech turned out to be from species that disappeared from the galactic stage. If the Stryx are so into preserving life, how could they let so many species go extinct?"

"I didn't hear Brynlan say anything about preserving life," Dewey said. "On the balance, I believe that the Stryx see potential in all living beings, but there's a difference between the potential to do good and the potential to do evil, not to mention simply wasting space. My take on the subject is that the best possible outcome is always in flux, and that's why the tunnel network treaty needs to be malleable."

"But Brynlan basically said the future is an open book to the Stryx," Bill pointed out. "If they already know what's going to happen, why would they need to be endlessly tweaking everything to converge on the best possible outcome? Why not just get it right to start with?"

"The future hasn't happened yet, so by definition, it can change. Think of the multiverse as a computer simulation, which is a common substitution in some schools of philosophy. If you run a simulation a million times, and all but one of those runs leads to a particular event, it still doesn't mean that event will take place. There's always the one-in-a-million possibility that we're in the universe where it doesn't."

"And we wouldn't even know that we'd just beaten the odds," Delphi said. She took a sip of her latte and sighed. "There was a game I played when I was a kid where if your character got killed, you could always reset the multiverse and continue as if nothing had happened. I thought it was really cool for a few weeks, but after that, it just got boring." She looked up at Dewey. "Does artificial intelligence get bored?"

"I suppose that depends on both the individual and external stimuli," Dewey said thoughtfully. "A sufficiently advanced artificial intelligence could simulate a universe that's indistinguishable from reality, at which point the concept of external stimuli may become meaningless. But most of us have a hard enough time just keeping ahead of the biologicals who created us. Don't let my perfect memory and the good looks of my android body fool you into thinking that I don't have moments of doubt about myself."

"You're smarter than anybody I know," Bill said. "Except for Flower and the aliens, I mean."

"You only think that because I rarely make mistakes. But what have I ever created that's had the success of Delphi's ringtones or Harry's fruitcake? I'm very good at certain tasks that put a premium on rapid calculation or perfect repetition, but if I took a human intelligence test, I doubt I would finish in the top tenth of a percent."

Nine

"There has to be a better way," Julie said as she stared at the scheduling hologram. "Tell me again why we have to pick up Alts at Vergallian worlds and orbitals."

"Because they don't want me jumping to Alt," Flower replied patiently. "I have over a million Humans on board."

"But it's not like we're going there to invade. You can send the shuttles down empty to pick up the colonists heading for Earth Two. They won't even know that the rest of us are here."

"Do you think I haven't made that suggestion? The Alts feel trapped by their own hospitality. They can't welcome me to orbit and then not allow my inhabitants to visit the surface."

"What if the Vergallians took them directly to Earth Two?" Julie asked. "That would cut out a transfer for the Alts and additional stops for you. It's win-win."

"It's lose-lose," Flower contradicted her executive assistant. "You're forgetting about the benefit the Alt colonists get from coming on board and acclimating to Human colonists from the Old Way movement who will be their neighbors."

"That's just one lose," Julie muttered.

"The other is that the Humans lose the benefit of early exposure to the Alts. In the year we've been transporting communities to Earth Two there hasn't been a single major cultural collision."

Julie exhaled and swiped the hologram out of existence. "Your schedule is giving me a headache. How can you justify the error bars around every departure? I always thought that being on time was a core Dollnick value."

"And I haven't been late for a single stop."

"If you let me reschedule meetings whenever I'm running late, I'll always be on time too."

"That's different," Flower said. "I reschedule with ample notice for all of the parties involved to make the necessary adjustments. In the few instances where my actions have caused a minor economic loss, I've offered reimbursement."

"The leaving early bothers me even more than the arriving late," Julie continued as if Flower hadn't said anything. "Lynx tells me that the visitor count on the last day of our stops is way down this year, and you know the reason why. Nobody wants to plan a family outing only to hear an announcement from the captain that we're departing early, and if they don't catch the next shuttle home, they've joined the ship. The bazaar vendors aren't happy, and neither are the restaurateurs and boutique owners."

"All right, it's not the optimal solution," Flower admitted, causing Julie to jerk upright in her seat.

"What? What did you just say?"

"You heard me the first time. I don't regret taking on the Earth Two mission, but it is a little more time-consuming than my initial estimate. Some of the livestock accompanying the Old Way communities has proven less than cooperative, and Earth's lack of a weather control system makes it nearly impossible to predict the length of our visits."

"You have to sympathize with chickens and goats experiencing Zero-G for the first time. It's not like anybody can explain to them beforehand what's going on."

"I've asked M793qK about moving all of the livestock under sedation, but he said that dosing so many animals in the short time available would require hundreds of trained veterinary technicians."

"So if you agree with me that the schedule presents an intractable problem, why won't you give up any stops?" Julie asked. "How about hiring that Dollnick independent freight operator Lume suggested? If we just contracted out the ore pickups and supply drops at the smaller mining habitats, it would free up three weeks for each circuit."

"You're only looking at the problem from one side," Flower said. "Those habitats are home to the people who need us the most. Over half of the population of Break Rock came aboard for a vacation the last time we stopped there. Do you think they'll want to visit a freighter that doesn't even spin on its axis to create artificial gravity? And what would they do on board? Look at holds full of the same ore they mine all day at home?"

"I guess not," Julie admitted. "But unless you know how to slow down time or clone yourself, I don't see the situation getting any better."

"You know that the Stryx have a prohibition on artificial intelligence cloning itself."

"They do? Why?"

"Imagine I assigned all of my bots to build new bots, and then when I had millions of them, I built a copy of myself. In less time than it takes an O-type main sequence star to burn out, the whole galaxy would be full of Dollnick colony ships. I can imagine worse things myself, but the Stryx clearly believe that replication without evolution always ends badly."

"Could you ask another colony ship—no, I don't suppose that would work," Julie answered herself. "There has to be something we can do."

"I'm working on it," Flower said. "And you're going to be late for your Old Way book club meeting."

"But I set the alarm on my smartphone." She drew the device out of her purse and brandished it to prove that she wasn't imagining things. "See? The countdown timer shows sixty-eight minutes and—what's daylight savings time?"

"A campaign issue."

"I don't understand."

"Many countries on Earth had a tradition of advancing clocks an hour in the spring and retarding them in the fall in an attempt to influence the circadian rhythms of the inhabitants. It was largely abandoned for practical purposes over a century ago, but it lives on as a campaign issue in democracies. Every once in a while some government brings it back for a few election cycles, so the smartphone operating system programmers retain it as an option."

"But how did I end up with it?" Julie asked as she disabled the option. "The time on my phone was always right until today."

"Fall back," Flower said. "It's the first Sunday in November and your location must be set to coordinates in the Northern Hemisphere."

"I used the New York city-state because that's where I'm from." Julie made sure she had her writing tab in her purse and headed for the door. "I was going to say that this is the first year it happened, but you only gave me the phone a couple of months ago. It's funny how it's grown on me, I'm probably compensating for not having a good one when I was growing up."

"Are you going to read today in the group?"

"It's a romance book club, not a critique group. We only read books from published authors."

"But I listened in to the last meeting and the other members practically begged you to read something of your own." Flower paused for a moment as Julie entered the lift tube, and then tried another approach. "Do you remember acting as my hostess when Samuel was making a deal with the Alts to share Earth Two?"

"Of course, I remember it, but before you go asking any questions, I was so nervous that I didn't pay much attention to the details," Julie said. "Wasn't the use of money a big sticking point?"

"Money and barter alike. When a family in the Old Way movement offers lodging without cost to a traveler, there's an expectation that the guest will pitch in to help with chores. The Alts have no such tradition of unspoken contracts around giving and receiving."

"How did they work it out?"

"With difficulty," Flower said. "But the point I'm trying to make is that these women have been helping you create character histories and teaching you about their traditions. They may feel that a sneak preview of your novel is a fair exchange for their efforts."

"But I didn't—oh," Julie said. "Now I see how unspoken contracts can cause problems. But I don't have anything ready."

"According to your tab, you have over a hundred thousand words. Were you writing a novel or an encyclopedia?"

"I'll read something if they bring it up, but you have to promise not to prompt them."

"I wouldn't dream of it."

Julie exited the lift tube on the ag deck where the Old Way encampment was located and started for the meeting tent. "But I can't read to them after all," she subvoced triumphantly. "They don't use tab technology."

"They don't use tabs themselves, but they aren't allergic to them," Flower replied over her executive assistant's implant. "How many times have you been here with Vivian helping her register families for GenePost on her tab?"

"You have a question for everything, don't you?" Julie said with a scowl, and then she laughed. "I like that line. I have to use it in a book someday."

There were only five women in the meeting tent, all of them grandmotherly types. It turned out that there was a field day in progress to celebrate Daylight Savings Time and the book club had canceled the meeting.

"But you guys aren't from Earth," Julie protested. "Why would you keep Daylight Savings Time?"

"We don't keep the time, just the holiday," a woman named Elsa told her. "The five of us stood around watching for a few hours, and then we thought of the chairs in the meeting tent and decided to have the meeting after all. I'm sorry you didn't get the message. One of the younger women talked with your ship."

"Flower has been overworked lately and she must have forgotten," Julie said, wondering why she was lying to protect the manipulative artificial intelligence.

"It's a good thing you came because we realized after we got here that it wouldn't be fair to the others to discuss Dark Prairie without them."

"Dark Prairie: The River's Revenge," another woman corrected Elsa. "It's the sixth book of the cycle, and that's usually the one where the triangle gets resolved."

"So we thought you might read us something of your own," Elsa continued. "But only if you're comfortable with it."

Julie looked at the eager faces of the women, the youngest of whom would never see seventy again. "I'm not used to reading out loud," she warned them. "I'll probably make a lot of mistakes, and I've never practiced doing character voices."

"You'll be wonderful," another of the women insisted. "Do you need more light, or will your fab provide it?"

"It's a tab, Annabelle," Elsa told her. "A fab is a semiconductor fabrication plant, where they make microchips."

Julie stopped with her tab halfway out of her purse. "How long have you been a member of the Old Way movement?" she asked.

"I joined with my family after I retired. It's taken me ten years to stop missing our immersive entertainment system, and my late husband was a big fan of the Grenouthian news."

"Gloria is the only one of us here who was born in the Old Way movement," Anabelle said. "How many communities were there eighty years ago, Glory?"

"Don't get me started talking about the past or I'll get confused about where I am today," a woman who looked like she'd lived in the sun and weather for the last ninety years said with a dry chuckle. "You don't want me to forget that we're on a spaceship and try to open a window."

Julie cleared her throat self-consciously and began to read from her tab. *"My first impression of Cold Mountain made me wish I was still home in my grandfather's cabin. When the bearded giant of a man who drove the buckboard announced that we'd arrived, my heart fell into the sensible leather boots that my husband-to-be had sent as a betrothal gift."*

"I can tell already that he's going to be one of those practical men who doesn't understand anything of a young woman's heart," Gloria said. "My first husband was like that. For our first anniversary he gave me a mangle."

"A what?" Julie asked.

"You've seen one at our laundry tent," Annabelle said. "The iron frame with the two rollers and the wheel on the side?"

"Oh, the clothes wringer. That's not very romantic."

"Let her continue, you two," Elsa said. "I want to hear what he looks like."

Julie looked back down at her tab to find her place, which wasn't that difficult because she'd only gotten through two sentences. *"The horse came to a halt at a word from Mathias, and he immediately hopped down and came around to offer a hand. I couldn't recall having felt more tired in my thirty-five years of life, and I would have collapsed on the ground without the support of his strong arms."*

"She likes him, you can tell," Elsa said.

"It's always the teamster," one of the other women added sagely.

"I remember the first time I took a long trip in a buckboard," Gloria said. "There was a single large spring of sorts below the bench seat, but it's nothing like traveling in a fully sprung wagon. I sat on a folded blanket because there wasn't any padding, and I swear I still had bruises on my butt for a week."

"I like the way you write in the first person," Annabelle told Julie. "It creates a sense of intimacy, like I'm seeing the world through your character's eyes before I even know her name."

"What is her name?" asked the fifth woman who hadn't yet spoken.

"No, don't tell us," Elsa said, gesturing at the tab. "Just keep reading."

Julie looked back at her tab and struggled for a moment to remember where she'd left off.

"She's just fallen into his arms," Gloria said with a gleam in her eyes.

"They're not in a clench or anything like that," the author said. "Mathias is just holding her up."

"Did he lift her down by the waist?" Annabelle asked. "When I was a girl, the boys would line up for a chance to hand me out of a wagon, but I'd just jump down myself and laugh at them."

"I was trying not to overwrite the scene," Julie said. "My mentor warned me that too much detail is worse than not enough when describing a change of state."

"Like her legs turning to jelly?" Elsa asked, and all of the women laughed.

"That comes later," Julie said, wondering whether her audience was more interested in hearing the story or talking about craft. "When my mentor talks about a change of state, she means going from riding in a wagon to standing on the ground or walking from the kitchen to the living room. You don't want your readers to think that the characters are constantly teleporting between locations, but nobody wants to read a blow-by-blow description of climbing a staircase."

"What's the next sentence?" Gloria asked. "Maybe we'll find out where he put his hands."

The five women looked to the author in anticipation.

"Will you be all right, Miss?" Mathias asked in a bass rumble that reminded Hyacinth of her deceased father. "I can hand you back up if you want to sit for a while. I'll just unhitch the horse and get him watered and fed."

"Hyacinth! That's my name," one of the women said.

"I thought it was Cindy," Elsa said.

"That's what I started telling people after somebody shortened my name to Hya. Like two words. Hi Yah."

"That's a shame, it's such a pretty name. Where did you get the idea for the name, Julie?"

"Uh, Flower," Julie admitted.

"So Hyacinth lived with her grandfather because her father is deceased," Gloria said. "It's amazing how you can pack that much information into just a few pages."

"I feel like I already know Hyacinth," Annabelle said. "I'll bet that her grandfather recently passed, and she responded to a matrimonial ad in a farming journal, but now she's having second thoughts."

"Second thoughts about a big, strong man who owns a buckboard."

"I hope it isn't too late," Cindy said. "What if the man she's coming to marry meets her in town and takes her directly to the preacher or the clerk to get hitched?"

"I've heard of marriages like that," Gloria said. "If you ask me, she'd be better off proposing to Mathias. At least they have a wagon trip in common, and he doesn't sound like the sort of man who would send a woman work boots for a betrothal present."

"Did she come with anything other than the clothes on her back?" Annabelle asked. "Did she have to sell her grandfather's farm to care for him in his final sickness?"

"Julie never said that the grandfather is dead," Elsa pointed out. "Or that he was a farmer."

"But he had a cabin. If he lived in town, she would have said it was a house."

"Maybe he was a miner," Cindy said. "We know that my namesake has just moved to a place called Cold Mountain, so the whole story could be taking place in a mountainous region."

"How many Old Way miners do you know?" Elsa asked.

"I've heard of communities on Drazen open worlds. Maybe the grandfather isn't dead, but he had debts, and Hyacinth has sold herself to be married to pay them off."

"Should I summarize what happens for you?" Julie asked. "It's not like I could have read more than a chapter or two in an hour."

"Oh, no. We want to hear it the way you wrote it, and we'll buy the book when it comes out," Elsa said.

"As long as it's on paper," Gloria added.

Julie hesitated. "I guess I can tell you that her grandfather died without spoiling anything."

"I knew it," Annabelle said triumphantly. "An old man doesn't send his only family away to become a mail-order bride. Read on."

"I don't know what came over me," Julie read. *"I've never been the fainting type."*

"I'll bet she isn't," Gloria said. "I can see her working in her grandfather's field with an old iron plow that leaves you feeling like your shoulders have been pulled out of their sockets after just an hour."

"I thought she was a small woman," Elsa said.

"Mathias is a giant. Hyacinth is average."

"Don't mind them," Annabelle said to Julie. "Keep reading."

"Old Henry should have been here waiting for you," Mathias said, glancing up at the darkening sky. "It's going to be pouring buckets within an hour."

"Old Henry?" Gloria demanded. "You're going to force Hyacinth to marry an old man? Better she should enter service and pay off her grandfather's debts."

"What debts?" Cindy asked. "For all we know, Hyacinth could be wearing a money belt stuffed with gold pieces below her traveling dress."

"Old Henry is—" Julie began to say, but Gloria cut her off.

"In for a surprise if he thinks he's going to get away with marrying a woman in the prime of her life. Mark my words, Julie won't let him."

"Old Henry drives the wagon for the Old Way community," Julie explained. "He was supposed to meet Mathias in Cold Mountain to pick up Hyacinth."

"If Cold Mountain isn't her destination, why was she so disappointed when she saw it?"

"Because Hyacinth used to work in—"

"Don't tell us," Cindy interrupted. "Just read it the way you wrote it."

"I looked up at the heavens and confirmed that the clouds were darkening. 'I'll wait in the general store until he comes.' For a moment, I thought that Mathias was going to say something, but then he nodded and hoisted the old chest holding all of my worldly goods out of the buckboard and balanced it on his shoulder."

"If Mathias isn't from the Old Way community, why is he driving a buckboard?" Gloria asked. "It's not the sort of wagon that a teamster would operate. They're just for light duty on the ranch or a trip into town."

"Maybe he's from the Old Way community near her grandfather's cabin and they made a deal," Elsa said.

"I think Mathias volunteered because he wanted to tell her how he felt but he couldn't find the words," Cindy said.

"There's nothing in the text to suggest that Mathias ever met Hyacinth before today," Annabelle pointed out.

"Maybe he admired her from afar."

Before Julie knew it, the time allotted for the book club was up, and five women declared that she had a bright future as an author. Back in the lift tube, she vented her frustration to Flower.

"First they push me to read, then they don't let me finish the first chapter," Julie complained.

"The important thing is that you tried, and next time it will be easier," Flower told her. "I've witnessed hundreds of book readings, and the more intimate the setting, the easier it is to lose control. I would have recommended that you stand instead of taking a seat in their circle, but I didn't want to make you nervous."

"But they were all so interested in Mathias, and he doesn't appear in the book after the first two pages."

"He seemed kind to me," the Dollnick AI said. "Hyacinth could do worse."

"Thanks a lot," Julie grumbled.

Ten

"You can't do your best for humanity if you don't take care of yourself," Vivian told Samuel. "It can wait until tomorrow."

"I'll be home in an hour," he promised. "Nikos is already waiting with his students in the café."

Vivian let out a sigh of frustration as she moved Rose to the stroller. "I'll wait on dinner until you get home, not because you deserve it, but because I don't trust you to eat without me watching you. And I still think this is really about your mother. You're afraid that if the Human Empire keeps taking *All Species Cookbook* money, the aliens will say that you're still tied to her apron strings."

"The aliens take nepotism for granted," Samuel said with a laugh. "They'd think it was weird if she wasn't supporting me, and the same goes for you and your mother. I don't expect us to create a revenue stream that will let us build the infrastructure for an empire anytime soon, but it's important for our students, who are the future of the empire, to start thinking in terms of self-sufficiency. A government that exists on charity is only as good as its biggest donor."

"Whatever," Vivian said. "I'm off the clock and I don't talk shop after hours. I wish the same was true for you."

"Good night, Rose," Krey said, crouching to pat the baby on the head. "See you tomorrow, Vivian."

"He promised one hour," Vivian told the Human Empire's mentor. "I'm counting on you to send him home."

"Then we better get going," Samuel said. He bent to kiss the baby and then tried to plant one on his wife's lips but she turned at the last second, so he ended up kissing her ear lobe. He shot Krey a helpless look and then headed for the nearest lift tube. The Cayl emperor's granddaughter padded silently behind him, while Vivian moved off in the opposite direction to do some shopping.

"Bill's café," Samuel told the lift tube capsule.

"Your mate is angry with you," Krey observed.

"It's the same as always. She thinks I work too hard."

"If her point of reference is other Humans, she's correct."

"It's not like I'm packing shipping containers all day or working in the fields," Samuel protested. "My job is ninety percent reading, and if I take a few EarthCent Intelligence reports home with me, it's just less time spent watching immersives."

"Do you read the reports to Vivian?"

"She won't let me."

"And you feel that she's being unreasonable?"

"We only have a few years to start meeting benchmarks or the whole empire launch could be pushed off for another century," Samuel said. "As soon as our School of Government starts graduating students, I'll delegate everything."

"There's always more to read than there is time to read it," Krey commented as the capsule doors slid open.

There were around thirty students in Bill's café, most of them eating dinner, but a dozen were sitting at the longest table, with Nikos at one end and the Zerakova twins at the other. There was an empty seat next to the Macro professor and Krey pushed Samuel ahead, indicating that she would sit at the next table and use her directional hearing to listen in.

"You told us not to wait to order," Nikos greeted Samuel apologetically after swallowing. "There's a nice casserole in the steam table I can recommend."

"My wife is making dinner," Samuel said, not seeing the need to add that Vivian's specialty was asking Flower what people were saying was good that day and ordering takeout. "It looks like most of you are still eating, so I'll just describe the challenge unless you've already done so."

"All I told the students was that anybody with an interest in how governments raise revenue was welcome to join us for a free dinner."

"Kat and I happened to be here because we heard about the casserole," Sabina said. "Nikos told me that you were going to talk about collecting taxes, and I made a bet with a Drazen back on Corner Station that it wouldn't happen in my lifetime."

"How were you planning on collecting if you're right?" a student asked.

"It's an honor bet. There's not any money involved."

"Fortunately for your honor, I don't see taxation in our near future, because everybody would quit the empire before we even get off the ground," Samuel said. "The whole tunnel network knows that our current source of funding is the royalty stream from the *All Species Cookbook,* which the Stryx conveniently awarded to EarthCent shortly before modifying the tunnel network treaty to favor the early creation of the Human Empire."

"Doesn't EarthCent have plenty of other places to spend the money?" a girl asked.

"Strangely enough, EarthCent has always run on a shoestring. Not having an independent source of income kept them from expanding much beyond the embassies and consulates that were fully funded by the Stryx."

"What about EarthCent Intelligence?" a young man asked. "All of the case studies we've looked at in class so far are based on their business database and collecting that sort of data must be expensive."

"It is, which is why EarthCent Intelligence sells subscriptions to the database," Samuel said. "I was going to bring it up as an example of a self-funding governmental agency."

"But wouldn't there have been large upfront expenses before they got to the point that they could sell database subscriptions to businesses?"

"My mother-in-law gave them a helping hand. Look, before you say anything, I know it's a bit much to swallow that my mother ended up publishing the *All Species Cookbook* through her embassy and my wife's mother made a fortune with InstaSitter and funded EarthCent Intelligence."

"Anything else?" a different young woman asked.

"Vivian's aunt owns the Galactic Free Press," Samuel said. "There, that's everything. Sometimes the Stryx work in mysterious ways and sometimes it seems pretty obvious after a little time passes. But none of that changes the fact that at some point in the near future, the Human Empire needs to generate a source of funding, or it will fizzle out."

"Are you going to ask us to sell stuff?" one of the students asked suspiciously. "I did the door-to-door cookies when I was a kid to raise money for our soccer team, but I don't think it would work for an empire."

"There aren't enough cookies," Katya said.

"So this is what brainstorming is all about," Samuel told them. "I want you all to throw ideas out there without overthinking them. Selling cookies door-to-door probably isn't the answer, but maybe there's some other human tradition for raising money that we're missing."

"Taxes," Nikos said.

"Customs?" another student asked. "I worked for Human Burger to get the scholarship, and they sent me to a different alien world every summer. There was always somebody waiting to meet us at customs so we wouldn't have to pay a bribe, but it seemed like a pretty good way to raise money."

"Most alien customs services are self-funding," Sabina told them. "Plus they provide a sort of safety valve."

"To prevent drugs and stuff from coming in?"

"For the aliens who work as customs agents and would probably have fallen into a life of crime otherwise."

"You should ask the people who came up with Human Burger to help out," the student who had worked for them said. "They have arrangements with all of the tunnel network species and—what?" he trailed off as the Zerakova twins dissolved in laughter.

"Has anybody explained to you guys who hired Flower to go around visiting sovereign human communities?" Samuel asked.

"Human Burger?"

"One level up. Human Burger is operated by Eccentric Enterprises which, on paper, is Flower's employer. But it's a front for EarthCent Intelligence, the same way Astria's Academy of Dance is a front for Vergallian Intelligence."

"Meaning his mother-in-law financed Human Burger," Sabina said, wiping her eyes. "She copied the scholarship program from InstaSitter."

"Could we do that to raise money for the Human Empire?" a girl asked. "Start a human-themed business?"

"Maybe your mother-in-law would sell us Human Burger," another student suggested.

"Or give it to us, since she seems to be into philanthropy," the first girl said.

"I don't think it makes much money, what with the employee benefits and all," Samuel said. "It's more of an outreach business, so the aliens who live on those worlds can see that we exist outside of Grenouthian documentaries."

"Does EarthCent Intelligence use it to spy on the aliens?" another student asked.

"They tried to recruit me after I finished my undergrad on Earth, but I told them I was applying to the School of Government," said the student who had brought up working for Human Burger.

"My wife knows a lot more about it than I do, so you can ask her," Samuel said.

"The local governments on Drazen, Horten, and Frunge worlds all raise revenues on a fee-for-service model," Katya said. "The Frunge charge businesses for access to infrastructure that's free to regular citizens, and the Drazens and Hortens charge everybody."

"But don't the aliens own the infrastructure on the open worlds where the sovereign human communities that make up the Human Empire are hosted?" Nikos asked.

"It's an issue," Katya agreed cheerfully.

"What about the Dollnicks?" a student asked.

"The princes pay for the public infrastructure, it's practically a competition with them," Sabina said. "They just have a different way of looking at the universe than most of the other species. And the Grenouthians handle everything through their clans."

"The truth is, none of the advanced species offer good examples for how to fund basic government services or infrastructure because they put it all in place long before they developed interstellar travel, and they all generate excess wealth," Samuel said. "Flower was constructed almost twenty-thousand years ago. I don't know if humanity had even discovered basic agriculture when she took her first jump, and she's completely self-sustaining. Power plants on alien worlds run so long with so little maintenance that if you amortize the cost over all of the users it comes out so close to free that it's not worth billing."

"How come you haven't been teaching us any of this in Macro?" the girl sitting next to Nikos demanded.

"Because we aren't aliens," he replied patiently. "When I was in graduate school, the faculty and students were evenly divided between those who study the way alien economies operate and those who believe it's irrelevant to humanity—the group I ended up joining. The simple fact is that we aren't aliens and we don't have their resources. Any advanced society that goes hundreds of thousands of years without a war ends up immensely rich."

"But if the wealth is concentrated—"

"We're getting off-topic," Samuel interrupted. "I need ideas for the Human Empire to bring in enough revenue to pay your salaries and benefits, to rent you office space, to let you hire the employees you need to manage whatever it is we eventually end up managing."

"Are you sure we need a bureaucracy?" one of the guys joked. "It sounds like we're going to finish school and nobody is going to need us."

"All of the empires have bureaucracies," Katya told him. "They probably started out thinking they could avoid it, but then a bridge somewhere collapses, and everybody wants to know who is supposed to be inspecting bridges. Soon you've got building permits, zoning regulations, environmental impact statements…"

"The Fleet Vergallians have a Department of Aesthetics that gets final approval on all construction projects that are bigger than a regulation dance floor," Sabina added.

"How big is that?" the guy asked.

"Small enough that they have one in every embassy for parties. I miss embassy parties."

"Anybody interested in dessert?" Bill asked. Telescoping legs shot out of the large tray he was carrying to create an instant stand. "Pretty neat, huh? A Drazen on the light industry deck has started manufacturing them for export."

"Let me see that again," Katya demanded.

The café manager tapped the button on one of the tray's handles with his index finger, and the legs retracted into short stubs, and then telescoped out again on a second tap.

"How about you, Bill?" Samuel asked to get the discussion back on track. "We're brainstorming ideas to generate revenue for the Human Empire, ideally something repeatable."

"Everybody back home said that the New York city-state would have gone broke without the lottery even before the Stryx opened Earth," Bill said, handing out plated desserts to the students as they pointed at their choices. "And that was just the local ones. There was a whole-Earth lottery that all of the governments shared."

"Did you ever win anything?"

"Me? I never played. Do you know what the odds are for those things? Somebody once told me that buying a ticket doesn't make a statistical difference in your chance of winning because the odds are so low."

"He's got a point," Nikos said. "The odds of winning the whole-Earth lottery are worse than a billion to one."

"So who would buy a ticket?" Samuel asked. One by one, the students slowly raised their hands, and in the end, Nikos joined in. "But you just said it's impossible to win."

"No, I said the chances of winning were vanishingly small. But somebody always does win, and when they do, it can be over a billion eBucks if the pot has been riding a while. That's around two hundred million creds."

"Real money," Sabina said, pointing at a brownie.

"So what do the governments get for running the lottery after they've paid all of their expenses?" Samuel asked. "A few hundred thousand eBucks to split?"

Nikos laughed. "I can see you don't have much experience with government lotteries. It's usually a fifty/fifty split, so even after the monopoly lottery agencies take their cut for management, there's still somewhere in the high forty-percent range for the government."

"So it's not expensive to run?"

"Just paying all of those quasi-government employees. There aren't any physical tickets if that's what you were thinking. The whole thing is handled through a smartphone app."

"What if somebody doesn't have a smartphone?" Samuel asked.

"Then they aren't really from Earth and they're out of luck."

"EarthCent owns an old lottery machine with ping pong balls they would probably give us," Sabina said. "They used to use it to choose the ambassadors for sabbatical, but everybody accused the president of rigging the results, and now the choices come from a Thark casino."

"My uncle bought me a season ticket for my birthday," one of the girls said. "He's kind of a lottery addict."

"And there's the whole issue of stepping on Earth's toes," Nikos said. "If you want to stay on good terms with the governments there, you'd either have to come up with a way to keep the lottery from being played on Earth or cut them in on the sales."

Samuel reluctantly waved away Bill's offer of Boston Cream Pie and thought for a moment. "I'm not crazy about funding the government with gambling, but at least it's an idea. Anything else."

"Me?" Bill asked again. "You know I used to work with my mom on the pushcart that the cult she belonged to assigned to us. We used to get tickets and fines for not having a legitimate vendor license or for setting up in areas where pushcarts were prohibited, but the cult had worked out that paying the penalties as they came in was cheaper than going legit and working in less profitable areas. You could write tickets."

"I don't know if the Human Empire will ever have that sort of jurisdiction anywhere, or that we'd even want it," Samuel said. "I'm hoping to eventually run the empire on the fee-for-service model because that's how the governments of worlds with sovereign human communities usually operate. It means coming up with services people need."

"Food services?"

"We already suggested Human Burger," one of the students said.

"Then I'm out of ideas," Bill said, retracting the legs on the tray. "And Flower told me to tell you that you're down to twenty minutes."

"My wife is waiting for me," Samuel explained to the students. "What else do governments on Earth do to raise funds? It's not something I've studied."

"Licenses are big because the thing they're licensing usually doesn't cost them anything," Nikos said. "They get a pretty good cut of the smartphone charges between the use of the spectrum and all of the other fees."

"Earth governments charge phone companies for using the electromagnetic spectrum? Why not charge them for using the visible light spectrum because that's what makes the phones different colors, or the audio spectrum for the talking and ring tones?"

"It's a little more complicated than that. Smartphones are one of the three protected legacy technologies on Earth, which means they can't be replaced with superior alien products that make more efficient use of the bandwidth. The result is an artificial shortage of spectrum because all of the service providers are limited to a small number of relatively narrow bands."

"What are the other two technologies?" Samuel asked.

"One is the global positioning system that uses satellites," Nikos said. "The other slips my mind."

"I'm from the Copenhagen city-state, and our government gets most of its funding from a value-added tax," a girl said. "They take twenty percent off the top of every eBuck that changes hands."

"We don't want to do a tax," Sabina said. "You have to remember that the representatives of the sovereign human communities who voted to go ahead with the Human

Empire only did so because they were promised that it wouldn't cost them anything."

"How long is the revenue from the *All Species Cookbook* expected to last?" Nikos asked.

Samuel sighed. "Probably longer than any of us will be alive, but that's not the point. For one thing, the other tunnel network species notice stuff like that, and if we don't figure out a way to fund ourselves by the time we take over from EarthCent, we'll end up being known as the Cookbook Empire."

"They'll probably pick a single recipe that sounds funny," Katya said. "Like the Chopped Liver Empire. Or the Vegan Sheezle Bug Substitute Empire."

"We would end up sizing our government to match the cookbook royalties rather than meeting the needs of our people," Samuel continued. "And the editor of the cookbook would become the de facto emperor."

"Could you start charging for the GenePost app?" one of the students asked. "I mean, not a lot, but I signed up when I found out about it, and I think most people will like the idea that they won't just lose track of their family and not be able to find them again. If you can get just a cred a year from billions of people, it adds up."

"We're trying to register the maximum number of people, and our focus group research reported that any fee would cut adoption by around eighty percent."

"How about after you get everybody signed up, say in five or ten years? And rather than just starting to charge everybody a cred a year, you could offer an enhanced version that does something people want."

"Like adding a free subscription to the Galactic Free Press," a serious-looking young man said.

"It's already free," several of the students told him.

"It's free with ads, and you have to scroll through all the navigation to see what's new," he said. "I'm talking about the paid version, where they curate the news you see and send alerts on the stories you choose to monitor. It saves me far more time than the cost of the subscription."

"The Galactic Free Press doesn't belong to the Human Empire," Samuel reminded them.

"But your wife's aunt started it," the serious student said. "I thought you implied that the Stryx were building up your in-law's fortunes as a way to help humanity without appearing to violate the non-interference clause of the tunnel network treaty."

"Maybe, but if everybody who subscribes to the paper also signs up for GenePost, which is our goal, there wouldn't be any paid subscribers left to pay the reporters and keep the business running. And it would be tantamount to a government takeover of humanity's main source of news, which is never a good idea."

"If we're going to make the effort to get everybody signed up for the GenePost app, I think it makes sense to put it at the center of a voluntary revenue collection scheme," Katya said.

"You mean like the old public Wikis on Earth, where every few months they pop up a message on your screen asking for donations?" Nikos asked. "I give them something once in a while, but I don't like it. Lots of people may go years at a time without using GenePost, because they aren't looking for family members, and nobody is looking for them."

"I meant voluntary as opting into other services, not as a charity. If nothing else, I bet we could raise a lot of money if you just combined it with the Human Lottery. And I'll bet you could get a lot of fence-sitters signed up for the app because they're more interested in winning a billion creds than finding out what happened to Aunt Harriet."

Eleven

"I still can't believe you get the whole week off while we're stopped at Earth," Julie said as Bill poured her a refill. "I'm stuck juggling GraphicXCon with meeting the leaders of all the Old Way communities who are coming on board for transport to Earth Two."

"It's not my fault the School of Government is on vacation and the spies from Harry's cafeteria will all be down on Earth checking up on their sources," Bill said, trying to hide a grin. "Almost half of the students are from Earth, so they'll be visiting family, and the ones who have never been there are going on a group tour."

"Why didn't you sleep in?"

"Because I wanted to make you breakfast so I could watch you eating."

"If you're trying to be romantic, it came out kind of gross," Julie said, though she couldn't help smiling at the same time. She hesitated a moment and then asked, "Are you going to take a shuttle down and look for her?"

"For who?" Bill asked, sounding genuinely confused.

"Your mom."

"We agreed not to talk about our mothers."

"But now you're a married man on your way to being a father," Julie said. "If my mom was still alive, I'd visit her, even if it was just to show how well I'm doing despite the lousy start she gave me."

"If my mom isn't out with a pushcart selling junk to tourists, she's back at the Sun Cult temple trying to get the attention of that fraud who convinced her he's a reincarnated Pharaoh or something," Bill said, and then he froze for a second. "Did you just say that you're pregnant?"

"No, but we're trying. If you're not going to see her, you might send a note. What if she wants to get away from the cult but she doesn't have anywhere else to go?"

"She had me when she was a teenager, she's not even forty. If she wants to live a normal life, there are plenty of jobs. Why is this so important to you?"

"Because you're my husband," Julie said. "I'm worried that at some point in the future you'll start regretting that you didn't try to reach out to her and then it will be too late."

Bill opened his mouth to respond but he was cut off by the bing-bong of the latest doorbell sound Julie had chosen for their cabin. Seizing on the excuse to end a conversation he didn't want to be having, he skipped asking Flower who was there and went to manually release the door. He expected to see Samuel or Vivian, since they lived right across the corridor, but instead it was the Farling doctor.

"Shuttle leaves in five minutes," M793qK rubbed out on his speaking legs. "Come on, Flower is holding the lift tube."

"I'm on vacation," Bill protested.

"And that's what we're doing, taking a vacation," the alien said, grabbing Bill by the shoulder and pulling him out of the apartment. "Good morning, Julie. I'll have him back by dinner, probably."

"If you're going to Earth, take him to see his mom," Julie called from the kitchen.

"Are we picking up products to test for the *All Species Cookbook* seal of approval?" Bill asked, breaking into a jog to keep up with the surprisingly rapid strides the Farling managed while upright on his hindmost set of limbs.

"There are countless shipping services capable of delivering packaged food products, and it's all paid for by the manufacturers who are seeking approval," M793qK said. "Now hold up a minute."

"What's the problem?"

"You're having a dizzy spell." The Farling doctor caught Bill as he began to collapse, and then pushed past the people waiting for the lift tube, which seemed to be taking much longer than usual to arrive.

"Medical emergency," Flower announced as the doors opened. "Please clear the way for the doctor."

The people who were waiting all stepped back while offering expressions of sympathy as M793qK rushed into the capsule carrying his patient. The second the doors closed, the alien stood Bill back on his feet and said, "All better now."

"What did you do to me?"

"I merely demonstrated the power of suggestion."

"I don't believe you. I think you actually stunned me with something. And I can't believe you went along with it, Flower."

"It was either fake a medical emergency or hold a shuttle with eight hundred and seventy-four passengers, all of whom would have seen you boarding late and wondered why you deserve special treatment," the Dollnick AI replied. "And you were already collapsing when M793qK picked you up."

"That doesn't mean he didn't puff knockout gas in my face or do some telepathic trick," Bill said. "There's no way I almost fainted just because he said I would."

"Don't think about Earth," M793qK said.

"What?"

"Now, what are you thinking about?"

"Earth, but that's only because—never mind."

"Take the back ramp," Flower said as the lift tube doors opened on the docking deck. "You're going to have to keep a limb on him, Doctor. He's not wearing his boots with the magnetic cleats."

"That's because I'm on vacation," Bill said, but he didn't shrug off one of the Farling's upper limbs that settled on his shoulder, and the two of them rapidly shuffled towards the ramp of the shuttle. "Hey, I don't know why I never noticed before. How come you don't need magnetic cleats?"

"I generate my own magnetic field," M793qK explained. "Most of the advanced species with wings evolve multiple strategies for flying, often with the aid of genetic engineering. Given my size and wingspan, it would be difficult to remain airborne if I wasn't capable of interacting with magnetic fields, along with a few other tricks."

"Do species have to have wings to evolve magnetic abilities?"

"I assume you're asking about Humans, and some of you can sense magnetic north as a part of your subconscious navigation wetware. I don't see it evolving much beyond that because there's no compelling need."

"You don't think being able to walk on the docking deck without doing accidental backflips is important?" Bill asked as he started up the shuttle's rear ramp with the doctor's limb still pressing on his shoulder.

"You've adapted to moving about in low gravity better than I realized," M793qK said. "You may have taken a few silly-looking high steps if I wasn't holding you down, but nothing as dramatic as losing contact with the deck. And evolution doesn't select traits that you only occasionally use in situations that your species encountered for the first time less than a century ago. Your low weight on the innermost deck of a colony ship or a large space liner doesn't impede your chance of breeding, and in some instances, may even offer a bonus.

"That's hard to believe," Bill said as he slipped into the rear row of the shuttle's central seating area. "How can the inability to walk properly in low gravity be a bonus to anything?"

"Humans have a marked propensity to engage in breeding activities while horizontal," the doctor said, easing his carapace down on four of the wide seats and drawing his lower limbs out of the aisle. "Fasten your seat belt."

"Welcome to Flower Transportation Services," the Dollnick AI announced a moment later. "This shuttle to Earth will be departing in thirty seconds. Please remain in your seats until we enter Earth's atmosphere and I make an announcement that it's safe to move about the cabin. We will be landing at the New York city-state mass-transit hub in approximately twenty-seven minutes."

"How come you never wear a safety belt?" Bill asked the giant alien beetle, whose multi-faceted eyes had taken on the unfocused look the Farling displayed when he was in his resting state.

"Have you already forgotten about my biological magnetism?" M793qK asked. "A crane couldn't lift me right now." He reached for the black medical bag he had shoved under a seatback of the row in front of theirs, pulled it closer, and extracted a tab. "Here," he said, extending it to Bill. "I've programmed it with some basic cryptography for you to practice. I'm going to meditate until we land."

Exactly on schedule, Flower set the shuttle down with barely a bump. When the doors opened forty-five seconds later, M793qK was ready, with his black bag dangling from one limb, and a drowsy-looking young man by his side.

"You should have taken advantage of the trip to rest up," the Farling said. "You look exhausted for somebody on vacation."

"It's the cryptography," Bill said, handing the tab back as they started down the ramp. "That kind of math just makes me sleepy."

"Then we'll have to try you on a different kind of math today. Where are you headed?"

"For the bus to the terminal. Aren't we going to catch the subway into town?"

"Our ride is already here," M793qK said, gesturing at a floater van with a soaring gryphon painted on the side in lifelike detail. It seemed way too close to the shuttle for safe spaceport operations.

"ReproMan?" Bill read off the van. "Have you gone into the finance business?"

"Art reproductions. You can pick something out for your apartment while we're there."

"Meaning that you're not paying me."

"The least expensive reproduction they sell is worth hundreds of creds," M793qK said in exasperation as he pulled open the rear door of the van. "We're talking about unique works of art painstakingly reproduced by Human artists using the same techniques employed by the original painter. They aren't copies, they are literally reproductions, as in, produced another time."

"Who would pay that much for a handmade copy of a painting?" Bill asked.

"Enough discerning sentients that I can employ half of the artists in the New York city-state, including ninety-nine percent of the ones who make a living at it." The doctor set his black medical bag on the floor and pulled a lever on the side of the padded bench seat which folded down into a Farling couch. "You can sit up front if you want to see how the city has changed in your absence."

"Who's driving?" Bill asked, glancing at the curtain that separated the back of the cargo area of the van from the front.

"Do you think I would trust my carapace to a Human driver in New York traffic? It's a self-driving van, of course, but there's a seat for you, unless you'd rather stay back here and practice your—"

"I'm going, I'm going." Bill hit the button to close the cargo door, slid aside the curtain, and climbed through the space between the bucket seats.

"Close that after you, I'm going to rest my eyes," M793qK rubbed out on his speaking legs. "And put on your seatbelt, you never know."

The floater van took off at a horrifying speed and made a beeline for Manhattan. It navigated smoothly around the other vehicles darting about the area of the transit hub, which was located at a terminus of the Elevator Transit Authority monorail to the north of the city. Once they got into city traffic, the van rose to the height that was reserved for emergency vehicles, giving Bill a view into the second-story windows of the buildings they flashed past.

In less time than seemed possible, they were pulling into the basement parking lot of an enormous skyscraper.

"We're here, but I think there's something wrong with the autopilot," Bill said over his shoulder as the van descended from level to level. "I see plenty of open parking spaces and we're still going down."

"I have a reserved spot," M793qK replied. "In the future, I may send you here to make a pickup if I can't get away myself, so pay attention to everything."

"It's very clean."

"Of course it's clean. Do you think I'd let a building I own fill up with litter and discarded chewing gum?" The van came to a halt and all of the doors opened simultaneously. "Now we're here."

"Did you really come all the way down to Earth to show me where to pick up reproduction art?"

"The art I can have delivered from the catalog, though I find it pays to put in a showing twice a year and remind my managers who they're working for," M793qK said, joining Bill outside the van. "First the vault, and then the elevator."

"There's a vault down here?"

"It's the safest place in case of a cataclysm."

"But the building has to be fifty stories," Bill pointed out. "If it collapsed, you'd never be able to get down here."

"It might take a few years of digging, but never is a gross exaggeration," the alien rubbed out on his speaking legs. There was a small glassed-in lobby right next to the parking spot, with two elevators and a fire door leading to the stairwell. M793qK approached the elevator on the right and pressed the call button. A panel slid aside and revealed the outline of a handprint. "Place your hand there," he told Bill.

"Is this going to hurt? You promised me that there wouldn't be any DNA-coded courier cases that draw a blood sample."

"I don't recall making that promise, but this is a scanner—no DNA required."

Bill placed his hand in the outline, which turned out to be a perfect match, and then shut his eyes tight as a bright bar of light passed down behind the glass.

"Now voice identification," M793qK said.

"Bill."

"Wait for the beep."

A moment later, a long beep sounded from the panel.

"Bill."

"Now the password," M793qK said as another panel slid open. "Put your hand in there and locate the buttons, but don't press any of them yet."

"Do you promise it's not a blood draw?"

"Cross my carapace, hope to molt," the doctor rubbed out impatiently. "Either you trust me or you don't."

Bill put his hand in the dark opening and gingerly felt around until he located five buttons that ended up corresponding with the locations of his fingertips.

"Now, here's the trick," M793qK said. "It's a time lock. Bring up the stopwatch on your heads-up display, and when you feel me pressing on your shoulder, hold down all five buttons and start the stopwatch. When I stop pressing, and I'll do a quick tap so you're sure, stop the timer and take all of your fingers off the buttons, but don't remove your hand. Then, without saying anything, moving, or changing your expression, count to thirty."

Bill followed the instructions, held the buttons down for seven seconds, counted to thirty after releasing them, and then pulled out his hand. "Is that everything?"

"Press the call button again."

As soon as Bill pressed the button, both panels closed and the elevator doors opened on what appeared to be a tunnel.

"Let's go," M793qK said. He led the way into the vault which was crammed with paintings, statues, and pottery.

"I don't get it," Bill complained. "All of that complicated security and then the vault turns out to be protected by an elevator door anybody could pry open with a crowbar. And why worry about any of this stuff when you have a building full of artists who can make more? Is this one of those double-blind things you were telling me about where the real vault is underneath this one or something?"

"No, this is it," M793qK said, flipping open a chest that looked like it was full of fake gems. "Here, help me fill this. I didn't bring a cup and my limbs aren't ideal for scooping."

Bill took the medical bag from the doctor, set it on top of the fake gems, and began scooping them in. "You don't even care which colors I grab?"

"You think those are fake, don't you? They're not, and neither is the art. I promised not to exchange the eBucks I earn through my pharmaceutical businesses for Stryx creds because it would distort the exchange rate, so I'm forced to settle for what I can get. Gems are of limited value to species that are capable of synthesizing them, but there is a market for certified natural gems, and I estimate the full bag will be worth close to two million creds."

"And you keep them behind an elevator door?"

"Look up as we leave. The real vault door retracted before the elevator door opened. And don't forget the number of seconds you held the buttons. It would be dangerous to get it wrong if you're here alone."

"So you're going to take these back to Flower and sell them for creds," Bill said.

"You're going to take them back to Flower. I have several important meetings to attend this morning. Just bring the bag by my clinic and put it in the fridge. The door will open for you."

"What if I get mugged?"

"Don't. The van will take you directly to the mass transit hub after I get out, and you can wait inside until Flower's shuttle returns."

"I don't know how much time you've spent in New York, but there are plenty of people who would kill me for a lot less than millions in jewels," Bill said nervously. "How about I just come along to your meetings and hold the bag?"

"That would turn you into a target," M793qK said as they exited. He hit the call button again, and the vault door descended even as the elevator door that hid it from sight closed. "I'm not asking you to sacrifice yourself if somebody holds a syringe to your neck and demands the jewels. As you've seen, there's plenty more where those came from."

"You're sure you didn't make them yourself?"

"I'm sure they'll pass the certification test for natural gems," the Farling hedged. "Now let's go upstairs and you can pick out a nice painting for your apartment."

"I'd be too nervous," Bill said, clutching the medical bag to his chest.

"You're afraid that Julie won't approve of your choice?"

"I don't have ice water in my veins the way you do. I'm not going to relax again until I'm back on Flower and the bag is in your clinic."

"Very well," M793qK rubbed out on his speaking legs. "I'll pick something out for you." He opened the glass door to the parking lot and escorted Bill back to the van. "As long as you don't panic and throw the bag out a window, everything will be fine. I'll see you later."

Bill found that his nervousness ebbed as the van navigated its way back to the mass transit hub and nothing untoward happened. Flower's shuttle arrived in less than an hour, and he forced himself to walk normally to the front ramp. The seats rapidly filled with cosplayers who were clearly on their way to spend the day at GraphicXCon, and Bill couldn't help recalling an ancient movie about jewel thieves at a costume ball that he'd watched with Julie.

"I'd prefer the aisle," a woman's voice spoke almost in his ear.

Bill tore his eyes away from the medical bag stowed under the seat in front of him just in time to see Dave sitting down next to him.

"Welcome back," the retired salesman said with a grin. "I tried speaking to you twice but you were just staring at M793qK's bag like you're delivering a replacement organ for him. I know that feeling myself."

"No, it's not an organ," Bill said reflexively, and then changed his mind. "I mean, I didn't ask."

"He usually grows replacements from cells, but a lot of people on Earth sign up to become organ donors when they get their floater license because it's the default choice, and M793qK hates to think of perfectly good body parts going to waste," Dave said. "June, this is Bill. He was a principal anime scaffolding actor on the set where I stood in for the Farling doctor."

"Pleased to meet you, Bill," June said, reaching past Dave to offer a handshake. "I hope we aren't invading your space."

"I'm glad to see a familiar face," Bill replied honestly. "These shuttles usually fill up to the last seat during stops, and while I like anime and graphic novels, I was never that comfortable being around strangers wearing masks."

"I know what you mean. People often misbehave when they believe they can do so without risk of identification."

"Did you come down with the doctor?" Dave asked. "He usually books appointments weeks in advance for our stops at Earth, and I can pick up easy work at his clinic."

"Like a nurse?" Bill asked.

"As a greeter. I meet the patients as they arrive and tell them what a great doctor he is and not to be freaked out by the fact he resembles a giant insect. M793qK says that when they see me in costume first it reduces their anxiety levels by over sixty percent."

"I've noticed you have that effect on people," June said, smiling at Dave. "You certainly know how to cut the red tape in officialdom." She looked past him to Bill and continued, "I had some unresolved parking tickets when I moved from Earth to Bits four decades ago and I was afraid they would arrest me as soon as I set foot on the planet. Dave came along to court in case I needed bail."

"The clerk came up with this ridiculous amount that included forty years of penalties and compound interest," Dave said. "I suggested to June that she excuse herself to go to the bathroom and wait for me outside. Then I told the clerk that June was on her way back to Flower and wouldn't return to Earth for another forty years, but I was authorized to settle for the original amount. After a little bartering, I got them to accept thirty-two creds."

"But standing in the street with all of the noise and smells, I realized I'd already had enough of Earth," June added. "So here we are."

Twelve

"This is the Captain speaking. We have arrived at Earth Two and will remain in orbit for five days while transferring colonists to the surface. Tourists are advised to return to Flower a day prior to departure as the planet is not yet connected to the tunnel network and you could be stranded for months if you miss the last shuttle."

"Doesn't apply to us," the Grenouthian director told his documentary crew as they piled into the bookmobile. He checked the clamps on the camera cases and tapped Harry on the shoulder. "Where's Dave?"

"He has a girlfriend now," the baker explained. "We saw them at breakfast, and he sent his apologies he wouldn't be coming, but he found you a substitute."

"If he wasn't a volunteer I'd fire him. And who did he find to take his place? An invisible Human?"

"Me," Belle said, climbing into the back of the bookmobile. "Sorry I'm not early, but I had some things to take care of and Dave didn't give me much notice."

"How do you know him?" Dewey asked the clone.

"I don't, really. Dave asked Flower to suggest somebody and I wanted to visit Earth Two. Maybe I'll get a story out of it for Gem Today."

"You can't use footage from the documentary," the Grenouthian director warned her. "The festivals would throw me out the door if they catch something that's already been broadcast."

"I brought my own equipment," Belle said, displaying the top-of-the-line smartphone she'd acquired on Bits. "The frame rate is sufficient for my species, and my editor prefers video from the field that looks a little raw."

"I guess it's too late to make changes now. Find a seat."

"Sit next to me," Harry said. "The more bodies there are between me and any portholes the less likely I am to look outside and get sick."

"Thank you," Belle said, relieved that she wouldn't have to sit next to somebody who wasn't comfortable around clones, which included pretty much all of the other humanoid tunnel network species. "Have you been to Earth Two before?"

"Every time Flower stops," Irene told her. "Jorb and Razood usually spend the whole week with the Alt colonists, and Dave accompanies them for the first day because he gets along with everybody. Harry and I try to get human-interest interviews, capturing the impressions of new arrivals, while the Grenouthian director does all of the technical shots. I'm also here to study the director's technique and clear up any little misunderstandings he may have with the subjects."

"The documentary has entered the maintenance stage," the Grenouthian director told them. "I've already submitted a feature-length version that's based on the initial landings to all of the relevant festivals. It's been short-listed in the colonization category at the upcoming Echo Station awards."

"In other words, if it strikes a chord with audiences, he'll be in a position to rush out a sequel, if not a miniseries," Jorb said, twisting in his seat to join the conversation. "If it turns out there's no audience for Alts and Humans colonizing a new world together, he'll turn all the video over to a historical archive and we'll stop shooting."

"They aren't exactly colonizing Earth Two together," Razood pointed out without turning around as Dewey slipped into the pilot's seat. "There's a border running through the middle of the continent, and the vast majority of people on both sides never go anywhere near it."

"Is it true that the Humans agreed to abide by the rulings of Alt debate masters?" Belle asked.

"Ask them yourself," the Grenouthian director grunted. "Change in plans for today, Dewey. I'll be working on the Alt side of the continent with Jorb and Razood. You can drop us off and then work with Irene, Harry, and Belle until it's time to bring them back."

"You're promoting me?" Irene asked. "I'm the unit director for the day?"

"That's right. I don't expect anything exciting to happen at this point, but keep your cameras running and ask a lot of questions."

The day passed as the Grenouthian director had predicted, with no excitement, and Irene focused all of their cameras and efforts on documenting a barn-raising. The building was standing before dusk, a testament to the Old Way carpenters having marked all of the boards prior to disassembly back on Earth. The posts and beams were numbered from the original construction, and the barn almost seemed to assemble itself.

"I hate to say it, but that was the most pleasant day we've spent on Earth Two," Harry said as the shuttle began its trip back to orbit. "It's not that I dislike the Grenouthian director, but he's a bit too excitable when we're shooting."

"I was impressed by your directorial decisions," Belle said to Irene. "Were you involved in the industry before moving to Flower?"

"Harry and I did some plays in college, and I shot plenty of video of our children while growing up, but nothing professional," Irene said. "I've been volunteering for the Grenouthian director every chance I get, and I'm also taking courses in documentary making at the Open University. But I never expected him to make me a unit director, even for a day. And he didn't say anything about it ahead of time."

"Does it mean you'll get paid?" Harry asked.

"My name will appear by itself in the credits rather than being included with twenty other volunteers. Dewey would be in trouble with Flower for letting me work all day if it was a paying job, but I may be in line for a fraction of a residual payment if the documentary gets picked up by a major distributor."

"I checked with Flower at your lunch break," Dewey spoke up from the pilot's seat. "She said that technically, since you were on Earth Two and the Alts don't use actuarial tables to limit the hours worked by the elderly, it won't reflect badly on her if you get paid for the day."

"Elderly?" Belle asked, turning in her seat to examine Irene more closely. "I noticed that Harry was dragging a bit at the end of the day, but you looked like you could have worked all night."

"Harry gets up a couple of hours earlier than I do," Irene said, surprised by the compliment. "It's a baker thing."

"Combining that information with all of the times I saw you visit the facilities, Harry, it sounds more like a prostate thing," Dewey said. "You should see M793qK."

"I like to stay hydrated on shoots," the baker retorted. "What are you doing for dinner, Belle? You should join us at Flower's Paradise. You said you wanted to have a look at our setup to pitch a story for Gem Today."

"Are you sure it won't upset any of the residents?" the Gem asked.

"They're used to being in commercials for the independent living deck, and we've been written up in the Galactic Free Press several times. Maureen, our public relations person, says that all publicity is good publicity."

"I meant my being a clone."

"Why would that bother anybody?" Irene asked. "You're not our clone."

"I'm not sure I understand your logic," Belle admitted.

"Earth made cloning people illegal even before the Stryx opened the planet, but that didn't stop some people from doing it, especially with their pets. In some cases, wealthy people created younger versions of themselves for estate planning purposes."

"We had a saying that you can't take it with you, but with a clone, you can leave it behind for yourself," Harry interjected.

"Except it doesn't really work that way since clones grow up with their own personalities," Irene said. "Some rich people who were obsessed with the idea of living forever tried creating blanks—adult clones with empty minds so they could have their memories and personalities transferred—but fortunately, it didn't work."

"Strangely enough, some of the advanced species theoretically allow such cloning and transfers in certain medical emergencies," Belle told them. "The Farlings are capable of creating a blank clone through the 3D cellular printing process and then transferring the essence of an individual, but I'm not sure if any of the tunnel network species have developed the necessary technology."

"That reminds me," Irene said. "You won't be the only non-Human if you come to eat with us tonight. Nancy was contacted last night by several Zarents who have started a sort of vocational school for Flower. She invited them to an informal dinner in the common room so they can talk to us about educational opportunities."

"The Zarents want to attract retired people to take vocational training?" the clone asked. "That doesn't sound right."

"One minute to Flower," Dewey announced. "I'm turning over control to her."

"You're welcome to come too," Irene said to the artificial person. "I'm never sure whether or not to invite you to meals since you don't eat."

"I'll take you up on that. I'm fascinated by everything about the Zarents, and I've been involved with the negotiations Flower holds with them."

Harry was surprised by the low attendance when the four of them arrived in the small commons where the original members of the independent living cooperative typically took their meals together. Jack and Nancy were at their normal table, along with Dave and his new girlfriend, but fewer than half of the seats in the room were occupied.

"Everybody, this is Belle," Harry introduced the clone. "Belle, this is Jack, the president of the cooperative, his wife Nancy, who runs our educational programs, Dave and uh—"

"June," Belle said. "We met on Bits."

"And Brenda, who is on our executive committee and does legal work for Flower."

"Earth legal work," the lawyer said, offering the clone a firm handshake. "I study tunnel network law as a sort of retirement hobby, but I'll never qualify to practice."

"How was Earth Two?" Jack asked.

"We shot a nice barn-raising that I think you'll enjoy," Irene told him. "I was unit director for the day."

"Where is everybody?" Harry asked. "I was actually worried we wouldn't be able to find seats for Belle and Dewey with the Zarents coming. We've never had them before."

"One of the Alt colonist groups that's going down to the planet later this week is holding a picnic to thank all of the retirees from the independent living deck who participated in the outreach program to help them acclimate to humans," Brenda said. "They're performing a concert as well."

"I should really be there with a camera," Irene said, beginning to rise. "I'll grab the one from my cabin and—"

"Your whole class is there," Nancy told her. "When I heard about the concert, I took the liberty of sending them all a notification through the continuing education alert system that they could earn extra credit by attending."

"Stay standing," Harry told Irene. "Come on, Belle. It looks like self-service tonight. I don't know why we brought you over to the table without getting food first."

The four-armed maintenance bot behind the steam table serving up food from one of the larger cafeterias was a sign that there was no surplus labor looking for work that night. Harry and Irene both went with comfort food, spaghetti for him, and chicken pot pie for her. Belle chose the vegetarian meal, which seemed rather heavy on steamed zucchini, and quickly moved onto the dessert cart, where she liberated a fudge brownie and a chocolate pudding. A fleshless limb terminating in a pincer reached past her and took the wicker basket filled with single-serving bags of potato chips that seemed to have been placed on the dessert cart as an afterthought.

"I don't know what's gotten into Flower," M793qK said through the external speaking pendant he was wearing on a necklace. "Potato chips are definitely not on the dietary recommendations list I drew up for this facility."

"We never get them," Harry said as he moved past the aliens to the hot drinks table. "Flower must have known you were coming."

"Stop drinking coffee at dinner and you won't wake up in the middle of the night and break a toe walking into a table leg," the Farling scolded Harry.

"It only happened the one time, and Irene and I both drink tea at night."

"Tea is also a diuretic unless you stick with the herbal blends. Is there any Earl Grey?"

Harry thumbed through the box of teabags. "Yes, but it's caffeinated."

"It's for me, not you, unless you'd like a cup also, Belle?"

"If you're recommending it," the Gem said graciously. "Are the Zarents who are coming tonight patients of yours?"

"I haven't had the pleasure of treating the individuals in question," M793qK said, accepting the first cup of Earl Grey and passing it on to Belle. "But the Zarents wished to show their respect by inviting me to their first public speaking event, and of course, I reciprocated that respect by showing up."

"Can you explain why they're always riding those little unicycles?" Irene asked. "I've spoken to a few while volunteering at the bazaar, but it's so awkward holding conversations when both sides have to wait for a translation through an external speech pendant."

"They'll learn to understand English quickly when they spend time around Humans. And they ride the unicycles for several reasons, including exercise. Having eight limbs, they can alternate the pair of tentacles they use to pedal, and they can make much better speed than walking about on their tentacles, which are optimized for Zero-G."

"What I don't get is how they can be so smart with those little bodies," Harry said as he handed the second cup of Earl Grey to the Farling. "It doesn't look like there's enough room in there for a big brain, not to mention much else."

M793qK's wings popped partially out of his carapace in a show of amusement. "You don't think that we engineered the Zarents with Human grey matter, do you? Their brains are a model of efficiency, and don't get me started on their memory systems."

"They're here," Irene called from the table, waving impatiently at her husband. "Come and sit down."

Harry quickly made two cups of herbal tea, added them to his tray, and returned to the table as a pair of Zarents riding unicycles headed past him in the other direction on their way to meet the Farling doctor. Everybody watched as M793qK tore open a bag of chips and offered them to the small aliens. Each Zarent fished out a single chip with a tentacle, took their time examining the snack food with devices attached to their tool harnesses, and then politely returned the potato chips to the bag.

"Don't know what they're missing," Dave said with a longing look. "Where did those chips come from anyway? They weren't up there when I visited the dessert cart."

"Does anybody know if the Zarents ever get off of their unicycles?" Nancy inquired. "When I asked Flower to send a table and a stand for the speakers, she said it wouldn't be necessary."

"I imagine she can patch them directly into her public address system for the room," Belle said. "I don't know anything about Zarent traditions for making public appearances, but I suspect it comes up so infrequently that there's no etiquette involved."

"Aren't they going to eat anything?"

Belle pointed at her ear for a few seconds to indicate she was communicating over her implant. "Flower says they ate before they came," she said. "Just tell them when you're ready, and if you want to make introductions, the one with the white star shape on his fur is Third Engineer Rokdim, and the other is First Educator Matzor."

Nancy rose to her feet and made her way through the tables to where the Farling doctor and the two Zarents seemed to be playing with the coffee stirrers. First Educator Matzor didn't notice the retired schoolteacher's approach, and M793qK reached out with a limb to stop the unicycle and prevent it from rolling over Nancy's foot.

"I'm sorry to interrupt," Nancy said, speaking slowly to give the Zarent's external translation devices a chance to analyze her voice. "Flower tells me that you're ready any time."

"Yes," the Zarent with the white star told her, casually sweeping away the coffee-stirrer tower with a tentacle. "Is there somewhere in particular you want us to circle?"

"Or we could rock in place like we're doing now," the other Zarent offered.

Nancy glanced at the Farling, who gave no indication that one course of action would be preferred over the other. "Whatever makes you comfortable. I believe everybody has a decent view of this area, and if they don't, there are plenty of empty seats." After the fact, she realized the implication of what she'd said, and added, "The Alts are holding a farewell concert and invited the cooperative. Otherwise, the room would be packed."

"You're Nancy, Jack's wife."

"Yes?"

"We came specifically to speak to you. The others are welcome to stay, but we take no offense if they wish to leave."

"No, they wanted to hear what you have to say," Nancy protested. She turned back to the tables, hoping that the Zarents wouldn't be offended by her looking away. "Our guests tonight are First Educator Matzor and Third Engineer Rokdim," she announced in a voice that carried without an artificial boost from Flower. "They're here to speak to us about the education program they've started."

"Thank you," First Educator Matzor said, rocking her unicycle gently back and forth to remain in place. "At the request of your Dollnick host, we have undertaken to start a vocational training course in deep space maintenance for interested Humans. While the physics of interstellar travel are currently outside the model of the universe that your species adheres to, some mechanical aspects of servicing and repairing a ship's physical plant are within your reach."

"The recent immigrants from Bits, with their understanding of low-level programming algorithms and crude machine controls, are demonstrating a remarkable aptitude for non-engineered life forms," Third Engineer Rokdim added as he rode in a slow circle around the Farling and the First Educator.

"But we have encountered certain difficulties in the teaching process for which Flower suggested we seek your help. In short," the Zarent extended all six tentacles that weren't on the pedals of her unicycle, "our tools and methods are poorly suited to bipedal humanoids, who also tower over us."

"Our understanding is that the residents of this deck have completed their primary careers, and in some cases, have entered a phase of their life cycle known as retirement. Flower assured us that some people in this retirement phase retain the memories of their professional lives, even if the skills have deteriorated through lack of practice. We're interested in hiring part-time instructors with experience in the trades who can serve as guides for the students. In addition to fair compensation, the instructors may enjoy learning some advanced techniques that are largely unknown outside of Zarent circles."

"Do you have a specific list of skills you're interested in?" Nancy asked when it became apparent that the Zarents had finished speaking.

"Welding, plumbing, and wired controls," Third Engineer Rokdim ticked off on his tentacles. "And anybody with a background in rigging."

"Rigging what?"

"Rigging anything," the Zarent told her. "On planets, they would likely have experience with erecting cranes, installing large pieces of equipment, jobs involving moving and erecting custom assemblies."

"Construction workers," Nancy suggested.

"Few construction workers have experience with rigging beyond basic scaffolding. Riggers are called upon to deal with complex situations that are likely unique to a particular job."

"Anyone with experience working on a freehold as a subsistence farmer would also be welcome to apply," First Educator Matzor said. "They should have a generalist skill set."

"And you want to train these people to your current state of the art so they can pass it along?" Nancy asked.

Both Zarents lifted their bodies off their unicycle seats and emitted a buzzing noise, and M793qK had to tuck his wings back in again.

"We hope that they will be able to translate our instructions more readily into actions for the students to copy," Third Engineer Rokdim said. He stopped circling on his unicycle and tilted towards the Farling, evidently communicating something telepathically.

"No, not puppets," M793qK said out loud through his speaking pendant. "That has a bad connotation in English. Yes, marionette means the same thing. Servomechanisms refer to electromechanical devices, not people."

"Are you aware you're talking out loud?" Nancy asked.

"I was hoping you would take my meaning and jump in with the right word. Oddly enough, I can't seem to recall an English term for an individual of some middling skill level who follows the instructions of an individual of a high skill level in order to demonstrate a technique to individuals of a low skill level."

"I don't think we have an exact word for that."

M793qK rubbed something out on his speaking legs, causing the Zarents to again lift themselves from their unicycles and emit a buzzing sound.

Back at the table, Harry washed down a mouthful of spaghetti with a swallow of herbal tea and asked Belle, "What did the Farling just say?"

"He said 'I told you so,'" the Gem replied. "I gather the three of them had a bet. Some of the advanced species find your limited vocabulary to be a source of endless entertainment."

"The job offer is interesting," Jack said. "I can think of a dozen members who were in the trades and complain that the volunteer work Flower finds for them isn't challenging. Maybe they'd enjoy doing a little teaching."

"Just don't tell them that we don't have a word for what they'll be doing," Irene said. "They're likely to take it the wrong way."

Thirteen

The young woman working behind the counter at the School of Government café reached for an individual-size teapot before Vivian placed her order.

"Green Sencha," Vivian told her, even though it wasn't necessary. "How's your afternoon going?"

"Slow," Delphi replied. "It's one of those days where all of the core students are in their double-session class and most of the others have something scheduled at the Open University. How about yourself?"

"Samuel is babysitting Rose in the office this afternoon and I was trying to catch up with some stuff we've been procrastinating." She studied the pastries in the dessert case, reminded herself that she was back to burning a lot of calories dancing, and made a command decision. "I'm going to try the Gem cake. Want to join me?"

"Just for a minute," Delphi said. "My relief will be here soon, and then I have to get to my loadmaster class." She finished hand-filling the teabag with the green tea, topped it off with boiling water from the espresso machine, and passed it across the counter. "I'll bring out the cake and the cup."

"Cut a slice for yourself," Vivian said. "It's on me."

"The Gem cake is the most expensive dessert on the menu, and the richest too," Delphi warned her. "The students will split a piece three or four ways. I don't think I could eat more than half a slice myself."

"I suppose if you put it that way, I'll bow to your superior experience. One slice, two forks."

The handful of students studying in the café all said something polite as Vivian made her way to her favorite table, an industrial-looking construct of iron and copper pipes with a treadle that drove a flywheel without a belt. She put her large purse on the glass tabletop next to the teapot, slid onto the faux-wood bench, and absent-mindedly gave the treadle a few pumps to get the flywheel spinning.

"Here we go," Delphi said, placing a teacup and saucer in front of Vivian, and then setting the plate with the single thick slice of the incredibly rich cake which was heavily covered with chocolate shavings. "Bill says that Harry invented this cake for Belle. Do you know her?"

"The Gem who came on board with you at Bits," Vivian said. "She interviewed me for Gem Today, a piece about working mothers on board Flower. I met her at the Blue Tea Café and she ordered a hot chocolate."

"She says all of the Gem love chocolate." Delphi used her fork to take a small corner of the slice, brought it to her mouth, and groaned theatrically. "This is almost too much. I guarantee it will cheer you up."

"Do I look sad?"

"A little. Or maybe a bit stressed?"

"I've been falling behind on the Human Empire's to-do list," Vivian said. "The Old Way communities at Earth Two sent a delegation to Flower to remind me that I promised them stamps."

"Postage stamps?"

"It's a stupid thing to have procrastinated, and on any other world it would have been unimportant, because everybody just uses the same stamps as the host species. Earth Two is probably the only occupied planet in the galaxy without a native stamp."

"I don't get why any of the aliens would use stamps," Delphi said. "We printed our own postage on Bits, and it was basically just a QR code that gave Thark routing information so that whichever species was delivering the mail could charge the face amount to the Rules Committee account. I just assumed that all of the advanced species did something similar."

"I take it you've never met a philatelist," Vivian said with a wry smile as she took a forkful of the cake. Her face went slack for a moment, and she remained silent while the chocolate dissolved on her tongue. "You're right. If I tried to eat a slice of this by myself I'd end up in a coma."

"What's a philatelist?" Delphi asked. "I've never heard that one."

"A stamp collector. And they like their stamps to be more than a computer code or a numeric value. The Human Empire already prints pre-paid postage on metered mail to get the DNA samples returned for GenePost, but the delegation from Earth Two wants wildlife stamps, and that means hiring artists and making choices. I was going to take care of it while I was officially on maternity leave but it just never happened."

"Are you going to have a contest? I have a friend who's an illustrator, and there are probably thousands of video game artists from Bits who would jump into a competition. It might be a pain choosing the winner, but you can get the whole thing over with quickly, like tearing off a bandage."

"I did a little research into the stamp business when I should have been picking an artist, and I found out that most species produce a huge variety, in part to sell them to collectors," Vivian said. "Now that I think of it, if we come up with stamps that appeal to alien collectors, it might not be a bad source of revenue. But the other thing I learned is that they're supposed to be meaningful."

"Wildlife is meaningful, at least to people who grew up without any," Delphi said. "All of the kids on Bits loved children's books with animals."

"Nature themes are acceptable for a series, as are famous individuals from history, but every species is expected to produce stamps that capture the essence of their culture and philosophy." She drew her tab out of her purse, swiped it to life, spent a few seconds navigating, and then passed it across the table. "These are the premier stamps of the tunnel network species that we see the most of because they can breathe our air. See if you can guess whose is whose."

"But I can't read any alien—" Delphi broke off when she saw how obvious the illustrations were. "Verlock, Horten, Grenouthian, Frunge, Drazen, Dollnick, Gem, Fillinduck. I didn't get the white one or the pillar of flame."

"The white stamp is issued by the Cherts, and the gout of flame is Huktra," Vivian told her. "And that's just one example from each. Nobody keeps the same stamps for too long because the philatelists are always looking to add to their collections."

"And you don't know what you can put on a stamp to compete with space elevators or mathematical laws," Delphi mused. "Maybe Sabina and Katya could give you some ideas. I've never met anybody who knows as much about tunnel network cultures as they do."

"Thanks for reminding me." Vivian took another forkful of cake as if to fortify herself. "That's going to help. I should probably pour my tea into a to-go cup and get this over with."

"If you want to talk to Sabina and Katya, their class just started like twenty minutes ago. There's always a run on the Gem cake when it lets out."

"I promised Samuel I would go and sit in for an hour. Keep it to yourself, but we've had some complaints."

"I'm surprised. The students flock around the twins when they hold their office hours in the café."

"The male students?"

"Now that you mention it, yes, but even on Bits that platinum blonde hair would have turned heads," Delphi said, standing up and taking the teapot. "I'll put this in a takeout cup for you."

"Thanks. What am I going to do with the rest of this cake?"

"Don't look at me. I can almost feel my waistline increasing. I'll wrap it up and you can bring it home for your husband. My boyfriend moved in after we stopped at Earth, and I don't have leftovers anymore. He's better than a garbage disposal."

"I knew men were good for something," Vivian said, grabbing her purse and following Delphi to the counter. "But I shouldn't say anything because my husband is always willing to babysit."

"Why is it babysitting when a father watches a baby and just part of her day when the mother watches?" Delphi asked. She poured the green tea into a takeout cup, secured the lid, and wrapped the remains of the cake in biodegradable plastic.

Vivian laughed, put the cake in her purse, and took the tea. "I don't know the answer to that, and I'm practically babysitting royalty. Maybe it's because people are tacitly admitting that babies need their mothers."

After exiting the café, Vivian made her way with heavy feet to the classroom where Sabina and Katya were teaching Introduction to Tunnel Network Culture, and slipped in the back door. It was impossible not to notice that the front and middle seats were all occupied by young men, and the young women sat around the periphery, some of them looking at their smartphones rather than the instructors.

"The moral of the story," Sabina was saying, "is if you ever get invited to a Fillinduck party, don't go near the Rinty bubbles, and keep your clothes on."

The males all exploded in laughter, and a few of the women smiled, but Vivian couldn't help noticing that a couple of girls, including the two who had come to complain to her about the class, looked like they were drinking unsweetened lemonade.

"Now, you won't have those problems with Verlocks," Katya said. "I worked in their embassy for a year and none of them realized I was female."

"I doubt that," a young man sitting in the front said.

"No, I'm serious. The Verlocks seek out harsh living environments, especially hot volcanic worlds, and they can't look at us without thinking how much of a burden it would be if we came to visit them at home. They're extremely hospitable, but—that reminds me of a party they hosted for the new Drazen ambassador."

Vivian saw the male students nudging each other and grinning in anticipation of another party story, but again, the girls looked far less interested.

"It was one of those last-minute things that the aliens settled by drawing names out of a hat because the new ambassador showed up a full cycle early—something about having already sold his home and having nowhere else to go. Anyway, who did I go with, Sabina?"

"That guy from the mining family with the missing pinky," her sister replied. "Everybody kept asking him why he didn't get a new one, but he said it showed that he'd worked the claims."

"I couldn't get used to it when we danced," Katya said. "But anyway, my point is—what was my point?"

One of the girls Vivian was watching groaned out loud, but it was largely covered by the laughs of the young men who were apparently witnessing a familiar routine.

"But how should we act when meeting a Verlock for the first time?" a young woman called out.

"You don't have to act at all," Katya said. "Verlocks think that everything we do is strange and immature, and I'm not just talking about me and my sister in this case. You can't really sink in their estimation because there's no lower to go. The most important thing about dealing with Verlocks is not to make them repeat themselves."

"Because you'll be old by the time they finish," Sabina chimed in.

"True, but they don't speak until they've fully considered what they're about to say, and if you've asked them a question, that's the answer you're going to get. It's not going to change, and if you try rephrasing the question to get a different answer, they'll take it as an insult to their analytical ability."

"But what if they're wrong?" one of the students asked.

"They aren't wrong," Katya said. "At least, I've never seen it happen. It's one of the things you'll have to get used to if you work around aliens. They aren't omniscient, with the possible exception of the Stryx, but thanks to their cultures or their education systems, they've learned not to go around offering bad advice just to hear the sounds of their own voices."

"Like we do," Sabina said, drawing a general laugh from the class. "Maybe the best way to get the point across is with a little role-playing. Katya?"

"What species should we have them do?"

"Flower?" Vivian subvoced without pointing at her ear. "Can you pass a message to Sabina and Katya that I'd like to see them get the girls involved with the role-playing?"

"Done," Flower replied as the males again exploded in laughter at something that one of the twins said.

"Volunteers," Katya said, and all of the hands at the front and center of the room shot up. "No, we're always getting boys. How about some girl power for a change? Lisa? Denise?"

The two young women who had separately complained to Vivian rose uneasily to their feet, and Denise started blushing before she even reached the front of the class.

"Perfect," Sabina said, and she whispered something in the shy girl's ear before standing her directly across from Lisa. "Denise is playing a Horten clerk for us, and Lisa, I want you to be a representative from the Human Empire who is visiting the Games Authority on the Horten deck of a Stryx station. You're trying to figure out what it will take to get some local humans approved as judges for an upcoming tournament."

"Hi," Lisa said, doing her best to offer a sincere smile. "I'm here from the Human Empire to ask about getting some of our people approved as judges."

Vivian cringed out of sympathy when Denise, whose nervous blush had taken on fire engine proportions, failed to answer. All of the students stirred uneasily.

"It's, uh, we're pretty good at gaming," Lisa attempted to improvise. "If there's a fee or something. No?"

"You can let out your breath now," Sabina said to the red-faced girl, and as Denise exhaled and sucked in a lungful of fresh air, her color started to fade. "Now what did Lisa get wrong?"

There was a long silence, and then one of the students suggested, "She should have started by offering money?"

"Maybe she's dressed immodestly and that embarrassed the Horten," a guy said.

"What did we tell you about Hortens and their emotions?" Katya asked.

"You didn't," Lisa said. "It's on the syllabus for today."

"Right, so we're doing it now," Sabina said. "If you ever visit a Horten office and the clerk starts to turn red, just turn around and leave. It means that they're angry, and the redder they get, the angrier they are. It might not be something that you did, though it probably is, but it's also not something you're going to resolve by guesswork."

"Usually it's because you either didn't make an appointment or because you're late," Katya said. "You can download a color guide for your tab that explains what Hortens are feeling for all of the shades of the rainbow. And the important thing to remember is that they expect everybody to be able to read their color changes. If you can't, you're missing over half of the content of what they're saying."

"Or not saying," Sabina said, glancing at the back of the class where Vivian sat. "We probably should have included that color chart with the syllabus."

"Now, with upper caste Vergallians, it's almost the opposite," Katya said. "They have enhanced perception, including truthsayers who can easily detect when most species are telling lies. When you talk to them, you should keep in mind that you're telling them more than you're saying."

"I heard that they only have that effect on men," Denise said. The color immediately began to return to her cheeks, though this time it stopped at an attractive pink.

"Mature upper caste Vergallian women, basically the ones from royal families who have been through the training, can secrete pheromones that put most males and some females into a sort of hypnotic state in which we're vulnerable to suggestions," Sabina said. "I can't explain the biology, but the more a humanoid looks like a Vergallian, the more likely it is to work."

"Panspermia, Stryx style," Katya said. "It's widely accepted among the tunnel network aliens that the Stryx visited our worlds and did some creative genetic engineering on our forebears to cause our evolution to converge toward near-compatible species. In fact, the Vergallians themselves are a mix of races that evolved on different worlds."

"But that's all in their pre-history and none of them like talking about it much."

"What about that academy of dance that the imperial couple told us about in ballroom practice?" asked one of the guys who hadn't seen Vivian slip into the back of the class.

"Astria's Academy of Dance," Katya said. "There's even a branch on Flower now if you want to crib extra lessons and make Samuel and Vivian think that you have talent."

"But why would an advanced species want to become known for a string of dance studios, or gaming tournaments, for that matter?"

"Or math academies, a news network with a penchant for making fun of primitive species, or a half-dozen other cultural specialties I could name. Do you see the common thread?"

"They make money?" asked the student who had suggested Lisa offer money to the Horten clerk in the role-playing exercise.

"They're all aimed at the common people," Sabina said. "The advanced species don't waste their time doing outreach to alien elites, there's nothing they want from each other enough to put up with egomaniacs from another species. But they're happy to win the hearts and minds of a segment of each other's populations, and they do that by picking a couple of things from their culture with crossover potential and pushing some money into them."

"Weirdly enough, humans have much more exposure to the other species than most aliens do at this point. More than half of humanity left Earth for work, and the people who remained behind are getting deluged with alien tourists because we're a new species to them," Katya said. "The other thing about the alien specialties—but I forgot what I was going to say again."

"Are you guys getting anything out of this?" Sabina asked, glancing towards Vivian again. "Neither of us have trained as teachers, and I'm beginning to think that it's harder than it looked."

"Today wasn't bad," Denise said.

Fourteen

"I envy you," Rayne said loudly to get Julie's attention.

Flower's executive assistant looked up from her sewing machine, stopping the needle instantly by ceasing the rocking motion of her feet on the treadle.

"Me? I can teach you to sew if you want. It's only taken me a year to get this far, and Flower is manufacturing new machines with some updates that make them easier to use."

Rayne's poker-face relaxed. "I wasn't talking about sewing, though maybe I could use a hobby. I envy you that with all of the jobs you do for Flower, you can put it all aside and do something else during your lunch hour. What are you making?"

"Another shirt for Bill," Julie said. "I'm experimenting with different looks for when he opens his own café. It's going to be a sort of uniform for all of the help."

"Hercules would think I'd lost my mind if I tried to sew something for him," Rayne said. "I tried knitting a stuffed rabbit for my daughter once and she thought it was a bear."

"What did you tell her?"

"That she was right. Do you have a minute?"

"Strangely enough, I have all afternoon, or at least until the thing at the shipyard," Julie corrected herself as she reached down and pulled the lever that unlocked the wheels on her office chair so she could move back behind her desk. "I was just going to go over the schedule for our stops again, but I can do that any time."

"That's what I wanted to talk to you about," Rayne said, settling into the guest seat. "I've been spending a lot of time with Lynx the last few weeks to get a feel for how the bazaar merchants and other businesses on board operate. Their number one complaint is how Flower has been making last-minute schedule changes to shave time off stops."

Julie nodded. "I was talking with Dewey the other day and he said pretty much the same thing. He'd be the last person, well, the last artificial person, to criticize Flower, but he's taken over running Next Stop Deliveries when he's around, and early departures wreak havoc with shippers. They prefer to save up all of their outgoing packages for one pickup at the end of a stop."

"That's just it. I wasn't with Flower a couple of months ago, but all the merchants I meet talk about the good old days before she took on the Earth Two colonization business. They say that Flower used to keep to her schedule like clockwork. Now she puts them off with double-talk about dynamic reverse rescheduling, like they should be happy that she's creating new logistics challenges."

"I'm not that bad," Flower interjected via an overhead speaker grille. "I hope these same merchants tell you that I compensate them for any losses directly attributable to early departures."

"Yes, but they don't want handouts," Rayne said, glancing up at the ceiling. "They want to live on a colony ship that sticks to its schedule."

"There has to be another way, Flower," Julie said. "What if we dropped one of our Earth Two stops so we're only going there three times a year instead of four? That would save a full week, and if you and the captain drop your elective stops, that would get us most of the way back to normal."

"I won't pretend that keeping the colonists on board for another month would be any burden, but my commitment to supervise the terraforming work requires quarterly visits to Earth Two," the Dollnick AI said.

"Who's the counterparty for that agreement?" Rayne asked. "EarthCent? The Alts? The Container Prince? Could you renegotiate?"

"There's a political aspect. I have to submit regular reports to the Terraforming Subcommittee of the Planning Board that granted EarthCent and the Alts a variance to carry on with the work abandoned by the Container Prince. That means meetings, votes, public hearings—all of which give third parties a chance to seek favors and concessions that I'm not in a position to grant."

"What sorts of things would they want from you?" Julie asked.

"If it was money, we could work something out, but you're talking about tunnel network power politics, an arena in which I have no standing," Flower said. "The committee members basically trade votes—you smooth the ruffles on my feathered crest and I'll smooth the ruffles on yours."

"Could we ask EarthCent and the Alts to approach the committee?" Rayne asked.

"The Alts declined tunnel network membership in favor of accepting protection from the Vergallians," Flower reminded them, "and while EarthCent would likely cooperate, they already owe everybody favors. I'm not saying it's impossible, only that it would take more time than you might imagine. It also wouldn't address pending requests from the Human Empire and the Conference of Sovereign Human Communities to expand our current circuit."

"Excuse me?" Julie looked up at the ceiling, a frown on her face. "Why is this the first time I'm hearing about the requests?"

"I didn't want you to worry. Both Samuel McAllister and Daniel Cohan are aware that we're in no position to add stops at this time, but they've made the requests to give us visibility for planning. I was going to tell you before we reached Union Station since Daniel has offered to host a meeting on the scheduling topic at CoSHC headquarters."

"And you want me to attend to say there's nothing we can do?"

"There are always options if you keep an open mind," Flower said, eliciting a snort from Rayne. "Your idea to drop one Earth Two stop a year is worth exploring as a fallback in case nothing else pans out, but in the meantime, I'd like the two of you to work on a plan for someday adding a second ship. At least that will give the Human Empire and CoSHC a target."

"But how far into the future are you talking?" Rayne asked. "I know a hundred years is nothing to most species whose kids are just finishing school at that age, but you're talking multiple generations for humans. We just don't plan that far ahead."

"Then this will be a good experience for you. Base your plans on a jump ship that spins on its axis to create artificial gravity and hosts a few hundred thousand inhabitants."

"You're talking about a small colony ship," Rayne said.

"Ultimately, it's the only type suitable for the job," Flower said. "You might want to read up on the Colony One movement if you aren't familiar with it."

"Aren't they a scam?"

"Flower hosted a tour for their group a few years ago," Julie said. "I met the founder, Sally Nugget, a trader who discovered a solid gold asteroid in space. Colony One is her philanthropy. Dianne, our resident Galactic Free Press reporter, did a nice story about them."

"I thought it was a sort of a cult where you pledge to make a donation if they can convince one of the advanced species to sell them an old colony ship for refurbishing," Rayne said. "Wait, is that your plan, Flower? You're going to broker a deal between Colony One and some aliens you know with a colony ship for sale?"

"That would be convenient, but I'm afraid that most of the people pledging support for Colony One imagine getting a ship to explore the galaxy, not to provide support services on the tunnel network for established human communities," Flower said. "But there is a certain amount of overlap that we'd be silly to ignore."

"It sounds like a disaster waiting to happen. Not getting another ship working our circuit," Rayne corrected herself hastily, "but the idea of a bunch of human space-travel enthusiasts getting their hands on a jump ship and going exploring. Don't they know that the galaxy is already occupied?"

"Not the whole thing. There are hundreds of billions of stars, after all, and an even greater number of planets. Existing empires expand to star systems in physical proximity for practical purposes, and species are always coming and going. That doesn't even take into account ongoing star and planetary formation."

"You're saying the exploration is still a viable way of adding new star systems to an empire?" Julie asked. "I didn't realize that."

"Why do you think colony ships exist?" Flower asked in reply. "Only two of the worlds I helped colonize showed signs of previous occupancy, though a hundred million years on a geologically active planet can bury any signs of failed ecosystems pretty deep, especially if you're talking about gaseous or energy-based forms of life."

"Getting back to the issue at hand, you want us to create a plan for adding another colony ship to our circuit for the sake of having something to present at this upcoming meeting on Union Station?"

"We aren't trying to deceive them. I want you to look at this as two separate challenges. If a second colony ship fell into our laps tomorrow, it wouldn't immediately solve our problems because there would be nobody living on board, no working economy, and no reason for anybody at our stops to visit unless they were hitching a ride. I want the two of you to prepare a plan so that the Human Empire and CoSHC will know what we all need to do if a companion ship can eventually be obtained."

"I suppose that's reasonable enough," Rayne said, though her face couldn't hide her suspicion that the Dollnick AI was trying to put something over on them. "Do you want to work on this together, Julie, or should we break it into parts? I could take the tourist attractions and small businesses I've been learning about from Lynx, and you could address the events and major businesses that you already do for Flower."

"That works for me, but let's sit down at the end of the month, put the two parts together, and then take it to Captain Pyun to ask what we've left out," Julie said. "Most people think he's just the disembodied voice who gives travel updates, or the guy in the funny uniform who does weddings, but the captain is EarthCent's point man on Flower, and he's the one who negotiates with the authorities at our stops. I think he's also sort of responsible for all of the alien intelligence agents on board."

"Should we pencil in hosting spies on our hypothetical companion ship?" Rayne asked. "No, don't tell me. I don't know anything about it so I'll leave it to you."

After the comptroller left, Julie finished running the seam she was working on just so the piece wouldn't be hanging from the sewing machine with a needle in it. Then she started checking her desk drawers.

"What are you looking for?" Flower asked.

"My phone. I must have left it somewhere."

"I'll call you and listen for the ringtone."

"Can't you just trace the signal or something?"

"This is more fun, and with all of the signal reflections inside the ship, it's also more accurate. It wouldn't be very helpful for me to tell you that your phone is in the food court somewhere."

"I'm just surprised," Julie said, getting up again and checking the shelves. "Did you hear anything?"

"Blue Tea Café," Flower said. "You left it there when you met Vivian this morning. One of the waitresses found your phone and they have it at the register for you to pick up any time."

"I guess I'm going for a walk then because I want to talk to Dewey about this new project if he's free. He's on my contact list."

"Have you already forgotten how you lived before I gave you the phone? I'll be happy to ping Dewey for you."

"Only if he's not busy."

"So it's okay for you to call him if he's busy but not for me to ping him for you?"

"There's a difference," Julie said as she left her office and headed for the lift tube. "If I text him to call if he has time, he can ignore it or wait. If you ping him, he probably feels that he has to answer."

"You're overthinking it. Dewey is at the shipyard observing the new training program for Humans, but he'll be happy to meet with you."

"I'll just pick up my phone first and then I'll go there. I kind of feel naked without it now."

"I can't believe how addictive humans find those things," Flower said as the capsule doors closed. "It's a primitive version of a tab that weighs too much and has terrible bandwidth issues. Lume bought one, and he said he can't watch mitt-paddle-cup-ball on it because the ball seems to disappear in flight."

"Lume bought a smartphone?"

"All of the intelligence agents felt they had to when it became a thing, which just goes to show the danger of expense accounts. Now they're playing with secure messaging apps which make it that much harder for me to keep track of what they're up to."

"I thought you were all friends," Julie said, fighting not to break into a run when the doors opened in sight of the Blue Tea Café. She shifted to subvocing and added, "Swiping a screen is easier than navigating on a heads-up display, and small devices fit better in pockets."

"The fake wristwatch Lume wears can do more than the most expensive smartphone will be capable of in a million years if you keep making them," Flower said dismissively. "Buying smartphones is just an affectation, like one-time pads."

"Bill will take a secure app over a one-time pad any day of the week." Julie sighed with relief when she saw the familiar crocheted phone case that the Human Empire's Cayl mentor had presented her with out of the blue. "There it is."

"Julie?" the guy behind the counter asked. "Flower told us you were on your way."

"Thank you. Is Fandaz in?"

The counterman shook his head. "She left a couple of hours ago with some Frunge guy after explaining to everybody that it was strictly business. It sounded like she had a guilty conscience or something."

Julie checked her messages and saw that she had missed two texts from the owner of the café. "Funny, she was trying to reach me when my phone was right here."

She began wandering back towards the lift tube while looking down at her phone, smiled at the café owner's lame excuse for going to watch Razood teach some new students blacksmithing without consulting with her chaperone beforehand, and almost ran into Yaem, who caught her by the shoulders at the last moment.

"Those things are a pedestrian hazard," Yaem said, indicating the smartphone with a slight movement of his head. "Do you have a minute to talk anime?"

"Only a minute," Julie said. "Was there a problem with submissions I vetted for the festival? I try to be fair, but I have to admit that some of the violent stuff just grosses me out."

"That's why we have hundreds of volunteers watching everything they have time for," the Sharf said.

"I thought I was it!"

"What gave you that impression? I asked you because I value your opinion and because we worked together launching the conference business." He withdrew his eye stalks almost into the sockets in the manner of a Sharf who was about to say something serious. "You know all about Humans. Was there something wrong with the last batch Flower picked up at Bits?"

Julie took a moment to reply as she tried to imagine what Yaem was getting at. "They seem normal enough to me," she said finally. "Have you had a problem with your recent hires?"

"Yes. The quit rate is triple or quadruple our usual. It's normal for employees in the entertainment business to move on for better offers, but we're the only major employer of anime artists on Flower. Exit interviews indicate that the recent quits from Bits are leaving the entertainment business."

"Oh, I have heard something like that from a few people. I think the first group that moved to Flower from Bits a few years ago was highly motivated to get involved with state-of-the-art alien entertainment technology, and in fact, that's the main reason they joined us. The larger group that just came on board a few months ago was dedicated to preserving Earth's old hacking and gaming culture. It makes sense that they would have more issues with settling into new jobs for a business owned by a Dollnick AI and managed by an alien, uh—you."

"That's what I thought," Yaem said, "but—" he was interrupted by a strange wailing sound that seemed to emanate from somewhere behind him, a mystery that was solved when he pulled a phone from his back pocket and swiped it to life. "Yes?" he said, waggling his eyestalks apologetically at Julie. "Yes? Yes. All right. Yes. Five minutes." He looked at the phone like he wanted to throw it down the corridor and then returned it to his back pocket. "Sorry. I just have time to grab a cup of tea and get back to the studio. We'll talk later."

Julie smiled sympathetically as the harried alien was forced to reach for his back pocket to answer another wail as he made his way into the Blue Tea Café. Then she resumed her walk to the lift tube and subvoced, "Are you really doing that bad on retaining new employees from Bits, Flower?"

"Relatively speaking, yes," Flower replied as the capsule started moving inwards toward the shipyard deck. "In absolute numbers, the quit rate is probably no worse than the industry norms, though as Yaem points out, it's not like there's another major anime studio on board to support horizontal moves."

"Do you think I got the reason right?"

"Largely. My first batch of immigrants from Bits wanted to be here, while this second, larger batch simply accepted me as their best option at the time. I'll hold onto most of them, of course, but I won't be surprised to lose twenty thousand or so. You'll see when you meet Dewey."

"Are all of the students in the new training program dropouts from Bits?"

"They haven't left me yet, and where there's proximity, there's hope," Flower said. "But I will say that news of the training program spread like wildfire through the younger population from Bits who are dissatisfied with life onboard. The skills that the Zarents are teaching are both in demand and highly transportable, meaning it's an attractive option for footloose youngsters who want to see more of the galaxy before settling down."

"Are they working on the new assembly line for rental ships, or…" Julie trailed off when the doors opened. "Is this the right place?"

"The shipyard is up to the left, out of sight due to the curvature of the deck. The training program proved so popular that I had it all moved out of the shipyard proper so the students wouldn't get in the way of the production workers."

"What's with all the heavy curtains?"

"A lot of welding practice at this end of the training area. If you walk up and around to the right, Dewey is waiting in the plumbing section."

"Is there that much call for plumbers in space?" Julie asked. "I remember a lot of jokes on Earth about it paying better than drug dealing, but I've never heard of anybody's toilet overflowing since I moved on board."

"Of course not," Flower said indignantly. "But I'm using the term plumbing in the Dollnick sense, which applies to all aspects of fluid transfer, wastewater treatment, and irrigation. It's a catch-all term for anything involving pipes or waveguides."

Julie greeted the waiting artificial person and asked, "What are they doing, Dewey?"

"Simulating an emergency bypass for a cooling system," Dewey said, pointing at a pair of Zarents who were mounted on maintenance bots. "Those saddles include a servomechanism interface that allows the Zarents to operate the four arms of the robots by moving their tentacles in those sleeves. Those eight students are trying to accomplish the same task through teamwork, but they're unaccustomed to working together."

"Don't you want to stay and watch?"

"They've been stuck on the same decoupling procedure for the last hour, and there are ten more groups strung out along the deck working on the same lesson. I understand that the Zarents will soon be getting help from retirees who can give the students a two-armed example. We can talk over here," he continued, motioning at a collection of chairs arranged in a circle.

"Was this set up for some sort of therapy group?" Julie asked. "Positive thinking for space maintenance trainees?"

"The Zarents traditionally lecture to a circle," Dewey said, and glancing over to where the instructors were demonstrating the proper procedure for the fourth time, added in a low voice, "I'm not sure if they have fronts or backs."

"I'll have to ask M793qK. Did Flower tell you why I wanted to talk?"

"She's given you a new assignment. I hope you take time off for yourself at some point."

"Flower promised me a super long vacation next year," Julie said. "I'm working with Rayne to create a plan for adding another colony ship to our circuit. It's strictly hypothetical, depending on whether a ship can be found and funded."

"Are you looking for a library consultant?"

"The library! I'd completely forgotten about that even though working there was my original job on board. I just wanted to get your take on what we'd need before I start the outline, and I'll want to run it past you later in the month before showing Captain Pyun."

"Flower."

"You think I should show it to Flower first?"

"I think fulfilling our mission for EarthCent requires Flower. If you're going to spread the schedule over two ships, they'll need to remain in constant communication." Dewey assumed a thoughtful expression. "I don't mean to make this about me, but I'll require a bigger ship than the bookmobile. I picture a need for continual trips between the two circuit ships to transfer people and goods."

"I thought they'd just meet up on a regular basis," Julie said.

"If it's too regular, you'll lose the whole advantage of having a second ship. I think you should plan for independent operation, but supervised from a distance. And in the spirit of starting with the attainable and progressing to the ideal, I think putting a small jump-capable freighter at my disposal would make a good beginning."

Fifteen

Bill pressed against the ship-wrap artwork on the bookmobile with both hands spread wide, trying to keep it smooth while Dewey went around the other side to take up the slack. "I don't understand, Flower," he said, trying to make sense of the collection of small tentacles that crowned the central Farling figure's head in the illustration. "Why would you display M793qK's coat of arms on the bookmobile when we're going to a Dollnick orbital repair facility on your business?"

"Because he's paying," Flower said bluntly.

"To show his advertising?"

"We're doing a three-way deal, and not all Dollnicks are enthusiastic about working with a rogue colony ship, even if I've been officially rehabilitated."

"Do you need a hand with that, Bill?" Lume asked from behind the young man. The Dollnick station chief, who ran a salad bar in the food court for cover, reached over and around the young man with all four long arms and pulled the ship-wrap taut, removing the final wrinkle. "All set, Dewey," he whistled loudly.

A minute later the artificial person returned from the other side of the small ship, and all three of them stood back to admire their work.

"What's with the tentacles wrapped around M793qK's head?" Bill asked. "Is he being attacked by an octopus?"

"The body isn't visible, but it's a fair bet that those tentacles belong to a Zarent," Lume said. "Given all of the doctor's work with them, I wouldn't be surprised if they're willing to be counted among his retainers."

"I wanted M793qK to add me, but he said I'd have to convince at least ten percent of human-derived artificial intelligences to join his cause to get added to his coat of arms," Dewey told them. "He said the Farlings have a College of Heraldry that keeps track of these things, and there's no greater embarrassment for members of the hierarchy than to be caught out cheating."

"Other than losing one's place in the hierarchy altogether, but that's a story for another day," M793qK rubbed out on his speaking legs as he joined the group. He thrust his medical bag at Bill and said, "When I give you the word, you open the bag and pour out the contents."

"Is this the, uh, what we picked up on Earth?"

"You'll find out soon enough. Any problems loading the transfer unit, Dewey?"

"I had to remove all of the shelves and the rear seating again," the artificial person said. "I really need a bigger ship."

"Good," the Farling said, climbing into the back of the bookmobile. "I'll just lie down on top of it, and you're in the passenger seat, Lume. Bill, you can sit on his lap."

Bill looked at the Dollnick intelligence agent and shook his head. "I'll just crouch between the front seats and hold on. I can see the orbital through the atmosphere retention field so it can't be more than a few minutes to get there."

"We'll be under acceleration the whole way, not in Zero-G," Dewey told him. "I don't think you have the arm strength to keep from being thrown into the back."

"I'm too old to sit on anybody's lap," Bill said stubbornly.

"Then take my seat and I'll ride hitchhiker," the artificial person said.

"But how will you fly the ship?"

"I'll jack in wirelessly for the fraction of the trip in which I'm actually in charge," Dewey said. "Flower will handle our launch and the orbital will insist that we hand over control for docking."

The trip went as quickly as Bill predicted, but he hadn't expected a heavily armed detachment of Dollnick space marines to surround their ship on the other end.

"Remember," Lume said, being careful to keep all four of his hands in full sight as he eased out of the co-pilot's seat. "Let me do the talking."

Bill mimicked the Dollnick's actions as he exited the opposite door of the bookmobile, and he wasn't surprised when he was patted down by a marine who was probably worried that the human was concealing another set of arms under his shirt. Oddly enough, the Dollnicks showed no interest in the black medical bag, and they let Dewey pass without a search, perhaps because a precedent had already been established for two-armed humanoids.

Lume whistled something untranslatable, and then moving slowly, he circled to the back of the bookmobile and released the hatch. M793qK eased himself out from his cramped position on top of the transfer unit, and then moved aside as a Dollnick wearing a lab coat climbed into the ship and began inspecting the cargo.

"The transfer unit is certified by Prince Kurda's advanced intelligence division and the seals are unbroken," Lume said to the tallest of the marines, who was apparently the commanding officer. "I personally guarantee its authenticity and will remain with it until the transfer is complete."

The lab-coated Dollnick activated a display on the transfer unit, plugged in a logging device, and initiated a diagnostic procedure. All of the assembled watchers held their breaths until the logger emitted a long high whistle, signifying that everything was satisfactory.

"I don't like it," the officer said. "Kruik deserves better than to be exiled with a rogue."

"My understanding is that this transfer is being made at Kruik's request," Lume said mildly. "We're not all cut out for a military career."

The Dollnick in the bookmobile left the data logger connected and moved to the rear of the transfer unit. He simultaneously twisted what looked like several valve handles, first to one side, then to the other, almost like he was working a combination lock. Then a circular hatch opened, revealing a bundle of optical cables whose ends were so bright that Bill was forced to shield his eyes.

The Dollnick officer gave a long and complex whistle, and another group of marines appeared. They were accompanied by several scientists in lab coats who were shepherding a floater that Bill would later describe as indescribable. It combined art and technology in a dizzying array of light-filled components and connections that seemed to be pulsing with life. The Dollnick marines all stood at attention and saluted with both hands on their left sides as the scientists connected a bundle of cables from the floater to the transfer unit in the shuttle.

Bill desperately wanted to ask what was going on, but the Farling doctor placed a restraining limb on the young man's shoulder, and they watched in silence with the solemn Dollnicks as the pulsing life slowly ebbed through the connector and into the transfer unit. When the alien construct finally went dark, the officer gave a final long whistle, and the marines formed up around the floater and marched off.

"That went as well as it could have," Lume said. "I've never attended a resignation ceremony before, and I'm not even sure if there's been one in my lifetime. You can always count on the military to do these things properly."

"Can I talk now?" Bill asked.

"Yes, but it's better to hold your questions until we're back," Lume told him. "Now we're waiting for the—that must be him coming now."

A towering Dollnick dressed in well-worn coveralls approached with long strides across the docking deck of the orbital. He greeted Lume, acknowledged the presence of Bill and Dewey with a polite nod, and then turned to M793qK and tilted his head like a curious dog.

"My first Farling sighting," the Dollnick said. "Seeing is believing, but what you want with an old secondary pile is beyond me. Name's Clufsh, if you can pronounce it."

"Clufsh," M793qK spoke through his pendant. "As you can see from my coat of arms, I've acquired Zarent retainers, and they requested that I obtain a secondary pile in working condition for them."

"I can imagine that Flower prefers not to have them tearing apart her infrastructure for the sake of keeping busy, but even an obsolete secondary pile is an expensive toy. We have a saying in the used parts business that the customer is always right, so follow me."

Bill had to run to keep up with the Dollnicks, Dewey jogging alongside. When they reached an area of the docking deck that reminded him of a scrap yard, he finally noticed that M793qK wasn't with them, and looked back to see that the Farling was still standing next to the open hatch of the bookmobile.

"Looks like the doctor is giving his limbs a rest," Lume said, and Bill's implant gave the translation of the Dollnick's whistle a humorous overtone.

"Here he comes now," Dewey said.

A loud buzz that rose rapidly in pitch due to the Doppler effect reached Bill's ears as M793qK flew the distance in a matter of a few seconds. Clufsh clapped with all four hands when the doctor landed. "Thank you. Not only have I seen a Farling, but a flying Farling. You do me honor." He turned and led the way into the scrap yard. "Here it is,"

"It's from an old Class One colony ship?" Lume asked as he admired a giant metal sphere that Bill could only assume was the secondary pile.

"Along with all of these parts," Clufsh said, gesturing with the arms on his right side.

"Why do you have them?"

"Same old story. Hundreds of thousands of years ago this was the premier orbital for servicing Class One colony ships. At some point, they got one in for repair with severe structural damage, and the artificial intelligence moved on to take over a newly constructed Class Two. Somehow the repairs kept getting procrastinated, and every time a Class One came in for service, they cannibalized the old ship for working parts. By the time that Class Threes like Flower became the predominant colony ship, nobody saw the point of investing in rebuilding a badly damaged Class One that had been largely stripped."

"I see some engine components and a lot of bot parts, but I don't recognize any of that kit," Lume said, pointing at a collection of racks populated with modular components of some sort.

"Communications and controls," Clufsh said. "All perfectly usable and a million years behind the state-of-the-art. Mind you, most of these parts aren't original. When a ship is in service for hundreds of thousands of years, everything gets replaced piecemeal."

"Did you arrange for an appraiser?" M793qK asked.

"An expert," the tall Dollnick said. He led the way to a shiny new piece of equipment that looked badly out of place surrounded by the salvaged parts. "If you'll place your proposed payment on the belt, I think you'll find that our orbital's AI is able to provide a fair assessment without delay."

"Get them on the belt, Bill," the Farling instructed.

Dewey held the bag for Bill while the young man shoveled out handful after handful of gems. The belt began to move into the machine, not smoothly, but with an odd stuttering motion that indicated momentary pauses as some jewels required more time to scan than others. Lume and the other Dollnick wandered off to examine more parts and assemblies during the valuation process, which ended up taking the better part of an hour. When Clufsh returned, both he and Lume were smiling broadly.

"Our orbital's AI updated me on the running count and it's already exceeded the asking price for all of the Class One parts we have listed," the taller Dollnick said. "Do you want to prepare a list of what you'll take?"

"All of it," M793qK rubbed out on his speaking legs. "The Zarents are fond of puzzles and have long communal memories. I'll be surprised if they don't find a use for everything, even if it's just to give their young practice."

"In the hundreds of years that I've been responsible for selling salvage, this is the first time a buyer who expressed an interest in a particular generation of parts has taken everything on offer," Clufsh said. "I believe I shall put in for retirement as this is clearly the pinnacle of my career."

"Does the size of our purchase qualify for rush delivery?" Lume asked. "Flower is running a very tight schedule, and if we can't load everything in the next four hours, we'll have to arrange for a freighter to bring it to our next stop."

"I'll get every hand in maintenance working on it, and we'll have all of the smaller components loaded in standard shipping containers in less than two hours," Clufsh said. "Our cargo bots will bring the secondary pile halfway if Flower will send her cargo bots to take delivery."

"That's acceptable," M793qK said, and gestured to the gem scanner. "I believe we have some change coming?" A bin opened with a reluctant sound, and Bill scooped out a single handful of gems. The Farling rubbed out something untranslatable on his speaking legs, and there was a slot-machine-like noise as another measure of gems poured into the bin. "Quantity discount," he explained to Bill. "Better late than never."

The next day, after Bill finished his prep work in the School of Government café and made sure that Delphi was set with the specials, he headed to his second job at Harry's cafeteria. Even though lunch was a good hour off, Jorb and Razood were waiting, and dragged him over to sit at the table.

"I have to help Harry," Bill protested. "Whatever it is, can't it wait until you're eating?"

"Where were you last night?" the Frunge demanded. "You were supposed to be chaperoning my date. Flower had to send a bot to keep Julie company."

"I saw the cargo bots bring the secondary pile in, but one of my sources said that you brought back a transfer unit in the bookmobile," Jorb said. "Who is it?"

"I don't know, guys," Bill said, trying to struggle up from his chair, but between the blacksmith's grip and the martial arts teacher's tentacle, he wasn't going anywhere. "Lume told me to hold my questions until we got back, but it was so late that I forgot to ask."

"He'll be working at his lunch counter," Razood said. "All of a sudden he's discovered that it does a better business if he's there making the salads himself."

"Dewey was there too."

"He doesn't owe us any favors," Jorb said. "And don't suggest that we ask M793qK. He wouldn't have brought you along if he didn't expect you to tell us what happened."

Bill considered this twisted bit of logic for a moment and conceded the point. "I still don't know much," he said. "M793qK bought a lot of old ship parts to give the Zarents to use for teaching or something. Before that, there was a kind of military ceremony, and the light pulsing through this—I don't know—like a high-tech sculpture or something, got sucked through some glass cables into the transfer unit in the bookmobile."

"An artificial intelligence transfer unit? How big was it?"

"You've been in the bookmobile. It took up the whole back with the shelves and seats removed."

Jorb and Razood exchanged a significant look. "And there was a military ceremony?" the blacksmith asked. "How many marines?"

"Eight on each side, so sixteen," Bill said, thinking about when the marines had marched away with the floater. "And an officer who was really tall."

"That's full honors," Razood said. "We must be talking about a military AI."

"Like a funeral?" Bill asked. "Are we transporting it to some sort of AI graveyard?"

"Don't be morbid," Flower interjected herself into the conversation. "I'm hosting Kruik while he works a few things out."

"The same Kruik who was in the news a few decades ago for representing the Dollnick Junior AI Corp at the tunnel network joint exercises?" Razood asked.

"I'm surprised you remember. You would have been barely out of childhood."

"I went through a phase when I watched all of the military fleet news. I wanted to be a dreadnaught captain when I grew up."

"What was he in the news for?" Jorb asked. "Did he win one of the competitions?"

"Lost a ship and barely got out alive," Razood said. "Still, tunnel network militaries value aggressive AI, and if you're going to lose a ship, the best time to do it is in a training exercise."

"He took it badly," Flower said. "After the joint exercise, Kruik became increasingly conservative to the point where his simple navigation decisions dragged on for microseconds. He voluntarily moved from the frontline combat ships back through the ranks until he eventually asked for a hospital ship, except there hasn't been an opening."

"Did you say microseconds?" Bill asked. "That doesn't sound slow to me."

"It's like molasses for artificial intelligence," Razood explained. "The reason they're invaluable in military roles is that they can make decisions before a biological can even process the visual data their eyes behold. If Kruik requires microseconds just to determine which way to go, how could he react to incoming weapons fire that travels at the speed of light?"

"But what are you going to do with him, Flower?'

"Kruik is a sentient being with free will," the Dollnick AI said. "I'm not going to do anything to him. Thanks to the LARPing studios, I've recently built up my information infrastructure to the point where I can host an advanced AI, at least temporarily. It's the first time that my recovered rogue status has worked in my favor, though I imagine that it's also a test."

"You mean the Council of Princes asked you to take Kruik in because the Dollnick military doesn't know what to do with him?" Jorb asked.

"That's a blunt way of putting it, but yes," Flower said. "He's resting for the time being, but I thought I would start him off running my lift tubes, just to get a feel for the ship and meet some people."

"Do you mean I'm going to have two Dollnick AIs telling me what to do?" Bill asked. "I'm not ready for this."

"Go ahead and help Harry," Razood said, relaxing his grip on Bill's arm. "Let him go, Jorb. We need to tag team Lume again."

"What was that all about?" Harry asked when his assistant entered the kitchen.

"Last night's stop," Bill said. "Did it wake you?"

"A couple of folks in the dining room mentioned feeling the transition this morning and then realizing we were in a tunnel. I guess the captain didn't make an announcement because most people slept through both ends."

"We came out at a Dollnick orbital around midnight and returned to the tunnel after four hours. Flower woke me like fifteen minutes beforehand, but I only got a couple of hours of sleep last night because I went straight to the café to start prepping when we got back."

"Do you want to take lunch off and go home for a nap?" Harry asked. "I can put out a salad and some leftovers and nobody will complain."

"I want to see if Jorb and Razood get anything out of Lume," Bill said, stifling a yawn. "Besides, I finally have enough employees trained that I don't need to work the counter at all. I'll take a nap this afternoon and go back into the café for a few hours this evening."

"That's the spirit. Maybe Flower has been teaching you how to delegate by not leaving you any choices."

Bill paused for a second as he was reaching for his apron. "I hope it's not that. I prefer when she tells me what she wants rather than manipulating me into it."

"Good morning, Avisia," Harry greeted the Vergallian as she entered the kitchen. "I'm putting together a big salad for lunch if you feel like whipping up a dressing."

"It would be rude to work in your kitchen without prior notice," Avisia said, but her eyes strayed to the new drying rack for herbs. "Maybe I could take an hour and do something simple."

"A simple dressing takes an hour?" Bill asked, handing the Vergallian a clean apron.

"It's barely enough time to add a little flavor to a vegetable oil base. But I heard a rumor that you made the trip to the Dollnick military orbital. Did anybody pledge you to secrecy?"

"No, but I don't think it was a military base. I mean, there were space marines there, but Captain Pyun told me that everybody has a military presence on their orbitals. The Dollnick we dealt with said it used to be the top service depot for colony ships on the tunnel network."

"That could have been a long time ago, and things change," Avisia said, sniffing at the thyme. "But I suppose military orbitals don't usually have tunnel network exits. I was just going by all of the warships I saw docked on the outer arms."

"You were awake?"

"I awoke when we exited the tunnel. I don't understand how Humans sleep through it."

"Some of us have nightmares about falling, though that's more on jumps, and just the first couple of times," Harry said.

"So, anything you can tell me about the visit, Bill?" the Vergallian asked, her eyes as large as saucers.

"Hey, none of that," Harry said. "He's still a kid, and it's not necessary."

"Sorry," Avisia said. "It's hard to ignore training sometimes. Bill!" She snapped her fingers in front of his face. "Sorry."

"What?" Bill asked, taking a second to get his bearings. "Oh, right. What did you ask again?"

"If you can tell me anything about your trip to the orbital."

"I guess we were buying old colony ship parts to give the Zarents examples for the training course Julie told me about. Some of the people we picked up at Bits got tired of games and programming and want to make a career change."

"Interesting," Avisia said as she searched through jars of seeds. "Any sesame?"

"Next shelf," Harry told her. "And there's mustard seed next to it if you were looking for that."

"You've read my mind. Was there anything else, Bill, or just the secondary pile I saw the cargo bots bring in, and whatever parts were in the shipping containers?"

"We sort of picked up another AI," Bill told her. "Flower said his name is Kruik, and Razood recognized the name from the news. Kruik used to be a military type, but something happened to make him more cautious, and now he takes too long to make up his mind."

Avisia looked over sharply. "A military artificial intelligence who resigned his commission? It sounds like a test for Flower."

"That's what she thought. I didn't get to talk to him, but she said he's going to start running the lift tubes to get to know us."

"What happened to the mortar and pestle?"

"The spice masher set? I'll get it," Bill said.

The kitchen door swung open and the Grenouthian director hopped in. "I've got a new military AI and a lot of old colony ship parts that M793qK paid for," he said as soon as he saw Avisia.

"I didn't know about the Farling paying, but the AI's name is Kruik, and he'll be staying with Flower for a while."

"Whose turn is it to write Yaem's report for him?"

"I'm making a dressing. If you don't want to do it, maybe it's time to teach Bill."

"Great idea," the Grenouthian director said. "You were there, Bill, so you can write an eyewitness account as Yaem's agent and earn him some bonus points."

"I should probably check with M793qK first," Bill said.

"No need, I just came from him." The alien handed over a thin sheet of paper covered with groups of numbers. "He gave me these instructions for you."

Bill took the encrypted communication, pretended to decode it at a glance, and then crumbled it into a glass of water and drank it down. "Right," he said. "Let's go."

Sixteen

Krey stood at one end of the large oval conference table in the seminar room trying to contain her frustration. In addition to the School of Government students sitting at the table, the chairs around the periphery of the room were occupied by the alien intelligence agents from Harry's cafeteria, all of whom had already taken a turn as the guest lecturer in previous weeks. The students grew visibly nervous as several seconds ticked by in silence while the Human Empire's Cayl mentor tried to figure out how to break through their treasured preconceptions.

"What is an empire?" Krey suddenly growled at the students.

Everybody sat quietly, assuming the question was a rhetorical device to launch into a lecture. The silence began to stretch again while the Cayl emperor's granddaughter pointedly ignored the raised hands of several of the alien agents.

"Nobody?" she asked. "There is no wrong answer."

"A form of government with an emperor?" one of the students offered uncertainly.

Krey didn't hesitate. "Wrong. Anybody else?"

"A group of political entities under the control of a central authority, often bound by treaties, and sometimes assembled through political marriages," another student said.

"Better. But you're focusing on the Human definition of empire, and the topic of this seminar is the greater galaxy. Nobody? Mei?"

"A business that operates across many star systems is often referred to as an empire," said the instructor for Theory and Practice of Interspecies Development.

Krey nodded slightly. "That is true when the term is translated into Humanese, but the Cayl and most other species do differentiate between business and military empires in our native tongues." She waited expectantly for one of the students to jump in, and her ears drooped a bit when nobody took the hint. "Jorb?"

The part-time Drazen spy, who had been waving his tentacle back and forth over his head like a schoolboy who knew the answer, rose to his feet. "An empire is defined by the limits of its strength," he said. "That strength can come in different forms, including economic power, but ultimately, no empire can stand for long without the ability to defend itself."

"I'll accept that as a working definition," Krey said as the Drazen sat back down looking rather pleased with himself. "Now, what is the state of the Human Empire's military?"

"We have a temporary waiver," said one of the students who had been paying attention during the Verlock's lecture about the change in the tunnel network treaty which paved the way for the Human Empire to eventually take over from EarthCent. "Once we meet the other benchmarks for a start-up empire, we'll be required to invest a percentage of our gross empire product into purchasing ships for the tunnel network's joint defense."

"And how do you all feel about that? Nikos?" she pointed to the surprised economics professor.

"Since you ask, I think it's a terrible waste of resources," he said. "For one thing, it's clear that the Stryx have ample power to protect the species that have signed onto the tunnel network, so making us all maintain a fleet is just redundant. But more importantly, we aren't capable of constructing ships that could be integrated into the command-and-control structure of a tunnel network expeditionary force, which means we'll be compelled to purchase them from our allies."

Krey pointed to a student seemingly picked at random and said, "Argue the opposite side."

"Uh..." The young man glanced at Nikos, who gave him an affirmative nod. "If the tunnel network treaty requires us to contribute to the joint defense, then the Stryx must have a reason for it."

"And that reason is..."

"To spend money with other species?"

The Cayl emperor's granddaughter growled in frustration. "Razood?"

The Frunge blacksmith rose from his seat. "The goal of the tunnel network is to prevent us from warring with each other, not to turn us into Stryx dependents. Even if every species in the galaxy joins the tunnel network, and well over ninety-nine percent of them haven't, the Frunge will maintain the ability to defend ourselves."

A female student rose from the table and faced Razood. "Those who prepare for war will surely get it," she said.

"My people haven't been in a war for a million years. What's that number for Humans?"

"But the sheer waste of it all," Nikos protested. "Think of what you could have done with the resources you've poured into military technology, not to mention training and paying personnel. If the tunnel network species weren't spending so much on ships and weapons, maybe you'd be able to afford your own multi-species empires, like the Cayl."

The aliens sitting around the periphery of the room seemed to freeze for a moment, and then they all burst out laughing. Lume hugged himself with all four arms and seemed to be having difficulty breathing, while the Grenouthian drummed on his belly like he was trying to send a message over a long distance. Even Avisia failed to keep her composure, at first letting escape a few chuckles, and then losing her perfect posture as she slid down in her chair and politely covered her mouth with both hands.

Krey sighed deeply. "I take it that your academic training didn't include much information about alien civilizations."

"I specialized in what I teach, Macroeconomics for Government Administrators," Nikos said. "Both pre- and post-Stryx."

"Human government administrators."

"There aren't any decent programs on Earth for studying alien governments, at least not at the graduate level. Anybody who's interested either tries to get into an alien university that takes humans or an Open University on a Stryx station."

"The Cayl Empire spends more on its military, in terms of both treasure and lives, than any other species we're aware of," Krey told him. "The males of our species serve in the military throughout their peak physical years, though in peacetime, they typically manage to work at another career when not on active duty. The member worlds of our empire are required to maintain reserves, but our fleet is manned exclusively by Cayl warriors."

"I thought you were even more advanced in the sciences than the Verlocks," a student said in surprise.

"Such comparisons aren't useful, but we are older than the Verlocks, and building our scientific knowledge is one of the core values of our species."

"In order to construct better warships and weapons?"

"That's a secondary effect, but we pursue knowledge of the universe for its own sake," the Cayl emperor's granddaughter said. "I've noticed through my attendance at these seminars that the students harbor a Human-centric view of the tunnel network and a tunnel-network-centric view of the galaxy. That wouldn't be a problem if you were a normative species, but you aren't. I think it would be wise to institute an exchange program as soon as possible."

"We were going to bring that up at the end of the semester," Katya said, and she addressed the students. "My sister and I have been trying to expose you guys to alien cultures by telling stories and role-playing, but it's no substitute for full immersion. It's best to go somewhere you'll be the only human in the class or the office."

"Can't you just give us a summary of what we'll learn?" asked one of the male students who had settled into the role of the unofficial class clown.

"You'll learn that the military, even if it's never used in anger, is the backbone of every advanced species on the tunnel network," Krey said, perhaps stressing the word 'advanced' a little more than absolutely necessary. "I've listened to your questions when the guest lecturers—" she indicated the aliens sitting along the wall with a wave of her paw, "—explained how their societies function, and I've seen the knowing looks on your faces that indicate your belief that you can do better."

"But the Vergallians are ruled by queens, and the Dollnicks by merchant princes," one of the students protested energetically. "The Verlocks and the Drazens have hereditary emperors who wish they could be anyone else, and when I got home and looked at my notes, I realized that the Grenouthian had evaded all of our questions about who ran their empire."

"You asked imprecise questions," the Grenouthian director said dismissively.

"Do you know what all empires have in common?" Krey asked the students.

"A military?" one of the girls ventured.

"An administration," another student said.

"You're on the right track," the Cayl emperor's granddaughter said. "Keep going with it."

"A school of government," the same girl tried again.

"Offices," a different student chimed in, causing Krey to start making a rolling motion with one of her paws, indicating that she wanted more in that theme.

"Monuments."

"Holidays."

"Government buildings."

"A leader," Mei suggested. "A figurehead."

"Exactly," Krey said.

"Which?"

"They aren't mutually exclusive, but the latter is more easily provided by hereditary emperors than the former."

"But if the emperor is a figurehead, who rules the empire?" Mei asked. "The military? A shadowy figure behind the throne?"

"Let's try something for effect," Krey said. "I'm going to count to three, and then I want the non-Humans present to call out a single word that describes who rules their empire. One. Two. Three."

"Committees," all of the aliens in the room said simultaneously.

Mei turned to Avisia and said, "But last week you spent two hours telling us about royal training and insisted that the Empire of a Hundred Worlds is ruled by queens."

"The empire is guided by a council of queens," the Vergallian intelligence agent replied. "A council is another word for a committee."

"And so it is with the Cayl," Krey said. "My grandfather has the final word on everything brought before him, but it's rare for administrative matters to be deemed important enough for the emperor's attention. The member worlds in our empire are responsible for their own administration, and the only time we get involved is when a population petitions the local garrison for help, usually in legal matters. Most such requests involve complaints of corrupt judicial processes, which are a cyclical problem in many cultures, but anything more complicated winds up before a committee of experts."

"But who appoints the committees?" Mei asked.

"There's no simple answer because of the number of factors involved."

"Bureaucratic processes," Razood said. "I assume that's what this school is training you all to do."

"Appoint people to sit on committees?" a student asked in dismay.

"And sit on committees yourselves, though these questions could be better answered by Samuel and Vivian, who weren't available to be here this morning, though we should see them at lunch in a few minutes," Krey said. "Perhaps Sabina and Katya could tell you a little about the committees they served on while working in the embassies of other species."

"We were saving that for the last class," Sabina said. "Committee work is the pits, especially if you're an assistant to a committee member, which means you have all of the responsibility and none of the say in what actually happens. And depending on the situation, the committee chair might opt for consensus rather than a simple majority."

"Consensus sucks," Katya said. "The simplest matter can drag on for years when everybody has to agree. It's almost the same as a veto when the chair calls for consensus."

"So the committee chairs are the ones in charge," a student said.

"Depends on the committee," Sabina told him. "Some committees rotate chairs at every meeting, or at least, at every meeting where they have a quorum."

"Which is another way to slow things down if you're on a committee and you don't agree with where things are heading," Katya said. "Just get enough members not to show up so there's never a quorum and the chair can't move anything."

"But what if it's a matter of life and death and it gets tied up forever in committee?" Mei asked.

"Then the military gets involved," Krey told her.

"I didn't mean wars. What if there was a flood or an earthquake?"

"Military, military."

"An asteroid headed at—no, that's not a good one. How about a plague?"

"Military."

"Economic collapse?" Nikos asked.

"That's a uniquely Human problem arising from your old system of central banks and fractional reserves," Krey said. "Has there been an economic collapse since the Stryx opened Earth?"

"Some people would tell you that the planet has only come out of recession in the last decade."

"And you?"

"Well, I could argue it either way," Nikos said. "Technically, the planet was in recession because the economy shrank every year. But that was mainly due to the population shrinking as people left to work on alien labor contracts, and the money they sent home is what let Earth start modernizing."

"Shall we check with the non-humans?" Krey asked, pointing at the intelligence agents.

"Never," Brynlan said.

"Fah, the economy is always growing," the Grenouthian said.

"Many of our tech-ban worlds have reached a state of equilibrium, so there isn't much growth, but certainly no shrinkage," Avisia said.

"There was the tectonic plate catastrophe on Enthaka around a hundred thousand years ago," Lume said. "They had to evacuate the planet, so I guess that counts as an economic collapse."

"None with us," Jorb said. "The consortiums would never allow it."

"We had a rogue artificial intelligence problem that crashed the economy, but I think that was before we developed interstellar travel," Razood said. "In any case, it was a couple of million years ago."

"How frequent were economic collapses on Earth?" Krey asked Nikos.

"It's not a fair comparison," the economics instructor protested. "If we had your technology and resources—"

"—and your fractional reserve banking system, you still would have needed a full reset a couple of times a century," the Cayl emperor's granddaughter interrupted. "Periods of inflation and devaluation are baked into the system. If in a fit of insanity, my grandfather introduced fiat currency and central banking to our empire—well, he wouldn't survive to do it—but if he did, I doubt even we could maintain stability for more than a century or two."

"So are you on the Stryx cred?" Nikos asked.

Krey laughed. "I don't think I ever saw one before I moved to Flower and became the Human Empire's mentor. Trade in our empire is largely a matter of record keeping. We do have coinage for convenience, and coins are traditionally minted from precious metals, but the vast majority of commercial transactions exist only as ledger entries."

"Like cryptocurrencies?"

"No. But it's time for lunch, and we can continue this discussion in the café."

It took around twenty minutes for everybody attending the seminar to move to the School of Government café and get served. The students pushed together enough tables for their own number plus the instructors, and most of the aliens clumped together at a table to one side. Jorb and Razood joined Samuel and Vivian, who had come in late and were sitting a distance away with their baby.

"Krey suggested that you get an exchange program cranked up as soon as possible," Jorb reported. "Your students have such a Human way of seeing everything that it's interfering with their ability to understand how the rest of the galaxy works. I guess I saw the same thing when I did the seminar, but I'm so used to Humans at this point that it didn't really register."

"We have a way of growing on aliens," Vivian said as she fed a bit of cucumber from her salad to Rose, who was sitting in the café-supplied baby seat.

"Did the students participate in the discussion?" Samuel asked. "Krey can be pretty intimidating without even trying."

"It took a while, but she got them involved by shifting to the basic definition of an empire," Razood said. "Then we did a bit of military and a bit of economy, the stuff that kids get worked up about."

"We planned on an exchange program, of course, but the idea was to offer it in the second year," Vivian said. "Maybe that's a mistake and we should encourage applicants to apply for exchange positions in their first year. We've seen how the students who worked at Human Burger or attended an Open University are way ahead of the ones who joined us directly after graduating on Earth, but neither of those experiences can match being the only human in an alien environment."

"That's almost exactly what Katya said," Jorb told her. "And the students seem to be responding much better to the twins than they did during my seminar a few weeks ago."

"I think they're getting the hang of teaching," Vivian said. "There haven't been any more complaints, but we'll see what happens at the end of the semester when teacher evaluations come in."

"You ask your instructors to grade themselves?" Razood asked between swallows of a bean porridge that Delphi had served him in a salad bowl. "That's novel."

"The students do the evaluations at the last meeting. The academic experts from Earth who advised us on the startup said that it's surprisingly useful."

"To who?"

"To the administration and the faculty alike," Vivian said. "While anonymous feedback can get quite personal, wouldn't you want to know if your lectures were difficult to follow, or if your syllabus was misleading?"

"But how would the students know that?" Jorb asked while Razood's mouth was again full. "Drazen faculty is rated every year by inspectors who are trained to judge the quality of the lectures."

Samuel put down his fork and looked closely at his alien friend. "You're putting me on. Right?"

"Seriously. I have a cousin who did it for a few years to take a break from classroom teaching. A lot of all-expenses-paid travel, but you don't make any friends being an inspector."

"That's what Fandaz always says, though she was checking up on diplomats rather than teachers," Razood said. He pulled out a smartphone and tapped out a message.

The faint sound of falling rocks came from the table occupied by the other alien intelligence agents, and Samuel saw Brynlan take out a phone. The Verlock checked the message and ponderously typed a reply with one thick finger. Razood's phone made a sound like a hammer hitting an anvil in the distance.

"Brynlan says that their teachers don't need inspection because they're all above average, which makes you wonder who taught him math," the Frunge said. "I'll check with the others."

A brief cacophony of ringtones ensued, and all of the aliens took out their smartphones. A few seconds later, Razood's phone clanged again, Jorb's phone let out a grunt and a thud like a martial artist who had just been thrown to the mat, and Samuel's phone chimed as well.

"Belle said that Gem teachers in their old empire were all equally bad because they were just reading from the approved textbooks," Samuel reported. "She's not sure about the state of education now, but she says that anything would be an improvement. Oh, and she said they had informers rather than inspectors."

"The Grenouthian director says that parents and relatives often sit in the classes that their clan members are taking, so they're the ones who provide the most valuable feedback," Jorb read off his phone. "He says that to evaluate a teacher properly, you need to observe the progress of the student, not make checks on some arbitrary list."

"Avisia says they base their teacher evaluations at the university level on class outcomes," Razood said. "The theory is that any given group of students should perform about the same as the last, and competency test results follow the professors around."

Jorb's phone grunted again, and he looked surprised by the message. "It's from Yaem," the Drazen said. "One of the other guys must have sent the question along."

"How do the Sharf evaluate teachers?" Vivian asked.

"He doesn't know."

"Yaem texted you just to say that he doesn't know?"

"I suppose he was being polite."

Razood's phone clanged again and he sucked the air through his teeth. "M793qK," he said. "I wasn't thinking when I chose the intel icon for a group text."

"You can send group texts?" Jorb asked.

"I'll show you later. It's pretty useful if you take the time to categorize your contacts." He swiped up to read the text, and then repeated the motion three more times before reaching the end. "To summarize, the next time I interrupt him in the middle of surgery for a stupid question, I'm going to be the one on the operating table."

"When did you all get phones?" Samuel asked.

"A couple of the recent immigrants from Bits set up a boutique, and if you get three friends to sign up at the same time, one of them gets a free phone," Jorb explained. "We went as two groups and split our savings."

"Did you sign contracts?" Vivian asked him. "That free phone may end up costing you a bundle."

"Brynlan read it. He said it included so many violations of tunnel network law that we could just ignore the contract because it would be thrown out in any of our courts."

Seventeen

"Julie," Jack greeted Flower's executive assistant. "What brings you to Flower's Paradise this fine morning?"

"A little bird told me that you were all going down to Tzeba to visit a textile factory, and Flower wants me to take a look at their production facilities. She suggested I tag along with your group."

"Does that mean you've become an industrial spy?" Jack asked with a twinkle in his eye.

"I hope not," Julie said. "It's more that Flower has developed a reputation as an impulse buyer, and salesmen can see her coming from a light year away. She wants me to see what's on offer without ending up in the middle of a negotiation."

"We're just about to leave, and of course, you're welcome to come along. You can hand out the locator bracelets and carry the emergency water bottles."

"As long as I don't have to walk around with a yellow umbrella."

"That's strictly for tour guides. Nancy headed down to the docking deck early to get everybody loaded and left me behind to wait for stragglers. Grab the supplies knapsack and let's go."

A couple was already waiting at the lift tube dressed for an outing to the Frunge open world. Julie greeted Dave and said to the woman, "I'm sure I know you, but I can't quite come up with a name. Something to do with the weather?"

"June," the woman said with a warm smile. "It's more of a seasonal name. And you are?"

"Julie."

"Hopefully the capsule will show up before January," Dave said. "We've been waiting almost five minutes."

"It hasn't been two minutes, Dave," June said. "You're just impatient." She looked closely at Flower's executive assistant and asked, "Is it possible that you're the Julie who hired my daughter Rayne? You're much younger than I imagined."

Julie felt her ears turn pink and repressed the urge to ask what Rayne had been saying about her. "Your daughter is amazing with the accounts and your granddaughter is so much fun. I've been trying to teach her to sew when she visits our offices after school."

The doors slid open and the group moved into the lift tube capsule.

"Flower, why aren't we moving?" Dave asked.

"My name is Kruik and I'll be your lift tube operator today," a male voice responded. "Please state your destination."

"Docking deck," Jack said. "As near as possible to the shuttle taking the independent living tour group to Tzeba, please."

The capsule started, and Dave asked, "Is everything okay with Flower? Is she on vacation? We've never had a substitute lift tube operator."

"Flower has generously offered to host me in her infrastructure while I consider my career options," Kruik responded. "I've operated lift tubes on military vessels, but this morning has proved to be an interesting challenge.

Most of the inhabitants expect me to recognize their voices and know where they live and work, as opposed to providing a deck and corridor address. In many instances, I've had to consult with Flower to figure out where to take people. I apologize for any delays."

"That's all right," Dave said. "Flower will hold the shuttle for us since Jack is in charge of the outing and Julie is her executive assistant."

"If there's anything I can do to help, just ask," Julie added.

"Thank you," Kruik said. "Docking deck. Please activate your magnetic cleats, and if you need assistance, I can ask Flower to dispatch a bot."

"I think we're all good," Jack said, and the three others nodded. "Thank you for the ride, we'll be back this afternoon."

"Give me your arm, Dave," June said as they exited the lift tube. "I'm still getting used to this shuffling about in low gravity business."

"You're all J's," Dave observed as he proffered his right arm. "June, Julie, and Jack. I feel outnumbered."

"There's an 'N' telling us to get our butts in gear," Jack said after spotting his wife standing next to the front ramp of the shuttle and waving at them.

The four latecomers made their way up the ramp and took seats near the front of the shuttle in the section reserved for the Flower's Paradise outing. The trip to the surface took just over a half hour, and Julie found herself posted next to the exit ramp with Nancy handing out locator bracelets.

"The green floater buses are ours," Julie repeated for the fortieth time while passing over a bracelet. "They're taking us directly to the factory."

"What about lunch?" a woman inquired.

"We'll be eating in the employee cafeteria," Nancy told her. "The factory is a joint project between the Frunge and humans, the first of its kind on Tzeba."

"Do they have an outlet store?" another woman asked.

"They all have outlet stores. It's one of the few constants in the galaxy."

When the line of retirees exiting the shuttle petered out, Julie ran up the ramp and quickly checked to make sure nobody had fallen asleep in a seat and been left behind. As she headed back, she almost ran into a Zarent on a unicycle coming out of the front of the shuttle that was always closed off, since Flower piloted the craft remotely.

"Julie," the little alien greeted her through the translation device it wore on its tool harness. "Flower told me that you were coming along."

The artificially generated voice somehow clicked with Julie's memory. Combined with the Zarent's size and the large number of accouterments on his tool harness, she recognized Chief Engineer Miklat. "Snap. How are you?" she greeted him. "What are you doing here?"

"You remembered my nickname," the Zarent said, emitting a pleased buzz as he turned his unicycle sharply toward the exit. "I'm visiting Flower for the conference, but I came down to Tzeba because I have a strong interest in semi-metallic textiles. They have many uses outside of flashy clothing."

"Conference?" Julie asked as she followed the alien down the ramp. "I didn't know that Zarents were interested in gaming."

"Gaming? Generally speaking, we aren't, unless the action is driven by educational or training considerations.

I'm here for the First Engineers Conference, at Club Flower."

Julie racked her brain trying to remember if she had seen anything about it on her schedule and somehow forgotten. Then they reached the stairs of the bus. "Would you like to climb up and I'll carry your unicycle?" she offered.

"Thank you," Snap said, and to Julie's surprise, he leaned into her and then clambered onto her back. "Is this comfortable for you?"

"Uh, it's fine," Julie said, even though she had meant for the octopus-like alien to climb up the stairs of the floater bus, not her back. She grabbed the unicycle just under the seat and found that it weighed no more than her purse, which admittedly, was overloaded. When she reached two empty seats next to each other, she turned in, and the Zarent climbed down and took what would have been the window seat if the floater bus hadn't been open like a wagon.

"Good morning, Julie," Irene greeted her from the next seat back. "Would you like to introduce us to your friend?"

"Chief Engineer Miklat, this is Irene and Harry. Irene is the official documentarian for the independent living cooperative."

"Pleased to make your acquaintance," the Zarent said through his translation device, extending a tentacle over the back of the seat to offer a sort of handshake. "If you'll be capturing video inside the factory, I'd like to get a copy when we return. I plan to give a talk about the visit when I return to the Miklat."

"Are the Wanderers back?" Harry asked in alarm. "No offense, Snap, but the people you work for made a lot of problems the last time they were here."

"They make problems for everybody," Snap said. "It's the Wanderers business model. They extort goods and services that enable them to move on to the next target, but I'm here without the ship."

"Did you travel alone?" Julie asked. "I thought it was difficult for Zarents to be away from their community."

"It's not pleasant, but I traveled here in the company of the engineers from thirty-seven other vessels, and it's a short trip in a jump ship."

"Unless my memory is going, Flower didn't mention anything about the First Engineers Conference," Julie said. "How are all of the ships in your mob getting along without their First Engineers?"

"Ah, I see the ambiguity in Humanese," Snap said. "It's not a conference for First Engineers, it's the first conference we've ever had. Most ships sent younger members of the engineering department to observe."

"Could I get an interview with you later?" Irene asked. "The current group of Zarents staying on board Flower has been working with retirees from our cooperative to train humans, mainly recent immigrants from Bits, in the trades. I've been working on a documentary about it."

"You believe there will be an audience for a documentary about vocational training?"

"Maybe on Earth. I'll bet nobody living there has ever seen a Zarent unless it was in that anime show we saw at the awards ceremony. What was it, Harry?"

"*Wanderer Mob*, though if I recall, it was all about the Zarents trying to keep the ships going on a shoestring," Harry said. "I only saw the clips at the award show."

"Maybe I should view a few episodes just to find out how we're being presented to the galaxy," Snap said. "How was the animation quality?"

"It was fine," Harry said. "The little apprentice looked just like a Zarent, and she whipped around on a unicycle fixing things."

"I remember that now," Julie said. "The show was up for several awards against *Everyday Superheroes*."

"The anime about M793qK," Snap said. "I've seen excerpts."

"The Zarents seem to be quite fond of him."

"Other than the Stryx, he and Flower are the only powerful sentients who have ever taken an interest in our well-being. We wouldn't have agreed to a conference for anybody else."

"The Farling doctor and Flower are the ones who are putting on the First Engineers Conference?" Julie asked, her voice rising. "What are they after?"

Snap raised his body from the seat and made the buzzing sound that served as laughter for the little octopus-like aliens. "If I knew that, I would be a powerful sentient rather than a mere engineer," he said. "Zarents are still arriving from distant mobs that haven't contacted the tunnel network in many millennia, so even if it's just a friendly get-together, it's a historic event for our kind."

"That's the first time I've ever heard anybody refer to Flower or the Farling doctor as powerful sentients," Irene said. "I thought they were both outcasts of a sort."

"The galaxy is full of empires, and the power behind the throne is often the individual who operates outside the normal bounds of society and collects enough favors to get things done."

"Would you repeat that on camera?"

"Do you want to do our interview now?" Snap asked. He consulted an instrument attached to his tool harness. "I estimate seventeen minutes before we arrive at the factory, so there should be ample time."

Irene retrieved her borrowed immersive camera from under Julie's seat, activated the gesture controls, and then waved it around the seatback so it floated well above Julie's lap and focused on the Zarent. "Is that okay with you both?" she asked.

"As long as I'm not in the frame," Julie said. "Does the camera have a mode to compensate for the landscape flying by behind him?"

"Technically, the landscape is standing still and we are flying by it," Snap said. "I believe that's a standard Grenouthian immersive camera, so you'll be able to replace the moving background with stock art of your choice if that's what you wish."

"You've used Grenouthian cameras?"

"I've repaired a few over the years for the Wanderers. Every once and a while a group of them will convince themselves that they have what it takes to produce a feature-length immersive, usually some action thriller that couldn't be farther from the way they live. After a few weeks, they decide that it's too much like work and give up."

"How did such a hard-working species like the Zarents ever become the glue that holds the Wanderer mobs, or at least their ships, together?" Irene asked.

"You didn't know that we were engineered by the Farlings as a bribe for a long-ago Wanderer mob to go away?" Snap asked.

"I know, but the audience doesn't," Irene said. "I'll be asking questions based on what I think they'll want to know about you, rather than what I'm familiar with from your previous stay on Flower and what I've learned so far making the documentary about the training program."

"Ah, I understand. Should I repeat my answer?"

"Maybe I'll ask something a little different. What I was trying to get at was," she paused to put a break in the soundtrack, "how do you feel about doing all of the work to keep the ships moving for Wanderers who are living a life of leisure?"

"It's what we do," Snap said. "For us, work is life. For the Wanderers, pleasure is life. We have a sort of symbiotic relationship, and it's not all due to the way the Farlings engineered us."

"Can you explain a little more?" Irene asked.

"It's true that we were designed from the genes up to perform deep spaceship maintenance, and for that, we are thankful. But in the millions of years since the Farlings created the first of our kind in test tubes, there has been genetic drift, a slow evolution, if you will, and everybody agrees that we've become a legitimate species."

"Did the Wanderers used to treat you badly?"

"Like many of the advanced species today treat the Gem," Snap said. "And there's nothing artificial about them other than their reproduction process, but it's enough to put the other species off."

"Are there any Gem with the Wanderer mobs?"

"Yes, they often serve as the security details when we stop at sketchy places, but they live on their own ships because it's more comfortable that way for everybody. Oddly enough, a similar sort of creeping discrimination seems to be building around the inhabitants of the Miklat."

"The other ships in the mob aren't comfortable with you anymore?"

"Our Wanderer inhabitants are the ones who are making the other Wanderers uncomfortable. It doesn't matter which species they are, being associated with the Miklat now carries with it the whiff of the unclean."

"A metaphoric whiff," Irene said, to confirm that the Zarent engineer wasn't talking about a problem with the Miklat's environmental systems.

"Exactly," Snap said. "The issue is with Flower having claimed the salvage rights to the Miklat and then gifting them to us. I think the Wanderers expected that after a few cycles, a year at most, we'd come crawling to them on our tentacles begging them to accept ownership again. We're coming up on two years, now, and that hasn't happened and never will."

"So the other Wanderers have it in for your Wanderers because the Zarents now own the Miklat?"

"Yes. As near as we can tell, they're worried that it's communicable."

"Like a disease? They're afraid of losing ownership of their ships to their Zarent crews?"

"It's just a hypothesis," Snap said modestly. "You're talking about a dozen advanced species, and it's unlikely they would all suffer from the same fears."

"My directorial debut, if you could call it that, was borrowing a camera from the Grenouthian director to document our independent living cooperative planting fruit trees on the Miklat's ag deck. Can you tell us how they're doing?"

"Chief Agronomist Miklat is very happy with the progress of the orchards planted by the volunteers from Flower's Paradise. They were primarily seedlings, so it will be another year or two before they start producing in earnest. Thanks to all of the help from Flower, our ag decks are now growing sufficient cereal crops for approximately fifty thousand humanoids. We've been more conservative with vegetables because they don't keep well."

"So the Miklat's population is approaching fifty thousand?" Irene asked. "My memory was that there were around twenty thousand Wanderers brought on board Flower when she took your ship in tow."

Snap seemed to sag a little on his tentacles. "Sadly, the population has fallen since then, we're closer to fifteen thousand Wanderers now. It's the opposite of what you might expect as we are continually improving the facilities with the complement of reconditioned bots Flower procured for us. And her replacement of our primary pile means the Miklat is overpowered, allowing us to begin in situ annealing of structural components that haven't been maintained in generations."

"What is in situ annealing?"

The Zarent paused for a moment as if he couldn't believe anybody would be unfamiliar with the process. Then he remembered that Irene was asking questions for the sake of her audience.

"Metal fatigue is always an issue for structural engineers, and although the Miklat is a colony ship whose spokes and plates were the finest that Dollnick metallurgy could produce, hundreds of thousands of years is a long time to remain in service. In situ annealing is a process that allows us to renew the alloys in place, a combination of heat treating, electron activation, and electromagnetic field shaping. All of these require power, and thanks to Flower's gift, we've been able to catch up with the most critical pending failures."

"That still doesn't sound very safe for the inhabitants," Irene said with concern. "Are you sure that's not why the Miklat is losing population?"

"With all the new equipment, we're in better shape than most of the ships in the mob," Snap said. "Starships are overbuilt to an extent you would never go to for a bridge or an apartment building because there's no assumption that help will be available if something fails in space. The risk of living on board the Miklat for a year isn't much greater than the risk of living on board Flower, which is vanishingly small. Where the gap comes in is if you project the risk a few hundred years into the future without ongoing maintenance. The risk of living on Flower, in that case, will barely rise since she's in perfect condition, while the risk of living on the Miklat would go up a hundredfold."

"Would you and your community of Zarents move to a newer ship if you had the opportunity?"

Chief Engineer Miklat's tentacles all stiffened. "I'll answer that question in the spirit in which you asked, but please keep in mind that there's no greater insult to a Zarent than to imply he's considering abandoning his ship. The majority of us were born on the Miklat and all of us hope to be on board when our time is up. The only reason we move between ships is for mating, to keep the gene pool from forming a bottleneck. It's something we're very sensitive about because our starter population was relatively small."

"I think we're pulling into a parking lot," Harry said to Irene. "Bring back the camera and we can sit together on the way home if the chief engineer is up to it."

"Did you have any more questions?" Snap asked.

"I'd love to ask about this conference that Flower and M793qK invited you to attend," Irene said. "You don't have to make any promises. We'll see how much energy we all have after the tour."

"I'd be happy to try to answer your questions, but as the conference hasn't started yet, all I know about it is the name and that it's all expenses paid. Everybody is staying in Club Flower, of course."

"I'll ask Flower about it when we get back," Julie said. "It's odd she didn't mention it, but I keep telling her she gives me too much work, so maybe she's trying to ease up. She works too hard herself."

"Flower has a helper running the lift tubes now," Irene said. "Maybe she's taken your advice."

"Are you talking about Kruik?" Snap asked as the floater bus came to a halt in front of a Frunge factory that looked like it could contain a city. "Brilliant young AI, very technically oriented. Flower introduced him to us, and he's been making himself available to model all sorts of systems for the engineers who are comparing ideas. It's a shame that the Wanderers and artificial intelligence can't get along with each other because he'd be welcome by the Zarents of any ship."

Eighteen

Bill finished stocking the dessert case before Delphi arrived, but he didn't bother prepping the salad bar because he knew that the young woman from Bits would have plenty of time to get it done before the lunch crowd started trickling in. He glanced at the empty steam table and sighed.

"Was that your imitation of steam escaping?" Flower asked over his implant.

"I know that it's more efficient to fill the whole steam table with hot food delivered from the Open University cafeteria kitchen before the lunch rush, but it feels like admitting to failure," Bill said. "It's not like anybody was complaining."

"You were coming in too early and skimping on making desserts. By concentrating on baked goods, not only will the students get the benefit of more variety, your extra pastry production makes a fair barter for the steam table entrées and side dishes. It's win-win."

"Do you really keep separate books for the School of Government café and the Open University cafeteria?"

"I keep separate books for everything in multiple versions depending on the intended audience," Flower said. "Delphi just arrived. Try not to spend too much time talking, because Harry has the day off, and M793qK is waiting for you."

"Is that today?" Bill asked.

"It's always today when you're asking."

"You're talking to Flower," Delphi guessed as she came out of the kitchen. "You were moving your lips and whispering."

"I'm not great at subvocing, especially when there's nobody around to hear," he told her. "I'm going to work late at Harry's cafeteria today, so I'm delegating you to handle the shift change. Is that okay?"

"Sure, I'm happy to do it, but don't start counting on me too much."

"You're not thinking of quitting already."

"I'm going to finish my Open University certification course by the time we get to Union Station," Delphi said seriously. "Shadow and I haven't made up our minds yet, and there's his sister and our role-playing group to take into account as well, but if we could get work on an interstellar cargo carrier…"

"All right, I get the message," Bill said, taking off his apron. "I'll get Flower to find us a few more students so you can start training them. You're my best employee and I want them to learn from your example."

"Happy to help," Delphi said, tying on her apron. "So why are you working late at your lunch job today?"

"M793qK finally has some free time to start catching up with the products we need to certify for the *All Species Cookbook*," Bill said. "He's already there waiting for me, which means there's a lot to do. Hopefully, Harry cooked something yesterday that I can heat up and give the aliens who come for lunch or they're all going to end up with ramen."

"Aliens eat ramen?"

"Except for the Frunge, but I give him seaweed with the ramen flavor package as a consolation prize. And now that we're having all of the steam table food delivered, I only worked four hours before you came in this morning, so I can work six at Harry's café before Flower starts nagging."

"It's weird that she cares how many hours people work. It's caused a lot of friction in the Bits community because most programmers are binge coders, staying up all night at their keyboards when it's going well. My dad is in his fifties and he was working fourteen hours a day before we left Bits."

"In this case, I'm thankful, because M793qK would keep me working until I was falling asleep on my feet if it wasn't for the ten-hour limit Flower gives me."

"It's not the same for everybody our age?" Delphi asked.

"I haven't asked her for all of the details, but I know it depends on how many days in a row you work. I'm kind of on a short leash because the café is open seven days a week, even though I don't really work on Sunday, other than stopping by to make sure everything is okay." Bill pointed at his ear to let Delphi know he had an incoming message. "I heard you," he said out loud. "On my way."

"Flower telling you to get a move on?"

Bill nodded and jogged off for the lift tube. A capsule arrived and he entered, and then waited for fifteen seconds before remembering that Kruik was now running the system. "Harry's cafeteria, please."

"I don't understand why a manager would have another job as a helper," Kruik said. "If officers and enlisted personnel swapped back and forth, there would be no discipline. Are you having difficulty with finances? A question of extortion or blackmail?"

"Harry taught me everything I know about food," Bill explained, even as he wondered at the military AI's overactive imagination. "It's sort of an experimental kitchen. I'm going there now to do some product testing."

"Are you one of M793qK's retainers? He's one of my guarantors."

"I work for him sometimes, I don't know if that makes me a retainer. What's a guarantor?"

"Under Dollnick law, when an artificial intelligence leaves government service, two sentients of equal or superior intellectual capacity are required to sign on as guarantors of its good conduct," Kruik said. "It's a formality from the early years when there was more concern over AIs going rogue."

"What if there aren't two sentients that smart available?" Bill asked.

"The Stryx are always willing to take responsibility for artificial intelligence with no place to go. Please convey to the good doctor that I have considered his proposal and I'm willing to accept the job providing all other parties agree."

"Got it," Bill said as the lift tube doors opened. "Thanks for the ride."

When he reached the cafeteria, the only alien in the dining room was Belle, who was reading something on her phone and nursing a mug that was likely hot chocolate.

"I didn't see you at lunch again yesterday," Bill said. "Can I make you something special today?"

"I've been eating in the food court lately, but I came by to have a few words with M793qK," the Gem said. "He's waiting in the kitchen for you."

"Just let me know if there's something you'd rather eat and we'll get it. Specialty foods and drinks are part of the deal you guys receive when your governments, you know…"

"Yes, thank you. When we get to Union Station, I'll be consulting with our embassy over whether or not to remain on Flower."

"Oh," Bill said, putting two and two together. "Well, let me know if you need anything." He continued through the swinging door into the kitchen where he caught the Farling doctor in the act of polishing off a bag of barbeque potato chips.

"Terrible," M793qK rubbed out on his speaking legs. "I've disposed of these so you won't be tempted."

"The new AI running the lift tubes asked me to tell you that he'll take the job if everybody else involved agrees."

"So he's already worked out that you're one of my retainers. How much do you know about agriculture?"

"Farming? I worked for a year on an illegal picking crew, but that doesn't mean much because I only saw the orchards and the fields at harvest time," Bill said. "Flower has sent me to the ag decks a few times for an afternoon, but beyond knowing which end of a seedling to stick in the dirt and where milk comes from, I'm pretty clueless."

"And painfully honest. Our job today is to evaluate packaged foods that are intended for emergencies when fresh food supplies are limited."

"One of my café workers is from Bits, and she said that the only fresh food they had was salad. Everything else came packaged or frozen from Earth or ag worlds, and a lot of people ate out of vending machines that could cook a pizza in under two minutes."

"Piling injury on insult to the digestive system," M793qK said dismissively. "In this case, we're looking at a situation where some fresh food will always be available, but we want to make sure there are sufficient supplies to deal with population shocks, such as a sudden influx of migrants."

"Sort of like the situation we have on Flower, except our ag decks are producing so much that we can feed everyone and still export the surplus," Bill said.

"Imagine if Flower reduced her ag deck production to below what we need to feed the population and you'll have an analogous situation. We'll start with the powdered eggs."

"You can powder eggs?"

"You can powder anything, though you wouldn't necessarily want to reconstitute the result and try to ingest it," M793qK said. "Get those buckets up on the counter."

Bill looked where the Farling was pointing with one of his longer limbs and saw three plastic buckets, two of which reminded him of the five-gallon ready-made-plaster containers that his mother used to insist they bring back to the commune when they came across empties in the streets. Fortunately, the powdered eggs were much lighter than joint compound, and he lined them up on the counter.

"I don't get the color schemes," Bill admitted. "This one looks like military camouflage, that one is so bright that it almost hurts my eyes, and the middle one is square. Who makes square buckets? Wouldn't the corners need to be reinforced?"

"Excellent observation," M793qK rubbed out. "The reason for the fanciful artwork on the containers is that the biggest market for these products is a Human subculture of survivalists who are preparing for apocalyptic times. The camouflage artwork and the bright colors are two sides of the same coin. The former is intended to appeal to militant-minded survivalists, and the latter to those who are worried about locating food in the aftermath of a flood, volcanic eruptions, etcetera. Can you tell me the attraction of the square container?"

Bill thought for a moment. "I guess you can fit more of them in a smaller space."

"Like a bunker or a bug-out vehicle."

"Is the powder as good as real eggs for baking?"

"You have to adjust the recipes for the missing water content, though oddly enough, some Humans would be better off eating powdered eggs because the cholesterol is oxidized during the drying process."

"Is this the same process as freeze drying? That came up in one of my Open University courses."

M793qK pulled the lid from one of the containers and inspected the seal while replying. "Freeze drying is more expensive and therefore reserved for higher margin foods, such as coffee and strawberries. Spray drying takes place at higher temperatures and relies on a nozzle, pressure, and cooling tower. Taste this," he concluded, extending to Bill a long-handled spoon with a bit of yellow powder.

"How is that going to tell us anything about the quality?"

"It was just an idea," the Farling said, pulling back the spoon. "Open the other two buckets and fill these sample vials. I'll take them back to my clinic for analysis."

"That's it? We're not going to add water?"

"Not unless you want to make a few hundred servings of scrambled eggs," M793qK said. "Are you expecting guests?"

"So what are we going to do with three unsealed buckets of powdered eggs?" Bill asked after he filled the first sample vial. He reached for a label, peeled off the backing, and got his hand slapped by the Farling.

"How many times do I have to tell you to fill out the label before you apply it to a round vial? Your printing is atrocious enough as it is."

"Sorry, but I still need to know what to do with all of the leftovers."

"You're bakers—you'll work it out," M793qK said, already moving on to the next lot of test products. "Eggs require far less infrastructure to produce than dairy, which is why I'm hopeful about these powdered milk products. I'm going to mix a glass for you."

"I'm not a big milk drinker," Bill said.

"You should start, and that applies to Julie as well. I'll give you a prescription if it will help."

"How would it help?"

"Doctor's orders and all of that," the Farling said. "The effect is usually temporary, but I've noticed that most members of your species are more likely to act on advice if it comes on an official-looking form with an indecipherable signature."

"I'm not one of them," Bill said as he finished filling and labeling the samples.

"You can add chocolate powder to the milk. We have three containers to evaluate, and you can take one of them home. I promised the other two to Belle."

"I wouldn't want to take it from her. She looks depressed."

"You really are developing reasonable skills of observation," M793qK said approvingly. "But in this case, she's purchased all three brands of powdered chocolate in the past and she didn't care for the one with the children playing on the label. I don't know if it's due to the quality of the product or the artwork."

"So you want me to add bad chocolate to my powdered milk?"

"Here," the doctor said, opening the container in question. "I'll add it to the milk I just mixed and you can judge for yourself." He stirred a generous serving of cocoa powder into the glass of reconstituted milk and pushed it down the counter at Bill like a bartender in the Wild West. "Drink. I'll take samples for analysis from the other containers and then we can get onto the real work."

"It's pretty good," Bill admitted a minute later when he finished the glass of chocolate milk. "I guess I could drink one of these a day."

"I want Julie drinking at least two," M793qK told him. "My offer of a prescription stands."

"So what's the real work you're talking about?"

"Taste testing. Drazen Foods has set up a new freeze-drying operation on Earth for prepared foods, so we know that the labeling is accurate, and the quality control is first-rate."

Bill shot the Farling doctor a skeptical look. "I'm pretty sure that Drazen Foods has tasters, and unlike me, they probably know what they're talking about."

"That's why I got here before lunch," the Farling doctor said. "Just because the other oxygen-breathing tunnel network species can eat anything Humans eat doesn't mean they think it tastes good. These Drazen Foods meals would come in handy for any alien guests if they're as good as promised. That's why I tempted Belle here with hot chocolate and the promise of two buckets of cocoa powder."

"You're losing me, but don't explain," Bill said. "Where's the stuff?"

"Around the other side of the counter in the large box. We don't need to test them all today, but pick out a variety."

The box in question proved to be the smallest standard Drazen shipping container, the type that was often used by travelers as a sort of oversized sea chest. Bill popped the lid and found that it was filled with packages that displayed photo-realistic images of gourmet dishes. They were surprisingly light, being dehydrated, but each package claimed to serve four when reconstituted.

"It's kind of all fancy," Bill reported. "Spaghetti Alfredo? Curried Roasted Eggplant with Smoked Cardamom and Coconut Milk? Peking Duck?"

"Grab that one," M793qK said. "I think we'd better work our way up to the roasted eggplant. I know that the Drazens are champions when it comes to freeze-dried foods, but it's hard to imagine complex combinations not coming out looking like something a Cayl hound threw up."

"How about Salmon Teriyaki with Rice and Broccoli?"

"That should work for everybody other than Razood and the Grenouthian director, who I believe has a salmon allergy."

"There's an Organic Spicy Red Bean Chili…"

"Sold," M793qK rubbed out on his speaking legs. "I'm going to go talk to Belle for a bit. You read the instructions, reconstitute the three packages we chose, and I'll ping the others to tell them lunch will be served in five minutes."

"Maybe the instructions will be too complicated to prepare the food that fast," Bill protested.

"Just add hot water," the Farling said on his way out of the kitchen, carrying two containers of cocoa powder. "And make sure to check the packages first and remove any sachets of chemical preservatives, usually something to scour free oxygen."

Bill read the instructions for the three meals M793qK had selected and saw that the Farling was essentially right. Since the Dollnick induction stovetop could bring water to a boil almost instantly, he took the time to look at the back of the gourmet eggplant meal and found that it contained multiple packages that had to be reconstituted separately before being combined.

Four minutes later, Jorb entered the kitchen with his nose held high. "What's that heavenly smell?" the Drazen demanded. "I get red beans with overtones of chili peppers, some kind of duck, and—salmon teriyaki?"

"I've been cooking all morning," Bill told him.

"You've outdone yourself."

"I was kidding. All I did was add hot water."

"You keep saying that as if it's nothing. I've tried making ramen and it never comes out as good as yours," Jorb said. "Can I help you bring out the food?"

"Each of these dishes is four servings," Bill cautioned the alien. "Put them in the center of the table, and make sure Razood and the Grenouthian get first crack at the chili."

"Razood eats duck and salmon," the Drazen protested. "I can scrape off the rice if it bothers him. Unless, if you have time to make up a few packages of ramen…"

"Give me three minutes."

The aliens had already helped themselves when Bill brought out a tray with four servings of extra spicy ramen, and he couldn't help noticing the empty seat next to Belle. M793qK was standing at the far end of the table showing something to Brynlan and the Grenouthian director on a

Farling device resembling a Dollnick tab. The giant alien beetle gestured for Bill to sit without looking up.

"Were you saving a place for Avisia?" Bill asked the clone as he took the empty seat.

"She couldn't make it today," Belle replied. "It's just as well since she's a vegetarian and doesn't care for spicy food. The Vergallian upper caste has a delicate palate."

"It looks like you had the salmon teriyaki. How was it?"

"Everything I eat that doesn't poison me tastes better than the nutrition drink I grew up on," Belle said with a sad smile. "I see Captain Pyun has joined us."

"Don't get up," Woojin barked in Bill's direction when the young man was already halfway out of his seat. "How many times have I told you that we're not in the military and you're not a subordinate?"

"I keep forgetting," Bill admitted. "I think it's the hat."

"You must be on official business to be wearing it," Razood said to the captain as he served himself another helping of the red bean chili. "Are we in trouble?"

Captain Pyun thought for a moment. "It depends on who you mean by we and what you mean by trouble," he eventually replied. "Did you all read the proposal I sent?"

"That was a proposal?" Jorb asked. "I thought it was a hypothetical scenario based on some numbers Julie worked up with that bean counter from Bits."

"Your employers have been pestering EarthCent Intelligence about the cyclicality of your reports. We make the same circuit of open worlds and orbitals with the largest Human populations twice a year. A smaller ship stopping at less populated open worlds once a year for shorter stays would triple the number of sovereign human communities visited."

"Where is EarthCent going to find an outside contractor like Flower willing to take the job?" Yaem asked. "Not that I'm against it, as long as it doesn't impact our anime productions and conventions."

"I'm working with Flower on a deal," M793qK rubbed out on his speaking legs. "It depends on a number of things going right and some bad decisions by a group of sentients known for their bad decision-making. It's not beyond the realm of possibility that all of you will soon be running a new field office, so you might want to recruit a friend before your respective agencies present you with some random agent in need of punishment duty."

"Is that why we're testing this food?" Bill asked.

"That and because Drazen Foods submitted it to the *All Species Cookbook* for certification," the doctor confirmed.

Nineteen

"Is this the meeting where they tell us the school is closing?" Mei muttered to Nikos as she took her seat at the conference table.

"It hasn't been going *that* badly, and our contracts pay us for a year either way," the economics professor said. "I insisted on that part before leaving Earth."

"I hope they give me the opportunity to redesign my course from the ground up. I've tried making changes on the fly, but I'm going to need to throw out the syllabus and start over from scratch. What made sense for the Theory and Practice of Interspecies Development when I was student-teaching on Earth just doesn't seem applicable when we're living on a state-of-the-art Dollnick colony ship visiting a different alien-owned planet every week."

"You're telling me. I started the semester teaching Macroeconomics for Government Administrators based on Earth's governments and economies. I can't figure out why they didn't hire somebody who studied at the Open University or on a Verlock academy world."

"It's embarrassing to get caught out so often by the students," Mei continued and lowered her voice. "I've started going over my lectures with Flower the night before so she can warn me if I'm going to say something that's too far from reality. I swear I'm learning more than my students."

"You too?" Nikos laughed. "I'd be dead without Flower. Not only has she read everything on economics published by all of the tunnel network species in the last century, she's been abstracting it for me. I spend most of my free time in my room talking with her."

"Every Monday, I ask the students if they have any questions from the Friday seminar. Then Flower arranges for me to meet with the alien who gave the seminar for a meal to follow up. They've all been very helpful."

"Look who's early," Sabina said as she and her sister entered the conference room. "Why the long faces?"

"We were just chatting about how unprepared we were for this job," Nikos said.

"Compared to Kat and me, you guys are consummate professionals. We're hoping that Samuel and Vivian fire us so we don't have to quit."

"We just aren't classroom teachers," Katya said. "Office hours in the café aren't bad, and I think we do decent role-playing exercises, but when it comes to preparing a lecture and sticking to the subject, we're the worst."

"Are you going to go back home?" Mei asked.

Sabina made a face. "Our mother would kill us. We're hoping to talk Samuel into letting us do something else for the Human Empire."

"Like outreach or public relations," Katya said, looking up as Vivian entered the conference room with Rose. "What do you say, Viv? Are you going to free us from our misery?"

"If you're talking about teaching, the two of you improved as the semester went on," Vivian said. "I even learned a few things when I sat in your classes."

"To keep an eye on us because you had complaints from some of the girls," Sabina said. "You don't have to deny it.

Flower told us that we were only teaching to half the class."

"Did she give you any advice for fixing it?"

"Get married. We told her to find us some guys and we're game."

Vivian laughed. "You don't know what you've let yourself in for. She's an obsessive matchmaker."

"Good morning," Krey said as she padded silently into the conference room. Before taking her stool, she removed a large flat box from her workbag, undid the hasp, and folded the lid all the way back flat. "I've taken up beading," she continued, displaying what looked like a hundred small compartments with different sizes and colors of beads. "Does anybody want a bracelet? I'm working my way up to a Usekh."

"What's a Usekh?" Mei asked.

"It's an Egyptian broad necklace, the closest term I can come to for the traditional collars worn by Cayl hounds of a certain rank. My two companions are overdue for a promotion."

"Just for the record, I'm early," Samuel said as he entered. "The meeting isn't scheduled for another five minutes, but if nobody objects, we can get started."

"Is the school closing?" Nikos asked bluntly.

"Not only aren't we closing, we can't close unless we want to give up on the idea of taking over for EarthCent in our lifetimes. What makes you ask?"

"There were only eighteen students in my class yesterday. That's a twenty-five percent drop-out rate over the course of the semester."

"Same here," Mei said. "I double-checked with Flower to see if anybody was out sick."

"I spent the first couple days this week interviewing all of the students about their plans, and in two cases, it was clear that they'd lost interest in the idea of government work," Samuel said. "It was pretty much the same story as with the four who dropped out earlier. Once they moved on board Flower and had the chance to attend a few business events, they found that the idea of working in private industry was too enticing to turn down. I'm hoping that the last two were the end of it, and we'll have a stable group going forward."

"How about the other students, the ones who took catch-up courses at the Open University this semester?" Nikos asked.

"Coincidentally, the drop rate was identical at twenty-five percent, so you can rest assured it wasn't the quality of your instruction," Vivian said. "My contacts on Earth tell me that the expected first year drop rate for a government school runs around half of what we're seeing. But we think we're doing pretty well considering that our government barely exists, and the campus is located on an interstellar spaceship that stops at so many interesting places."

"So what I was hoping to do today is get a jump on planning for next semester for the students who've been taking catch-up courses from the Open University," Samuel said. "We're sticking with a six-week break without any intersession courses because we don't want the students to feel that we're pressuring them to remain on Flower. In fact, we just received word of a grant from EarthCent that will pay the travel expenses for any students who want to visit an alien homeworld or orbital and write an essay about their experience."

"How many pages?" Mei asked.

"It wasn't mentioned in the grant."

"That's the first thing students will want to know when we tell them."

"Oh." Samuel thought for a moment. "I'll send a message to my mom's special assistant and ask her to tighten up the requirements before we announce the grant. I wouldn't want EarthCent paying for vacations and getting back bar napkins with a couple of words in return."

"We're out," Sabina said.

"Of napkins?"

"Of teaching. We don't want to come back next semester."

"I thought you were settling in," Samuel said, glancing at Vivian for confirmation.

"It's not torture, it's just not us," Katya said. "Besides, we're running out of material."

"You can get textbooks with teacher's guides," Mei told them.

"Thanks, but no thanks."

"I hope you're not talking about quitting the Human Empire," Samuel said. "Other than Vivian and me, you're the only humans with any experience in alien diplomacy who passed the civil service exam. If I haven't thanked you for all of the visits to the administrators of open worlds you've been doing in my place, it's because I'm not a great manager."

"We like handling the requests and complaints that come up at every stop," Sabina said. "We would have offered to do all of them but we didn't want you to think we were trying to take over."

"You like dealing with complaints?"

"Sure, it's a challenge. And they're almost always issues that we can actually do something about."

"Except for scheduling," Katya said with a scowl. "Everybody either wants Flower to come more often or to start making stops at some other world with which they have a business relationship."

"They want Flower to bypass them and go elsewhere?" Nikos asked.

"A lot of the older sovereign human communities have their own daughter colonies on other open worlds. But shipping goods and people back and forth on independent freighters is expensive, and the trips can include a half-dozen other stops."

"With Flower, they could go one way, drop off their merchandise, and return through the tunnels on a rental if their homeworld has a Tunnel Trips franchise," Sabina said. "And those long freighter trips are in Zero-G, which doesn't agree with most people."

"I don't know how that got past me," Samuel said. "I used to be good at listening to people."

"And now you're doing too much," Vivian said. "When we get to Union Station, I'm going to ask your father to beat some sense into you."

"But what are we going to do about faculty for next semester if Sabina and Katya stop teaching?" Samuel asked. "I was counting on Introduction to Tunnel Network Culture as a full-year course."

"I can teach it, and so can you for that matter," Vivian said. "But I think we'd do better to turn it into another seminar."

"Do you think the aliens would be willing to do two seminars?"

"Not with the aliens, with retirees from the independent living deck," Vivian said. "They've lived all over the tunnel network, including plenty who were born to parents who were working as alien labor. I've already heard from a few retirees with university-level teaching experience who would happily pick up a course. I think it makes more sense to bring them in one at a time for a guest seminar like we do with the aliens, to see who connects well with the students and really knows their stuff."

"How are you doing with the stamps?" Nikos asked. "I came up with some numbers for their revenue generation potential and the margins are better than printing paper money or minting coins. It's a wonder more societies don't use postage stamps for currency."

"You do realize that other than proof sales to collectors, we have to arrange for delivery of packages in return."

"I thought you were going to sell exclusively to collectors. The galactic market is larger than you might realize, and I can't imagine that we're in any position to start providing delivery services."

"We won't need to," Sabina said. "Every world, every orbital, has its own postal service, though many of them contract it out to private package delivery businesses. The revenue share from stamp sales is determined by a tunnel network committee that actively adjusts rates every cycle."

"That ensures an even distribution of the gross sales, but what if a participating species sells stamps below cost?" Nikos asked.

"The mail will be delivered with postage due—that's why stamps have values on them. Which reminds me, Vivian. You're going to need a postage-due design."

"Do collectors buy them, or can we get by with just a big number on the same background for every denomination?" Vivian asked, sweeping her tab to life to take notes.

"It's sort of a point of pride with all of the tunnel networks to have unique artwork for enough values so they can be easily combined to make up the difference," Sabina said. "It's a way of signaling that they aren't so bereft of creativity that they can't manage a dozen more designs."

"Is the status of postage unique on the tunnel network?" Nikos asked. "It seems ripe for arbitrage, given that all of the aliens have their own currencies."

"The exchange rates are pretty stable, and if you look in the corners of stamps that are denominated in a currency other than Stryx creds, you'll see the equivalent value printed in the corner. It's one of the rules for participation."

"We're going to denominate in Stryx creds, at least until the Human Empire has its own currency," Vivian said. "Earth already has stamps with values in eBucks, and I've heard that members of the rate-setting committee say that's the main reason they have to meet so often."

"What percentage of the students who took Open University catch-up courses this semester will be full-time with us next semester?" Mei asked.

"All of them," Samuel said. "I know we didn't explain this in detail, but dividing the incoming class the way we did was more about letting the more advanced students move ahead than holding the majority back. We didn't have the luxury of teaching three times as many courses to accommodate everybody, and the instruction at the Open University is excellent. It gave us the option to launch on the smallest possible scale without turning away applicants who were a little less prepared."

"We're going to need new job titles," Katya said. "You're the Human Empire's First Administrator, which could cover about anything, and Vivian is the Registrar, which works for the school and the GenePost app. But when Sabina and I were introducing ourselves at the meetings we took for you, all we had were our names and 'of the Human Empire.' If we had titles that worked with our last name we could do twice as much work."

"That's about the weakest request for a promotion I've ever heard," Nikos said.

"That's because you don't know how the aliens value consistency. You don't want to lie to them, because when they find out you'll lose all credibility, but they appreciate a good workaround. If Sabina and I could go places as Minister Zerakova, or Vice Chancellor Zerakova, we could split the meetings between us, and most of the aliens would think that they're dealing with one person."

"I still don't think you look that similar," Krey said as she slipped a tiny bead onto the thread.

"Everybody else thinks we're identical, even Avisia, and Vergallians have a good eye for human faces."

"Are there that many meetings to attend at each stop that you'd have to play that game?" Mei asked.

"No, but we could take turns doing advance work at the worlds that want Flower to stop that she doesn't have room for in the schedule. The fact that we're based on Flower will give the Human Empire a sort of artificial proximity. At least we could start figuring out their needs rather than leaving Daniel and his CoSHC office on Union Station to do everything long distance."

"That's actually a decent idea," Samuel said. "I'm not sure about the bit where you try to pass as the same person by using a title with your family name, though you're right that most of the aliens would think it was funny if they caught you out. Someday the Human Empire will want to establish a presence on those worlds, and if you can get us a head start, that would be a good use of your time and our money."

"Why not be ambassadors?" Vivian suggested. "Ambassador Zerakova."

"We checked the tunnel network treaty and it's a reserved word," Katya said. "We can't be ambassadors or consuls until the Human Empire takes over for EarthCent."

"We've been using the minister title for standard governmental departments, though the only one who does anything is Larry, our Minister of Trade."

"We've never met him," Nikos said.

"He's not full-time, or even paid," Samuel explained. "And he's the head of the Traders Guild, though that's also an unpaid honor. But he's gone on diplomatic tours when we've asked him, and I've got something coming up for him next month."

"On Flower?" Sabina asked. "Is he married?"

"Happily married with a newborn, and I'm going to ask him to spend a few months on Earth for us, which hopefully works out for his wife. Hildy Grueun, EarthCent's public relations and marketing guru, managed to get enough people together to agree on the first World's Fair in a century. I suspect they persuaded someone we all know to help foot the bill. When we stopped at Earth, we took proposals from events management consultants and hired one to build us a pavilion, but word through the grapevine is that it's a disaster."

"The EarthCent grapevine?" Katya asked. "It tends to blow everything out of proportion, like that classroom game where you whisper a secret to the person next to you, and by the time it gets to the teacher, it's all garbled."

"The alien intelligence agents grapevine," Samuel said. "One of the benefits of having them on board is that their information about what's happening on Earth is usually better than ours."

"That's embarrassing," Mei said. "How can alien spies know more about our world than we do?"

"They hire human sources, but they also get reports from their tourists and local businessmen," Vivian told her. "I think there's a bit of proofreading bias at work, where people who grow up speaking a language are so fluent at reading that their brains make substitutions for some types of errors in the text without them even noticing. Somebody who learned a language later in life isn't skipping ahead, so they catch those errors."

"So aliens are more likely to spot faulty construction?"

"Probably, but that's not what I meant. If you grew up in a city where every other storefront was closed, you'd stop noticing them. To an alien tourist, closed stores would be a potential subject for a Grenouthian documentary about Earth's weird economic system."

"Earth also smells funny," Krey said, holding a double strand of beads up to the light. "Too blue," she growled, and snapped the bottom of the cord so the beads all came off and fell into the lid. Then she began laboriously sorting them back into the compartments.

"Let me summarize," Nikos said. "We still have jobs, you're going to hire some retirees from the independent living deck to teach a seminar, and even though a quarter of the class quit, we're going to have more students next semester because we're getting the kids who were taking catch-up courses this semester."

"And we think you should break your courses into two sections," Vivian said. "We'd like to keep the same basic schedule, except now you'll both teach two morning classes four days a week, and the new students will be divided between them.

"You mean while I have half the new students in Macro, she'll have the other half, and then we'll switch."

"That's an idea," Mei said. "Instead of the students all switching classrooms, you and I can exchange. It's not like we're teaching lab courses."

"Same office hours in the café?" Nikos asked.

"I don't see why not," Samuel said. "Do you have any requests for the café that I should pass on to Bill?"

"I think it's about time they started serving alcohol, at least beer and wine in the evening. Some of the students who would rather be there end up in some noisy bar because they want a nightcap."

"Hey, can we keep going to the café when the semester is over?" Katya asked.

"Like, emeritus faculty," Sabina said.

"After one semester of teaching?" Samuel asked skeptically.

"That's a hundred percent of the School of Government's history."

"I knew that teaching one course was too good to be true," Mei said. "So now we'll be teaching two classes in the morning for the starting students plus an advance course in the afternoon?"

"About that," Vivian said with a grin. "We haven't announced it yet, but we're sending all your advanced students out for six-month internships after the break. We have offers from alien embassies on Stryx stations for over a hundred slots, so the students can even pick and choose."

"You're just going to spring it on them?"

"We warned everyone that the program is a work in progress. If some of the students can't get along with aliens, it's better that we find out now. And we're paying for all of them to get diplomatic-grade implants."

"That sounds reasonable," Krey said.

Twenty

"So you're saying I can't substitute five hundred days of writing two hundred words a day for fifty days of writing two thousand," Julie said, and she let out a sigh of defeat. "I had the feeling something was going wrong, but I didn't want to show you the manuscript before it was finished."

"You should still publish," Bianca said. "Every author has to write a first book, and most of us are relieved when it doesn't turn out to be our best. Who would want to start at the top and go downhill?"

"Skiers. When I tried reading my manuscript to an Old Way book group, the women kept on interrupting and I didn't get past the first two pages."

"Were you sitting with them?"

"Yes," Julie admitted. "Flower said that was a mistake."

"She's right," Bianca said. "There's a reason that battles usually go to the side that can hold the high ground. Standing while everybody else is sitting gives you a natural air of authority even if you aren't feeling sure of yourself. New authors often feel more comfortable sitting in a circle than standing in front of an audience, but a speaker needs to establish a degree of separation from the listeners or the whole event turns into a muddle."

"I'll add it to my list of things to work on. Thanks to Flower, I'm used to speaking in front of crowds, but there's a difference between standing up and representing her and standing up and asking people to judge my book."

Bianca took a sip from her blue tea and smiled at the delicate flavor. "I threw up the first time I had to give a book reading. And the second time. And the third time, though by then it didn't bother me. After that I was fine, but to this day I carry a toothbrush and a little tube of toothpaste in my purse."

"Really?" Julie asked, and Bianca opened her purse to produce the items in question, which were wrapped together with plastic film. "So what specifically did you hate about my book?"

"I didn't hate any of it, Julie. I just don't think it's the best you can do. If you want a specific criticism, I found some scenes uneven. I suspect you began writing about the thunderstorm that spooked the horse one day, your heroine getting thrown the next day, and a handsome stranger rescuing her on the third. Taken by themselves, those paragraphs were all well written, but when you put them together, they didn't quite meld."

"Those are exactly the points I stopped each day! You know, before I started this book I used to get up and do all of my writing before work, but then I read—"

"The Coffee Break Author," Bianca interrupted. "I know Geraldine, and she made more money on that book than on all of her novels combined. I can't imagine how many promising writing careers it's ruined."

"She was lying?" Julie asked in dismay.

"No, she actually did write all of her books in five-minute chunks during coffee breaks until the how-to guide made her rich enough to quit her day job. Strangely enough, she didn't improve after that. I think it's because she spends far more time selling consulting services to new writers than plotting her next romance."

"I didn't read any of her novels. I guess I should have."

"You're not alone. My point is that you have all of the tools you need to be successful. You can tell a story, you can solve a plot, and your dialogue is strong. What you need now is to set aside a solid block of time every day to work at it."

"Flower keeps promising me a long vacation next year. She's got something up her sleeve."

"If she has four sleeves like her Dollnick creators you might be in trouble," Bianca said, looking up and smiling as the Frunge owner of the café approached the table. "Thank you, Fandaz. The daily special was excellent."

"You're most welcome," Fandaz replied. "I was curious what you thought of the protagonists in Julie's book."

"I understand that she unconsciously based them on you and a certain Frunge blacksmith. I thought their relationship was very romantic."

"Do you think it would stretch to a series?"

"I don't know if—ah, I missed your meaning," Bianca cut herself off. "I wish the two of you centuries of joy together."

Fandaz's hair vines darkened with a rush of chlorophyll. "Thank you," she said. "Can I get the two of you anything else?"

"Three hours of free time every day," Julie said. "No, I'm just kidding. One thing about having Flower as a boss is I know she works ten times as hard as I do. She's at it around the clock, and her idea of multi-tasking is holding ten thousand simultaneous conversations while navigating interstellar space." Her phone began to beep obnoxiously and she swiped to turn off the alarm. "I'm sorry, but I have an appointment to see M793qK. I think he has feedback about a report I was working on for Flower."

"Hold on for a second and I'll give you something for him," the owner of the Blue Tea Café said. "It's a sort of substitute flour that Humans are making on a Dollnick world for the Frunge market, and he promised to check it for me to see if it contains any grains."

Julie took her leave from her writing mentor and followed Fandaz to the counter where the alien handed over a glass vial of coarse flour. M793qK was seeing a walk-in patient when Julie arrived at the clinic, so she asked Flower to ping her when the doctor became available and continued down the corridor to the library to do a little browsing. She changed course when she saw Dewey behind the main circulation desk.

"Julie," the artificial person greeted her. "You're early."

"Early is on time," she responded automatically, "but I wasn't coming here, so I don't think it's technically true."

"Early for our meeting with M793qK," Dewey said. "It's not for another half hour."

"But I set my smartphone alarm to give me five minutes to get here."

"There was a new operating system push last night. It restores the factory defaults if you only changed the setting on your user profile."

"Do you mean the original setting for the meeting notification app was a half hour?" Julie asked. "That was too long for me so I changed it to five minutes. Can you make it permanent for me?"

Dewey accepted the proffered phone, reset her personal advanced notification time, and then changed the default setting so the fix would be permanent. "Going by the number of apps you have installed, you must use the phone quite a bit," he commented.

"It's nice having something smaller than a tab, and I like all of the effects that go with the camera," Julie said. "And texting works pretty well with all of the people from Bits who are working for Flower now. They don't show any sign of abandoning their smartphones for tabs."

"Between you and me, I've invested in a manufacturer on Earth that makes phones," Dewey said. "It's a strange situation from the business standpoint as the Dollnicks make all sorts of universal devices that could emulate everything a phone can do for a fraction of the price. But smartphones are one of Earth's three protected technologies, and the brand name devices are building cachet with social signaling aliens."

"What are they signaling? Is it a way of making fun of humanity?"

The artificial person flashed a roguish smile. "It's a way to show that they're early adopters, quick to discover the latest thing."

"But smartphones aren't the latest thing. They were all rendered obsolete almost a century ago when—hold on, I have to take this." Julie swiped the connection as she moved back out into the corridor to take a rare voice call. "Rayne?"

"You told me to let you know as soon as I ran the numbers," the comptroller said. "It's not good."

"How bad?"

"I can't believe how expensive big ships are. We'd need to get every working-age human in the galaxy to chip in nearly a thousand creds just to get started."

"Then it's not going to happen," Julie said. "Thanks for the effort."

"It's probably my swansong," Rayne said. "I haven't broken it to Sarah yet, but when we get to Union Station, Hercules and I plan to stay on and look for a different opportunity."

"You mean to stay behind on Union Station? What about your mother?"

"I'm working on her."

Julie dropped the phone back in her purse and returned to the library. Before she could pick up her conversation with Dewey, she got a ping from Bill and pointed at her ear.

"I'm going to Flower's Paradise to act in a training video Harry's wife is shooting," he said. "I'll make dinner when I get back. Okay?"

"Takeout is fine too," Julie said. "I love the vegetarian lasagna from the independent living deck cafeteria."

"I'll see if they have it today," Bill said. "Love you."

"Me too," Julie said and broke off the connection. Dewey was busy with a library patron, so she started browsing the new releases in the romance section at the same time her husband was entering the common room at Flower's Paradise.

"Thanks for coming," Harry greeted Bill. "Samuel and Vivian are on their way, but Irene doesn't want to use them."

"Remind me that I'm supposed to pick up dinner," Bill said. "But it looks like you have plenty of volunteers."

"Look again," the baker said, making a sweeping gesture around the common room of Flower's Paradise, and accidentally sending the floating immersive camera he was controlling towards the wall where it stopped just short of contact and let out a plaintive beep. "You didn't see that."

"So what was I supposed to see?"

"Everybody in here is over sixty-five," Harry said. "This training video is Irene's first official commission, and she doesn't want to make GenePost out to be a geriatric service."

"Samuel and Vivian are young," Bill pointed out.

"They're going to introduce themselves and the Human Empire. Irene says the video will be more effective if the subjects look like regular people."

"I guess I qualify there. It's just that I don't know if I want to be findable."

"You haven't already signed up for GenePost? Almost everybody in our cooperative participated in the beta test last year so that M793qK could perfect the DNA scanner he built for the postcard samples."

"He mentioned something about one of his subsidiaries on Earth putting the scanners into mass production," Bill said. "The doctor is always complaining about having too many eBucks to get rid of, so he puts most of his pharmaceutical royalties back into other Earth businesses."

"My grandmother used to say that the poor have poor problems and the rich have rich problems," Harry said with a laugh. "Or maybe it was single people have single problems and married people have married problems. My grandmother wasn't the most optimistic person."

"There you are," Irene said, taking Bill by the arm. "Thank you for volunteering. When I realized I forgot to arrange for any young actors I almost had a panic attack. This is my first paid directing job."

"Harry mentioned that," Bill said. "Am I it?"

"For the generic young male age group. We aren't going to show the same procedure a dozen times because that would make for a boring video. I asked Lynx to bring her daughter, so that gives us a middle-aged woman and a ten-year-old girl. Hopefully, Em will bring a friend so I can get a reaction shot."

"Is there a script? I haven't been on camera since they dropped my character from *Everyday Superheroes* the second season."

"I'm planning to add a voiceover to your scene explaining the process. We'll show you filling out the postcard, reading the instructions, and giving the blood sample."

"So I shouldn't say anything?" Bill asked.

"Dave volunteered to work the desk, so if you chat and slip in a few smiles, that would work best. The set is a mockup of what we think the GenePost registration booths at the New World's Fair will look like, though the training video will work for anywhere."

"Well, I guess I'm ready then."

"Samuel and Vivian are bringing the blank postcards and the DNA scanner," Irene said. "There's coffee and pastry while—No!" she interrupted herself, turning toward the volunteer camera operators from her class. "Don't point the cameras directly at light fixtures or I'll have to manually reset the saturation levels."

"My wife, the director," Harry said with a chuckle. "It's hard to believe that a few generations ago people our age were moving into care homes."

"Here come Vivian and Samuel," Bill said. "I'll help them get set up."

Thanks to a year of beta testing, Vivian was an old hand at setting up a GenePost booth with a poster, an attractive display of sample postcards, and a basket of giveaways branded with the Human Empire logo. The new element was the special-purpose DNA scanner now being manufactured on Earth.

"Try not to wince when you press your finger on the green oval," Irene instructed the actors. "Most people find the blood draw to be painless, and we don't want to create the impression that it hurts."

Ten-year-old Em immediately ducked back behind her mother, where she was joined by Sarah, her friend from Flower's school. Bill glanced at Lynx to see if she wanted to go first and get it over with before he stepped forward.

"I'd like to sign up for GenePost," he said to Dave, who was acting the part of a Human Empire volunteer.

"We have two options for you," Dave said. "You can take a postcard home to fill out the information, or I can enter your data on this bonded tab. In either case, you'll use the card's touch oval that painlessly extracts a blood sample using the latest Farling technology,"

"If you enter the information on your tab, how does it get matched with the blood sample?" Bill asked.

"All of the postcards have a unique identifying code that the tab can read, so I can associate the sample you give with the information I enter. It reduces the chance of a transcription error later."

"Let's do that," Bill said. He pressed the ball of his index finger against the green oval on a postcard, doing his best to ignore the swarm of floating immersive cameras operated by Irene's students. He found that the blood draw tickled, causing him to grin. "That didn't hurt a bit."

Dave tapped Bill's basic information into the form and then scanned the code on the postcard with the tab's camera. Then he took Bill's picture. "You can install the GenePost app on any compatible device and register with your name and face. I'll just feed your sample into the DNA scanner and you're all set."

"Can I do it on my implant?"

"Tabs and smartphones, anything that runs an app," Dave said, glancing over at Vivian for confirmation. "I don't think implants allow you to install software for security reasons, being connected to your brain and all."

"Oh, that makes sense." He watched as his postcard was sucked into the scanner, and then disgorged a few seconds later with a hole where the green sampling oval had been located. "So that's it?"

"All set," Dave said. "Don't forget to check the GenePost app for future enhancements. I've heard they're planning on a Human Empire lottery."

After seeing Bill go first, the two little girls signed up together, both of them showing off neat printing when filling out their cards. Then Lynx took her turn, and couldn't help scrunching up her face when giving the blood sample.

"But it didn't hurt at all," Em scolded her mother.

"It's the thought of it," Lynx replied. "Do I need to do another take?"

"It will be fine," Irene said. "I'm only planning on a combined fifteen or twenty seconds of video from the four of you. The Grenouthian director told me that training videos for a situation like this should err on the side of brevity, and we don't want to risk discouraging people from signing up. They can always ask the volunteer if they're giving their information on the spot, and if they're just picking up a postcard to mail in later, they can read the instructions at home."

"But don't they have to hand the postcard in immediately?"

"M793qK says that the printable substrate will preserve blood samples for over a year, as long as the postcards aren't exposed to high heat or left in direct sunlight for more than a few hours. The amount of blood his equipment needs to create a DNA profile is minute, and the carbon nanotubes that collect the samples are self-sealing."

"The print-on-demand place next to the library does carbon nanotubes?" Lynx asked. "I had no idea they did anything other than books."

"They print the postcards, but the sampling substrate is added by a high-speed Dollnick 3D printer that M793qK specified," Vivian told her. "Flower has been doing them for us under contract, but we're buying printers for our pavilion at the New World's Fair. After that, the postcards for Earth will all be made locally."

Harry reminded Bill about buying dinner, and while the young man was ordering vegetarian lasagna in the largest independent living cafeteria, his wife was taking a ping from Flower.

"You have one minute if you want to be early," the Dollnick AI told her. "Dewey is waiting for you at the circulation desk."

Julie stuck the book she'd been reading back on the shelf, rendezvoused with the artificial person, and together they ran down the corridor to the clinic.

"Your manuscript is full of flaws, but I think it's worth trying," the Farling doctor said without any preliminary. "Flower agrees, Krey is on board, and we just need to get the go-ahead from the Stryx."

"You want to publish my Old Way romance?"

M793qK literally jumped back a step and extended all of his upper limbs as if to fend off evil spirits. "Where did you get that idea?"

"You said you read my manuscript, and the only other thing I've written lately—you were talking about the plan that Rayne and I worked up for Flower to obtain a companion ship."

"It lacked the detailed budgeting and timeline to qualify as a plan, and your writing style made me believe you were thinking of making it a novel or a screenplay. I don't read romance novels."

"That's what I tell everyone too," Dewey said. "What sort of timeline are we talking about?"

"It's up to the Stryx and the Zarents," M793qK rubbed out on his speaking legs. "If everything falls into place, we could start at Union Station, which would have the added advantage of seven or eight months to get everything running smoothly before Julie goes out on maternity leave."

"Congratulations," the artificial person said to Flower's executive assistant. "I'm an experienced godparent if you and Bill are taking applications."

Julie turned pale and stared at the Farling doctor. "You haven't even examined me."

"Do you think my scanners at the clinic's entrance would miss a pregnancy?" M793qK asked. "You can go out and come in again if you want a second opinion. No, that was a little medical joke—come back."

"I need to talk to my husband."

"Drink lots of milk," the Farling doctor called after her. "And make sure you brush your teeth twice a day. That tooth-a-baby business is positively medieval."

"M793qK says that I'm pregnant," Julie said out loud when she entered the lift tube. "I can't believe it."

"Do you wish to return to the clinic for another examination?" a male voice inquired.

"Kruik? I forgot you were running the lift tubes. No, just take me home, please."

"Do you wish to speak to Flower? I can get her for you."

"It can wait until I'm sitting," Julie said, feeling a bit unsteady on her feet as the capsule accelerated. "Are we going faster than usual?"

"I'm sorry if I made you uncomfortable," Kruik said. "I've been experimenting with variable acceleration profiles when passengers sound like they're in a hurry. In some ways, the infrastructure of colony ships is more flexible than that of warships."

Julie was still light-headed when she collapsed on her couch, though now she wasn't sure if it was from the news, a physical effect of pregnancy, or the lift tube. "Where's Bill?" she asked out loud.

"On his way home from the independent living cooperative," Flower responded immediately. "He's bringing lasagna for dinner. Don't forget you're eating for two now."

"Is that the big vacation you've been promising me? Maternity leave?"

"And it's mandated. You can catch up on your writing."

"How am I going to tell Bill?"

"Are you worried about his reaction?"

"It's not that," Julie said. "You're talking about a life-changing event for us. I don't want to just say it like I'm telling him about my day at work."

"I could send a fruit basket with a card," Flower offered.

"I'll come up with something. Don't you tell him," she warned.

"I wouldn't dream of it. I'll leave you to rest now, but I'm right here if you want to talk."

Julie was still struggling to wrap her mind around the change that was coming to her life when Bill returned with a large take-out container of lasagna.

"The guy working the steam table in the independent living cafeteria gave me twice as much as I ordered and said it was on the house because they made too much today," he reported. "Can I borrow your phone?"

"It's in my purse. What do you need it for?"

"You have the GenePost app installed, right? Vivian said I could add my profile to it if I don't want to fool around with downloading the app to my tab. If I don't do it now, I'll forget." Bill swiped the phone to life. "What's your secret code again?"

"Seven nine three one one," Julie told him. "I used the numerals from M793qK plus eleven for the last letter."

"GenePost," Bill said to the phone, and he was actually surprised when the app opened. "Add user."

"Please center your face in the box," a pleasant voice requested as the camera activated. "Positive identification for Bill. You have one new message."

"I guess it worked," Bill said, setting down the phone and starting for the kitchen. "What do you want to go with your lasagna?"

"Aren't you going to check your message?" Julie asked.

"It's just going to be one of those welcome things. I've already had enough of GenePost for one day."

"I didn't get one when I signed up." Julie picked up the phone and tapped the message. "It's from your mom," she called out excitedly.

"My mother?" Bill asked, his voice suddenly hollow. "What does she want?"

"Read it and tell me."

"No, you read it. I don't know if I want to talk to her."

"Reading isn't talking," Julie said as she began scrolling through the long message. "She says that she left the Sun Cult, and the first thing she did when she got a smartphone was to sign up with the GenePost beta. Her husband—"

"She married that whack job from the cult?" Bill interrupted.

Julie took advantage of the pause to read ahead.

"It's a different guy, the one who convinced her to—wait a minute."

"What?"

Julie waved him off to leave her alone while she was reading.

"Come on," Bill protested. "She's *my* mother."

"All right, that's not so bad. In fact, it would make a pretty interesting plot for a romance."

Bill sat on the couch, still holding the lasagna, and tried to read over her shoulder. "She found Gortunda? Isn't that the Horten religion that takes humans?"

"They had a big revival in New York, and she was selling bottled water from the pushcart when she met Torja. He's human, but he took a Horten name when he ascended to the second level."

"Is it a real marriage or some alien thing?"

"Both. She said they would have invited you if she knew where you were. And she says you're going to be a big brother!"

"But she's almost forty," Bill said, staring at the text. "What's she going to do without the Sun Cult compound? Sleep in the pushcart with Torja?"

"She has a job at a Horten gaming center now, but she says that after the baby is born, they're going to become missionaries. Hey, she thinks they'll be assigned to a Stryx station!"

"So what does she want from me?" Bill demanded. "She has a husband and a new baby on the way."

"She just wants to hear that you're alive and well. You don't even have to let her know where you are—the GenePost app lets you choose to keep your location secret."

Bill slumped on the couch, cradling the lasagna in his lap and staring at nothing for several minutes. Finally, he asked, "How should I reply?"

"Tell her that she's going to be a grandmother," Julie said, breaking into a wide smile. As Bill's face lit up with understanding, she subvoced to Flower, "Now this would make a good ending for an Old Way romance."

From the Author

The next EarthCent book will be **Bits of Flower**, the second book in the **EarthCent Metaverse** series. The timeline overlaps with **Double Living**, but ends later. If you haven't read **Bits of Anarchy**, the first book of the **EarthCent Metaverse** spinoff, it's not too late. If you're new to the EarthCent books, you can start back at the beginning with **Union Station 1, 2, 3**, a discounted three-book bundle.

For notifications of new releases, sign up for the mailing list at www.ifitbreaks.com. I also post new releases to facebook.com/E.M.Foner/ and respond to all temperate e-mail sent to e_foner@yahoo.com

Made in United States
Orlando, FL
08 March 2023

30860438R00146